THE VANISHING FOREST

Jaysee Jewel

THE VANISHING FOREST

Copyright © 2023 by Jaysee Jewel

All rights reserved.

Book cover designs by Creative Paramita

Edited by Noah Sky

Author: Jaysee Jewel

Subjects: Dark Fantasy / Horror / Action and Adventure

First Edition: August 2023

Ebook ISBN: 979-8-9872796-6-3

Paperback ISBN: 979-8-9872796-7-0

https://jayseejewel.mystrikingly.com/

Introduction

Ten years ago

The forest rang with the cheery chirps of birds, rustling leaves, and the angry chant of a lone squirrel trying to assert dominance over Cynthia, her husband, and the other eight hikers traveling through the Pukaskwa National Park. They'd been wandering through the Ontario wilderness for hours and Cynthia was falling behind once again. Her husband had to repeatedly stop and back up to keep her company so she wouldn't feel bad for slowing everyone down.

"How was Gabriel?" Cynthia's husband Dennis asked, referring to his brother and her brother-in-law. She had just called Gabriel to update him on where they were. He'd been planning to join them on this expedition but work got in the way, as it often did.

"Still miserable," she said with a laugh, shifting her backpack and ignoring the strain it put on her shoulders. "Still upset to be missing all the fun."

"He'll get over it." Dennis gestured to the trees on every side. "Besides, it's not like he's missing out on much." He took another step, then stopped and rested a hand on her shoulder. "What is that?"

Cynthia paused too.

"Grant!" Dennis called ahead to their leader. "Grant! You know what that thing is?" He pointed at something a quarter mile away. It was a tall wall of stone, though there weren't supposed to be any buildings or mountains around here. Anything beyond a tree, bear, or lake was out of the ordinary.

"I don't know," Grant shouted back, then quickened his pace. "But it looks like the most interesting thing we've found today." Grant had spent this whole trip complaining about boredom. This strange wall might finally free them from his whining.

"Dennis—" Cynthia gulped, forced to follow Grant with the others. "This wasn't on the map." She had a bad feeling about this. Had they wandered out of the park by accident? Were they lost?

"Maybe we strayed outside the border," Dennis suggested, confirming her fears, though his relaxed posture and smile proved he didn't share Cynthia's worry.

Her jaw dropped as they got closer. They hadn't merely stumbled onto some small building in the middle of nowhere. They'd found a fifty-foot-tall wall that stretched as far as the eye could see. Had they discovered a government or military facility?

A shiver ran up Cynthia's spine when they stopped in front of the wall. It was even more imposing up close.

Dennis pressed a hand against it. There was a hole twenty feet to their right—a square doorway granting access inside. It looked normal, though most traps did.

"This is so cool," Stephanie, Grant's sister, whispered in awe as she peered through the entrance. "Do you think it's, like, the Canadian version of Area 51?"

"They wouldn't have let us wander around freely if it was," Cynthia countered. She was the only one shaking with fear. The others looked like excited children planning to sneak into an R-rated movie. She wished Dennis's militant brother was here. He would have been the voice of reason.

"Let's go in," Grant suggested, pointing at the doorway. "It's not like there's gonna be anything inside. This wall was probably built to mark boundaries. That's all."

Dennis shrugged, then turned to Cynthia. "If you don't want to go in, we can stay behind."

Every fiber of her being was telling her to flee. It wasn't the wall that scared her—it was the complete silence within it. The animals had been so loud a hundred feet away but now she couldn't even hear the wind rustling the leaves. Then again, it wasn't like a single wall could hurt them, not unless there was some invisible forcefield within it that would zap them if they tried to sneak inside.

"I'll text Gabriel and let him know where we are first," she suggested as the others debated whether they should venture in. "That way if something goes wrong, he can tell the authorities where we last were."

"Works for me." Grant flashed her a smile, then stepped through the door. The debate ended once he did. If one of them went, they all did. No splitting up. That was the rule they agreed on when deciding to travel here.

Cynthia sent Gabriel the text, accompanying it with a photo of the massive wall, then she followed Dennis through the hole.

"I hope we don't regret this," she muttered, knowing it was just her paranoia talking but still hoping they weren't being stupid. She had a daughter to return home to, so taking risks wasn't something she could afford anymore.

"Don't worry," Dennis assured her, holding her hand and leading her forward. "We'll be fine as long as we stick together."

Episode 1

Present Day

*T*he Vanishing Forest is the name of a mysteriously walled-in wood located in Ontario's Pukaskwa National Park. It was discovered ten years ago by a crew of hikers in 2025, though no one knows how it got there or why no one found it before.

Its most defining feature is the large stone fortification surrounding it on all sides. The walls form a circle and are clearly manmade. They stand fifty feet tall and are incredibly smooth, making them difficult to climb without gear. As a result, any who enter must use one of the four doors on each side.

The speaker in the video stopped talking for a moment and listened to someone behind the camera, then nodded and smiled. *Right. Before I continue, we would like to remind our viewers that entering the forest is strictly forbidden. Any who attempt to go in without permission from the military will be arrested.* He nodded at the cameraman again, then returned to his original script.

The ten hikers who originally discovered the walls entered through the eastern door and vanished, leaving behind only a few personal articles at the entrance. There was an eleventh hiker, Gabriel Nilson, who originally planned to go with them but cancelled at the last minute. He was the one who alerted the authorities after they disappeared.

Personally, I would have gone after them, but this guy was clearly smarter than me. By staying behind and spreading the word about the walls, he saved himself and prevented others from vanishing too.

"It was common sense," Uncle Gabriel said to the video playing on Lili's laptop. She caught him rolling his eyes before returning his attention to his plate. "He talks like I was a coward. The fact is, I would have gone in after them if the government didn't intervene." To prove how annoyed he was, he stabbed his breakfast sausage with a fork, his military cap flopping forward as he tilted his head.

Lili paused the video so she wouldn't miss anything. It was titled "The Rural Rangers Tackle the Vanishing Woods". It wasn't the first video of theirs she'd watched in front of her uncle, but this was the only time he'd reacted.

The handsome, muscular man on the screen stopped talking and the pause button appeared over his face. "I'm sure he's just trying to be optimistic about what happened," she commented.

"You should feel insulted too," her uncle grumbled, taking a sip of his coffee before slamming it on the plastic table between them. He wasn't a violent man. He was just prone to getting annoyed when it concerned what happened in those walls ten years ago. "He's talking about the death of your parents like it was a good thing."

"That's not true," Lili countered, more quietly this time. "If it annoys you so much, I can listen to it in my room."

"Like that would help," he muttered. The trailer they lived in was so small that even a whisper traveled through the walls. "Besides, I want to hear what else he gets wrong."

She tilted her head, trying to come up with another defense for her favorite channel, then gave up and pressed play.

After more people vanished, including twenty soldiers and scientists, the military decided to exclusively send drones. However, any cameras they sent in shut down immediately and any machinery with cords connected to the outside world had their cables mysteriously cut.

A video of someone sending in a drone filled the screen. Lili watched as it moved past the walls, then immediately disappeared. She could see the grass and trees beyond the doorway but anything that moved past the threshold immediately vanished like magic.

It's super cool, right? The brown-haired hunk grinned and looked ready to rant about how awesome it was until a second young man playfully shoved him out of the lens. This second person had long blond hair and glasses that made him look like a model. He took over the voiceover from that point on.

Many theories about the wall have spread over the years. Some claim it's a government-funded experiment. Others assume it's some kind of natural or magical phenomenon. Regardless, due to the dangers the forest presents, the walls have been blocked off and are now guarded by both cameras and soldiers.

The camera switched to shots of deformed animals exiting the forest walls. They were the only things that came back out, unlike the humans, but their bodies were always altered and unnatural. One video showed a frog with only its hind legs, wandering about like a person. Another showed an owl with no feathers and a backward head. It walked forward as though nothing was wrong. *By the end of the month, we'll be able to show you—*

"They're just saying things we already know," Lili's uncle interrupted, motioning for her to turn it off. She obeyed. The video was almost over anyway. "Turn on something else, or better yet, start your schoolwork. Videos like that rot your brain."

"Okay." Lili shrugged and pulled her homeschool textbooks from a nearby drawer. "But they're not as dumb as you think. The Rural Rangers make a lot of great videos teaching people how to survive in the wild. They're explorers—"

Her uncle rolled his eyes. "I can teach you more about that than a few teens on the internet."

She was tempted to let him know that the two on-screen weren't teens anymore but in his eyes, anyone below thirty was young. Besides, the other three were still eighteen so he wasn't totally wrong. If he was thirty years younger, her uncle would have fit in with this group. With his buzz cut and muscular build, paired with the crisp grey military uniform, he was more fit than men half his age.

She didn't mind his harsh manner. Not only had he lost all of his friends when they entered the walls, but he'd also been tasked with guarding the Vanishing Woods until retirement, which he did with pride because he knew how horrible it felt to lose someone within it.

Since he was Lili's only remaining family—her parents had been part of the hiking party that vanished—Lili had moved into the camper stationed outside the walls and spent most of her childhood exploring the woods surrounding the Vanishing Forest. Growing up here had given her a morbid curiosity about the place that took her parents. She wasn't stupid enough to go inside but still spent countless days climbing trees in an attempt to peer over the walls. She never saw anything, sadly, with the exception of wingless dragonflies and two-legged spiders, but part of her believed her parents were still alive. She had always hoped to find them exiting those doors one day.

Most of her early years were wasted watching for people who never came. Then, six years ago on her twelfth birthday, her wish finally came true. She saw her mother.

On a normal day like any other, Lili had been sitting in a tree, reading a book while keeping an eye on the door. Then she finally saw movement.

Her mother used to look almost identical to Lili, with curly black hair that ran to the tips of her ears, dark skin, and large brown eyes. She'd always had a warm feeling about her, coupled with a paranoia that turned her into a helicopter parent.

However, the woman that exited the walls was nothing like the mother Lili remembered. She had greying flesh that was flaking away, like a reptile shedding its skin. She smelled of rot and dirt, the scent so strong that it filled Lili's nose and lungs from ten feet away. Lili also saw green buds popping from her eyes, like plants sprouting from the ground. It had terrified Lili so much that even though she'd spent years waiting for this day, she stayed rooted to the tree branch. When the woman's budding eyeballs turned on her, Lili felt ready to scream rather than shout for joy.

Not a word was spoken as her mother waited for Lili to come to her. Her fingers rose, gesturing for the child to follow. But when Lili didn't move, her mother turned back around and reentered the walls without uttering a word.

Lili relived that moment every night, wondering what would have happened if she had gone to her mother instead. Would it have prevented her from disappearing again?

Regardless, Lili avoided the walls after that day and didn't speak of what she saw. She tried to explain what happened to her uncle many times, even though she knew he'd get mad at her for being so close to the walls, but whenever the thought of confessing crossed her mind, something would stop her. Her heart would start racing or her throat would become so dry she'd start to choke. Her thoughts would race, convincing her that Uncle Gabriel would send her away if she told him about it. That, or he might enter the walls himself and be lost forever.

Regardless, even as she approached adulthood, she never managed to tell him the truth. Her body wouldn't allow it. On good days, she pretended the encounter hadn't happened at all. She would rather remember the healthy, happy mother from pictures than recall a walking corpse. On bad days, it was all she could think about.

"Lili?" Her uncle tapped her plate with his fork. "Maybe you shouldn't watch those videos anymore. It might tempt you to go beyond the walls."

"I would never do that," she lied, closing her laptop. The gentle hum of the fridge beside her filled the silence. Their kitchen was so cramped that any noise was amplified. "And you should be worried about other people trying to go beyond the walls. Not everyone's as cautious as you."

"How many people saw the video?" he asked, growing concerned.

"It has five million views right now."

"What?"

"They're a popular group. All their videos get at least a million."

"Perhaps I should tell someone to shut them up." Her uncle got to his feet, already reaching for his phone. Lili didn't try to stop him. He couldn't be talked out of anything he set his mind to. That was why she had no plans to tell him she was leaving today. Her eighteenth birthday was last week and now that she felt old enough, she had decided it was finally time to look for her mother. She believed—or rather, knew— her mom was still alive, and that meant Lili could save her. Ever since their last encounter, Lili's heart had urged her to enter the forest and find out what had happened to her parents. It needed to be her. Sometimes she chalked the eagerness up to being a teenager, though another part of her knew it was deeper than that.

"I'll see you tonight," her uncle said, phone in hand. He gave her a brief hug before heading out to patrol the walls. He did it every day and trusted her enough by this point to leave her alone to study.

That gave her ten hours to carry out her plan. It was more than enough to get behind the walls. By the time he realized she was gone, it would be too late.

She didn't like going behind his back like this, but the Canadian government stopped sending soldiers into the forest years ago. There was zero chance of her parents being rescued now, so it was up to her. Plus, if she got lucky, her departure might finally motivate her uncle to send an entire army into those walls regardless of the risk. He had talked about doing it for years, meticulously planning each detail, but he refused to leave her behind like her parents accidentally did.

During the last six years, she had studied the area surrounding the walls, memorizing the layout and distances. She had also learned survival skills from the Rural Rangers videos, though she knew who would never be completely ready. There was always more to learn.

Despite her concerns, she couldn't wait any longer. With each passing day, her mother felt further away. Ever since that horrible day, she had been filled with an aching need to enter the forest. She dreamed about it constantly and even had visions of its interior while awake. If she didn't go in now, it would drive her insane. Lili would rather enter the forest now, of her own free will, than accidentally sleepwalk there without any preparation.

Determined to see this through, she left a note explaining everything on the table for her uncle, then she packed up her food, water, clothes, tools, and matches. She also had a few seeds she could plant if she got desperate. If there was zero chance of leaving, she needed to ensure she could survive long enough to search the entire area, which could take months or even years since it was nearly two hundred miles across.

After retrieving a smiling photo of herself and leaving it with the note so her uncle could remember her in case she never came back, she headed out. She knew entering the Vanishing Woods might get her killed, but it was better than living a life of regret.

Episode 2

Lili knew the patrol routes by heart so it was easy to avoid the guards as she maneuvered through the pines and maples. Most of the guards knew her by name thanks to her uncle, so she could explain away her being there easily enough if she was caught. The only things that would draw suspicion were her backpack, thick coat, and steel-toed boots.

The woods surrounding the walls looked the same as any other forest in Canada—filled with vibrant green pine, maple, and spruce trees. This was the perfect time of year to enter the walls, the weather warm but not yet humid. The fresh scent of budding flowers and dirt filled her nose as her boots leapt over dead leaves and thin branches.

The walls stretched above her head, high and imposing, their light grey surfaces strangely smooth despite being exposed to the elements for years. The eastern entrance was ten feet high and was more of a square hole chiseled into the wall than a gate or door. It made it clear just how thick the walls were—at least five or six feet across.

Lili wasn't expecting to encounter anyone other than maybe a few guards, so she was surprised to hear unfamiliar voices near the walls. At first, she feared it was another zombie-like person from within but as she neared the sound, staying hidden behind bushes and tree trunks, she spotted the source. There were five normal humans standing thirty feet from the wall entrance, hiding from the cameras pointed at the doorway.

They weren't just any tourists or hikers, though. They looked familiar.

Her eyes widened. The Rural Rangers. What were they doing here?

It was impossible for the rangers to be here by accident. Did they plan to go inside or just film the exterior?

The loudest voice was Leon Sullivan, the tall and muscular member of the troupe. He was also the most handsome, hence him doing the majority of the talking. His brown hair was styled perfectly despite being in the middle of the forest and he was currently narrating to the camera while one of the other boys filmed. His British accent sounded as pleasing in person as it was onscreen.

The one holding the camera was Jacques Abreo, the brains of the group and unofficial leader. He had long blond hair and square glasses to fit his role and was almost as tall and handsome as Leon. He was currently waving one hand at Leon, warning him to avoid saying anything stupid on camera. Jacques was originally from France but most of the boys currently lived in England so his accent was a mix of the two.

Standing behind Jacques and currently peering through the eastern entrance was the short German redhead, Viktor Jansen. His legs were shaking and, judging by his constant grumbling, he was dreading entering the doorway. A huge pack filled with pots and plants hung off his back.

Leaning against some trees behind him were the identical twins, Aidyn and Kaidyn Myer. They had black hair styled similarly to Leon's but rather than sporting massive muscles, they had lean figures. They also had swords hanging from their hips, the type of flashy weapon she would normally see hanging on someone's wall. It made Lili's hunting knife look pathetic in comparison. The sight of the weapons also made her wonder how they managed to cross the border with them. Perhaps they bought them here instead, which implied just how much planning had gone into this trip. Even after watching them for years, Lili still couldn't tell the twins apart unless they spoke. One had a deep, monotone voice while the other was high and cheery. Their accents were also a mix of English and American, despite being born in Japan.

"It's been decided that Viktor will be the first to go through the doorway," Leon was saying to the camera with a huge grin.

"What? No way!" Viktor shouted back, his voice noticeably higher than the rest. He threw a rock at his friend and missed completely. "You're dead meat if you try to push me through there."

"Oh, come on. You always make me go first. Why don't you try it for a change?" Leon asked with a laugh, making a show of wrapping his arms under Viktor's armpits and lifting him completely off the ground. Viktor tried to punch him and failed.

"Okay, that's enough." Jacques sighed and turned off the camera, motioning for them to cut it out. "The audience doesn't need to see us argue about who goes first."

"But it's entertaining," Leon defended, holding Viktor away from his body like one would a feral cat, trying to avoid getting punched in the face.

As the boys loitered, chatting amongst themselves while they examined the door, Lili realized that the twins weren't the only armed ones. Leon had an axe strapped to his back—though she assumed it was for show. Jacques carried a bow and arrows and Viktor had a shield attached to his pack.

Since Viktor was the cook, he was known for running away instead of fighting. They supposedly stopped giving him weapons after he dropped an expensive gun into a pit while fleeing. It wasn't like he needed it anyway. Most of the places they explored weren't dangerous. The most they encountered were bears or deer, so she was surprised they were so well armed.

Should she wait for them to enter first? If there was something dangerous in there, it would be safer to follow them and let them kill any threats ahead of her. She nodded to herself, deciding that was the safest option.

When she moved her head, the twins turned toward her in unison. Their dark eyes studied her like animals determining if something was a threat.

"Shoot." She should have known they'd notice her, even if she was behind a bush. Should she run?

"Hold on," deep-voiced Kaidyn said, pointing in her direction. "Someone's here. Might be a guard."

Now all eyes were on her. She knew she couldn't outrun them, especially the twins. She might as well give up before there was a blade at her neck.

"I'm not a guard," she shouted back, standing and raising her hands above her head. "I won't turn you in."

She felt the hair rising on the back of her neck under the Rangers' scrutiny. She had only seen them through her computer screen so it was surreal for them to be standing before her now.

"I wasn't going to accuse a teenager of being part of the military," Jacques said after he got a good look at her. He stepped forward while the others took defensive stances. "But that doesn't mean you won't turn us in. Please identify yourself. We've come too far to let anyone stop us now."

"I'm not here to stop you. I'm entering the walls myself," she admitted. "If you'd like, I could guide you."

The young blond man raised an eyebrow, adjusted his glasses, then glanced at his companions. "Have you been inside before?"

"No." Obviously not. "But I've lived here for the last ten years. My uncle is in charge of monitoring the walls and ensuring no one gets in." She was tempted to let them know about the constant tug she felt in her heart, leading toward both the forest and her mother, but it would no doubt make her sound like a madwoman.

"So if you haven't been inside, you're just as clueless as we are." Jacques sighed and waved her away. "Sorry. We don't need a guide."

"Hey," Leon interrupted. "If she's going inside anyway, we can still take her with us." He flashed a bright smile at Lili, ever the charmer. "We could protect her."

She liked the sound of that but the others didn't seem impressed.

"She'll slow us down. We can't afford a liability in such a dangerous, unknown area," Jacques replied.

"I can take care of myself. I won't get in your way. I promise." She turned so he could see her backpack. "I came prepared."

Now he definitely didn't look willing to let her tag along.

She focused on the others, pleading with her eyes. Viktor looked hesitant to form any opinion—he was too focused on the door—and the twins looked split. Smiling Aidyn looked happy to have her but the somber Kaidyn had his arms crossed, ready to tie her up so she couldn't follow them.

"The more the merrier," Leon added.

"What exactly is your motive for coming?" Jacques interrupted his friend. "Fame? Wealth? Curiosity?"

"I'm looking for my parents," she admitted. "They went in ten years ago and I want to know if they're still alive."

"And you know the risks?" Jacques asked, though he looked more convinced now. Even the twins looked surprised. "If you don't prove to be an asset, we'll leave you behind."

"I won't be and I know the risks," Lili insisted, nodding enthusiastically. "I wouldn't dare go in there unprepared."

"Fine." Jacques turned away, satisfied.

Now it seemed like only Kaidyn was debating whether they should bring her along. He'd always struck her as the most cautious one, resembling a cat, so she wasn't surprised.

"Why are you guys here?" she asked. "Filming a documentary?"

Leon grinned. "Kind of. I'm here for the fame and riches our discoveries will bring."

"And to research the mysteries of the forest," Jacques added calmly.

"My brother and I are looking for someone," Aidyn said. "They went in a year ago and never came back, just like your parents."

"And Viktor was dragged along because he didn't want to get left behind," Leon said, grabbing the red-haired boy again and squeezing him despite the young man's protests. "We all have different motives so you should fit in just fine."

Lili tried to smile but could tell only two people wanted her in the group: Leon and Aidyn. Still, regardless of how they felt, this was the most advantageous option. Sure, she was using them, but perhaps she could prove useful in the future.

"I'll go in first," she offered. "So you guys won't have to argue about it anymore."

"Nah, that won't do." Leon pulled her into their circle. "We'll need one of the crew on camera for the first step. Have to keep up the illusion that we're all hot and single, right?"

Jacques rolled his eyes and sighed. "Leon will go in first, as he always does. Aidyn will follow in case there's a threat, then Kaidyn will go last to watch our backs. We've already discussed this. Leon was just bugging Viktor earlier to get a rise out of him."

"Wait, you weren't serious?" Viktor shouted and tried to hit the much bigger Leon again. He was unsuccessful, of course. Leon dodged his attack like it was nothing.

"Okay. If you need me to do anything, just let me know," Lili offered quietly, already fading into the background. "Otherwise, I'll hang back and stay away from the camera. Speaking of, are you sure your cameras will work inside the walls?" Whatever made the drones shut down might affect the cameras too.

"We're about to find out." Jacques motioned for the others to proceed.

"By the way," Lili ventured as Leon approached the door. "How did you guys get permission to come here? The military usually arrests anyone who tries to enter."

"We didn't get permission," Jacques answered. "We snuck in."

"Really?" She pointed over her shoulder at a camera hanging in the tree above them, currently filming them. "Then you don't mind being on camera?"

Jacques gasped and Viktor went white.

"You didn't know about the cameras?" she asked, a little surprised they weren't more thorough when researching the place.

"Of course we did." Jacques pointed at the more obvious cameras by the door, which they had avoided. Unfortunately, those were just the dummy cameras, meant to distract trespassers from the ones hidden in the trees.

Lili ignored the urge to tease them. "I assumed you deactivated it first," she said, referring to the one above their heads. "But if you didn't, there's probably a helicopter on its way to pick us up."

The glances the men shot at each other were hilarious. They'd been so confident a moment ago but now looked like children caught with their hands in the cookie jar.

"I think we have about five more minutes before they come after us," she offered. She'd already calculated that months ago.

"Dang it. Leon. Get moving," Jacques shouted, turning on his camera again and filming the entrance. "We don't have much time. Will they follow us in?" He directed the last question at Lili. She had become useful after all.

"No. They consider it a death trap. Anyone who enters is a lost cause." Even her.

"Ladies and gentlemen," Leon said, posing in front of the door and flexing for the camera. "You are about to witness the first man to ever enter the Vanishing Woods—" He paused dramatically. "—and survive."

"Just do it already, moron," Jacques said with a nervous chuckle.

Lili held her breath as Leon stepped through the door, all smiles, and vanished before their eyes. One second he was in front of them, the next it was like he had fallen through the floor or entered a portal.

"Well, that confirms that part," Jacques said. "Kaidyn, did you see anything strange happen when he went in?"

The twins, who had been standing closest to the door, shook their heads. "Other than him disappearing? No. He's just gone," Kaidyn answered.

"Curious. Maybe it's an optical illusion." Jacques motioned for Aidyn to go next, then followed after.

With the three talkative ones gone, Lili felt a little awkward, and it didn't help that Viktor was shaking too much to take a single step, even with grumpy Kaidyn trying to force him.

"Are you seriously chickening out now?" Kaidyn asked, leaning in front of the shorter guy and glaring at him. "Not even the girl is as afraid as you."

Lili wasn't sure if she liked being referred to as "the girl" but she hadn't given them her name so she ignored it.

She didn't know much about Viktor other than that he liked to cook so she wasn't sure how to encourage him. She knew he liked plants. Maybe that could work.

"There are lots of strange animals inside the walls," she told Viktor, drawing his attention away from the fear. "I've seen lots of strange things out here, like two-legged frogs and earless rabbits. I'm sure there are lots of strange plants in there too."

"Yeah," Viktor said in a wobbly voice. "*Venomous* plants that could eat us."

"Look, I appreciate the help." Kaidyn glanced at her. "But you don't need to get involved. You should go ahead. I'll take him with me." He frowned at Viktor. "I'll carry him if I have to."

"Fine by me." Shrugging, Lili brushed past them, not wanting to get caught by her uncle. She couldn't lose this one chance.

While she tried to pretend she wasn't nervous, she was biting her lip as she studied the entryway. The doorway towered over her and the sides were so thick she couldn't reach both sides with her hands.

After staring at the empty forest within, she put her hand forward, expecting to feel something like water or electricity. There had to be something that explained how the people disappeared when they entered.

But she felt nothing—only air.

"We don't have all day" Kaidyn warned.

His deep voice frightened her more than the doorway, so she did as commanded and stepped through. As soon as she moved past the wall, the three men who had entered ahead of her popped back into view. They were standing a few feet away, waiting for her. When she looked back, she couldn't see Kaidyn and Viktor, who had been behind her a moment ago. Strange.

But the weirdest thing she saw immediately after stepping through the doorway were statues, all of them in various stances and locations around the doorway. They were people clothed in various outfits, some wearing hiking gear and others in winter coats, t-shirts, or even long robes that looked like they belonged in history books. Every part of them, including their clothes, was made of light grey stone. Their faces looked so real, their expressions so lifelike, that it was terrifying. Some of them looked tired or without the will to live but most of them had mouths open in silent screams, their hands reaching for the exit.

They almost made her consider going back.

There were also a few broken drones at their feet. That answered one question, at least.

"We're trying to figure out what these statues symbolized," Jacques told her as she stared at the pieces of art. "Their feet look like they're growing right out of the grass. Whoever placed them here must have dug holes underneath so they wouldn't fall over with time."

"I think they're tributes to the people who used to live here," Aidyn told her, smiling brightly.

"Or they're the people who went missing," Leon said in a dramatic, almost silly tone.

"If that was the case, there'd be hundreds, not dozens," Jacques interjected, tapping the head of one of the statues. "Though we can't take that out of consideration. My personal hypothesis is that they might be a warning, though I couldn't tell you what the warning is."

Regardless of what they meant or how they got there, the statues creeped Lili out. Plus, she had the strangest sense she'd seen them before, as if from a dream she'd forgotten.

While they waited for Viktor and the second twin to arrive, Lili took her first look at the interior of the forest. While the trees outside were average with brown or white trunks—their green leaves no different from every other part of Canada—the trees inside had leaves tinged with purple and blue, though the green was still present. The bark on some trunks was white and crimson as well, though the red shades were so dark she wouldn't have noticed the color from afar. The musty scent continued past the doorway, though it had a tinge of acidity to it now.

There were a few yellow birds flying around the tree tops but their cries were warped, like they were singing backward. It sent a shiver up her spine.

"What's taking them so long?" Jacques asked, his voice overpowering the birds.

"I think Viktor's too scared," Leon said with a concerned laugh. "Should we go back out to help him?"

"Kaidyn will help him. He'd never leave anyone behind," Aidyn replied confidently, his faith in his brother unyielding.

Just as he said, Kaidyn stepped through the doorway with Viktor hanging over his shoulder, a scowl on his face and eyes closed in embarrassment. Kaidyn bore no expression but the others were laughing enough to compensate for him.

"Glad you made it," Jacques said as Kaidyn dropped Viktor on the ground. "So, now that we're all together again—" He pulled a map from his pocket while Aidyn recorded the statues with another camera. "It should take around ten days to reach the other end of the wall. We're hoping to encounter survivors on the way so we can interview them and figure out why no one ever leaves."

"You're sure there will be survivors?" Lili asked hesitantly, not wanting to mention the state she found her mother in back then. It might make them consider retreating.

Jacques shot her a dismissive look, like he didn't appreciate a total stranger questioning him. "There has to be. Look around. This is just a normal forest, albeit a strangely colorful one." Jacques pointed at the trees behind them, then put his map back in his pocket. "And if everyone's dead, I'm sure we'll at least find their remains."

"Jacques." Kaidyn pulled the leader aside so the other three boys couldn't hear. He was still in earshot of Lili but didn't seem to care. "What's up with these statues?"

"Leon thinks they're what remain of the people who came in," Jacques said, phrasing it like a joke but his voice wobbled at the last word, hinting at his true fears.

Kaidyn frowned. Lili could tell he'd thought the same. "What if Leon's right? What if they used to be real people?"

"What do you mean? I touched one of them. It was definitely stone."

Lili glanced at the statues again, still in awe at how lifelike they were.

"I'm just saying. If things are unnatural in this forest, why not these statues too?"

"Are you suggesting they might come to life when our backs are turned?" Jacques asked, chuckling darkly even as he continued studying them intently.

"I don't know, but we should be careful," Lili interrupted. Kaidyn glared at her as she said this, his expression the same as Jacques's earlier but with unrestrained malice.

"We'll have to keep watches while we sleep. I don't trust anything in here," Kaidyn said, his tone implying he included her in that statement.

"Understood." Jacques shifted his pack and took the camera from Aidyn, then brought the focus back to their journey. "Let's get moving. We only have eight hours before sundown. I want to document at least one important discovery before that happens."

"Roger." Both Leon and Aidyn saluted him comically while Viktor shivered, sticking close to the stronger members of the group.

Lili found herself hanging back again, staying at least a couple feet away from the team as they began their westward journey. Jacques led the way, using a compass in the beginning but getting frustrated when it became unreliable, the arrow refusing to stay in one direction for long.

Lili was sure about one thing now: there was a reason no one ever made it out. The air in here reeked of death. Now they just had to figure out how this forest worked so they could avoid getting themselves killed too.

Episode 3

The first sign of civilization they encountered was a red tent, or rather, its remains. The fabric was torn to shreds and next to it was a ring of rocks forming a campfire. A wild animal must have ripped the place apart. The question was, had someone been inside the tent when it happened?

Lili was the first to reach the tent so she bent down to move the cloth, hoping to find traces of its owner, but Jacques stopped her.

"Hold on," he said, motioning for her to step back and muttering a French word she didn't know. "We'll take it from here."

Lili nodded and stepped back, only now becoming aware of the camera in Jacques's hand. He didn't want her in the shot. Plus, they didn't have any reason to trust someone they had just met.

"Looks like whoever camped here was attacked," Jacques said as he pulled the tent open. "Kaidyn, Aidyn, Leon. Keep an eye out for any threats."

Lili watched Jacques uncover a small bag stuck in the mud, as well as a few discarded pieces of clothing next to it. One was a dirty bra and the other was a pair of ripped jeans. Inside the small bag was a wallet, though it was empty aside from a few credit cards and coins. The cards bore the name Daniel Athler and showed he was born twenty-eight years ago.

"Here." Jacques handed the wallet to Viktor, who put it in his massive pack.

"At least there aren't any bones," Lili commented, trying to lighten the mood. Kaidyn shot her an annoyed look.

"She's right," Leon said with a chuckle, facing away from them like a guard dog. "That's a good sign."

"If the owner of this tent was eaten, his body was likely dragged away by the animal that killed him." Jacques sighed and leaned away from the tent. "There's nothing else here."

Lili couldn't help feeling disappointed. She was going to ask what they should do about the campsite when Leon shouted.

"Something's coming," he warned.

Sure enough, Lili turned and spotted some dark figures several feet away, moving steadily toward them, their bodies low to the ground. It looked like a pack of wolves, their fur a dark grey. There was also something far larger and louder trailing along behind them.

Lili squinted at the threat, pulling her knife off the side of her pack and tensing her body as the bigger creature got close enough to identify.

Walking behind the pack of five was a massive wolf the size of a shed. It had long legs—three times the length of Lili's five-foot body—and its head was distorted like someone had broken its snout and never let it heal. Jagged cuts crisscrossed its body. The wounds were still bleeding, the crimson color overpowering the grey of its skin.

"Jacques," Leon said over his shoulder, pulling the axe off his back. "What is that?"

Jacques removed his glasses and put them in his pocket. "I haven't seen anything like that before." His eyes widened as the beast let out a wet, guttural roar that shook the ground. "It must be to blame for this camper's death. Explains why we didn't find the body. That thing could swallow a man whole."

"So, do we run?" Viktor asked, clearly hoping Jacques would say yes. He was already hiding behind his shield.

"We can't outrun it," Aidyn warned.

Leon grinned. "Then we'll have to fight it. You three should probably hide." He pointed at Lili, Jacques, and Viktor. The red-haired cook didn't need to be told twice and was already climbing up the nearest tree by the time Lili recovered from her paralysis.

The stench of blood and rotting meat wafted toward them. As Lili tried to climb a different tree, picking one with a thick trunk so it couldn't be knocked down easily, she noticed a hole in the beast's chest. Peeking through the open flesh was what looked like more skin and bones, though it appeared more human than bestial. She could see eyes inside, drenched in more blood.

"Lili, you need to stop staring and climb!" Jacques shouted. He had somehow already reached the top of his own tree and was readying an arrow to loose on one of the approaching wolves. The beasts were nearly upon the three fighters, who were armed and ready for battle.

"I got it," Lili shouted back, not wanting to appear weak like Viktor, who was clinging to his tree like a monkey. She had to prove herself useful or they might tell her to go back.

The regular wolves attacked first, leaping on the twins with snarls and lunging for their throats. Unfortunately for the beasts, the twins predicted their movements and dodged their attacks with relative ease, coming away with only a few scratches. At least, it looked that way to Lili's eyes. Watching them dodge the wolves and stab them in the back with their swords made them look nearly inhuman.

Leon was slower but managed to hit the wolves before they could reach him. He smashed two of them in the head, then when a third one bit his shoulder, Leon yanked the beast off with one hand and threw it against a tree. Lili heard the wolf's bones crunch on impact.

Now that she was seeing them move, the wolves looked weaker than regular ones. Perhaps that was a result of the forest's influence.

"These guys are incredible," she whispered, ignoring the wounds they'd already sustained from the wolves and focusing on how easily they had taken the beasts out. Each twin had killed one and Leon took care of the other three.

"I don't know what you're talking about," Jacques interrupted her awestruck thoughts. "Those morons almost lost an arm. They need to be more careful."

Lili didn't respond and began pulling some small branches off the tree so she could throw them at that giant wolf. It was a few feet away from Leon now. Its jaw dropped, ready to chomp his head off.

"Leon, behind you!" Jacques shouted. "And you're bleeding. Work together as a team from now on or you'll end up dead."

The three acknowledged him with nods, then Jacques loosed an arrow at the monster, hitting it in the eye. The wound did nothing to stop its movement. As it snapped at Leon, narrowly missing, Lili began to fear for the fighters' lives.

"You heard the boss!" Leon shouted and darted away from the beast. As he retreated, the twins circled around the creature. It took Lili a few seconds to notice but the twins were carrying a thin wire between them, which they were wrapping around the beast's long legs as they ran. When Jacques's second arrow embedded itself in the creature's shoulder, the wolf began to tilt, its legs completely tangled.

"Wait," Jacques shouted at Leon, who was glancing over his shoulder to see if he had time to hit the beast. "Not yet."

The giant wolf collapsed on its knees as the rope tightened around it, but then it lowered its head, grabbed the wire in its bleeding teeth, and bit it in two, releasing itself.

Lili gulped. It was intelligent.

As the monster turned toward the twins, who were still within range, Lili threw the sticks she had collected, hoping they would be enough of a distraction to help them escape. Unfortunately, as the pieces of wood bounced off its skull, the wolf didn't even flinch. It was too focused on the thin boys darting around it.

"Don't get involved, Lili," Leon ordered, pointing his axe at her as he turned to face the wolf. "I'm the one it should focus on. Just stay put."

Lili froze again, clinging to her branch and wondered if she'd somehow made things worse. Had her interference put them in greater danger?

She saw the twins make eye contact, then they started climbing the trees in unison. Her heart raced as they scrambled up the trunks, narrowly avoiding the long claws tearing up the bark in an attempt to grab them. Poor Aidyn yelped as one of the claws snagged on his ankle and nearly pulled him down but one of Jacques's arrows hit the wolf's paw and it released him.

Leon charged with a shout, his axe above his head and angled for the creature's back. "Get your paws off my friend, you bastard!"

"Leon, wait," Jacques shouted but it was too late. Leon drove his axe into the wolf's rear, embedding it in its flesh and carving out a spurt of blood that hit the young man in the face. The wolf turned and smacked Leon with a massive paw, sending him flying past Lili's tree. In that moment, the wolf's movements felt almost human, like it had thrown a punch. Lili cringed when Leon landed on his back, unconscious. He was still bleeding from his shoulder and there was a new cut across his face and chest.

"Moron." Jacques loosed another arrow, then turned his attention to Lili and Viktor. "Lili, that thing will eat Leon if we don't stop it. I need you to distract it while I think of a plan. Get down there and run in the opposite direction, away from the twins. I would ask Viktor to do it instead but he'd die of fright. Now go!" Viktor looked like he wanted to help but was too scared to move.

Lili pressed her fists against her chest, petrified. Even now, the massive wolf was approaching them with the axe hanging from its back. Its hind legs weren't moving anymore but it was dragging itself forward with its front paws. It would be upon Leon in seconds. He was still unconscious.

"Got it," Lili said. "I won't let you down." Leaving her pack hanging from the branches and taking only her knife, she leapt from the tree. Her ankle twisted uncomfortably upon landing but she ignored the pain and sprinted away from the wolf, shouting as she went.

She lost sight of the others as she ran, too busy dodging trees and listening to the crashes of the monster chasing her. It was fast and its painful groaning only filled her with more fear. It sounded like a man screaming within a wolf's growl.

"Cut off its head!" she heard Jacques shout. Her lungs stung and her feet ached, slowing her pace. The thing was almost at her heels now. Branches and dead leaves grabbed at her shoes, slowing her down. She expected to feel its claws in her legs in a moment.

"Mom," she panted. "Help me."

There was a yell from the twins behind her, then she heard a load bellow from the beast.

The snapping of sticks and crunch of leaves stopped.

She looked over her shoulder, still running. Her breath burned her throat.

The twins were standing over the monster's collapsed body. Both of their swords were embedded in the thing's neck and they were working together to saw off its head.

The twins' pants were drenched with blood by the time they finished and while Aidyn looked relieved, Kaidyn was glaring at the monster beneath his boots, like he wasn't satisfied. Lili only stopped moving when she saw the angry twin kick its head and it didn't react. Even when she acknowledged that the danger was gone, her heart refused to slow down.

"Nice job, Kaidyn," Aidyn said, high fiving his brother before running back to the others, who were crouching around an unconscious

Leon. Only Kaidyn remained with the monster, leaning down to study its body.

"Thank you," Lili said, doubling back and nearly gagging from the blood's stench.

"I didn't do it for you," he muttered, yanking his sword from the corpse.

Now she understood why Kaidyn never spoke on camera. He'd scare the fans away. "Okay—"

"I don't think you should be here at all. You're not cut out for this."

She frowned. "I know I'm not the most experienced but I just helped—"

"Running away won't work every time. We need people who have actual skills." His dark eyes turned on her. "You're dressed like you're on a camping trip, not a dangerous mission. I suggest you leave before you get yourself and the rest of my friends killed."

"What?" Now he was taking things too far. "What about Viktor? He didn't fight either."

"He's here because he's an expert when it comes to plants and animals. He provides our food and clean water. What do you offer, besides acting as bait?"

Lili stepped back, trying to figure out what she had done to anger him. Did he hate her simply because she wasn't an expert in something? Most normal people weren't. Besides, she had a reason to enter this forest.

The twin either didn't notice her discomfort or ignored it as he removed his brother's sword from the wolf's head and rejoined the others.

"Will I even last a day before they kick me out?" she muttered as she watched Kaidyn join the group. He started speaking angrily to the rest of them, voicing his feelings about her departure and pointing at Leon's injuries to emphasize whatever he was saying. His words prompted Aidyn and Viktor to look over at her sadly but Jacques was shaking his head and saying something in return. Was he defending her?

She took one last look at the giant wolf and the red flesh under its neck, where bones and grey skin were protruding. Doing so made her want to vomit.

"Leon's gonna be okay," Viktor assured her as she joined them. He was avoiding her eyes, focusing on Leon's unconscious body. "It's just a few cuts and bruises. Nothing that won't heal." He was currently rubbing a liquid on the wounds, cleaning them before bandaging them. As he opened his pack and rummaged through all the bottles, clothes, and smaller bags within, she understood why his backpack was the biggest out of the group.

"Let's get away from all these corpses," Jacques said. "Aidyn, Kaidyn. You carry Leon. We can cover more ground before it gets dark. Viktor, do you want to grab one of those wolf carcasses for food?"

Viktor wrinkled his nose. "We have plenty of food. I don't want to start eating those things until we get desperate."

"Fair enough." Jacques looked from Lili to Kaidyn, who was still scowling at her. "We'll discuss our future plans *after* we've made camp. It's too late to turn back today anyway."

Lili didn't like delaying the question of what would happen to her, but she wanted to get away from all the dead bodies too. The smell might attract more of those monsters.

She had a plan in mind already. If they decided to send her home tonight or tomorrow, she'd set out on her own. She didn't need them. They were just a safer alternative to going solo.

But going alone, even with the tug of her mother's soul leading her, would be a nightmare.

Episode 4

Leon was awake and walking around by the time they set up camp in a small clearing, far away from where they'd left the corpses. He was bugging the others for sympathy and receiving none except from Aidyn, who gave him some friendly pats on the back while they set up their orange tents. Viktor was preparing a campfire so he could cook some canned meat and vegetables for the group. Lili prepared her own tent, keeping it separate from the rest but close enough to avoid any risk of attack. They hadn't spotted any more wild animals on their way here, but she could sometimes hear distant cries and knew the animals were never too far behind.

Once everything was set up and the group was seated around the campfire, Jacques finally began the discussion of what they should do moving forward. Lili sat next to Leon this time, feeling the most comfortable with him and Aidyn since they didn't dislike having her around.

"On to our first order of business. Leon. Are you feeling okay?" Jacques asked, dipping a spoon into the cup of stew Viktor had created with his canned ingredients.

Leon shot him a thumbs up. "I'll be right as rain tomorrow."

"That reminds me, I think it'll rain tonight," Viktor muttered, already fiddling with some empty bottles in his pack. "I need to set some of these out to collect rainwater."

"Good to hear. Now then, it's time to discuss what we just saw." Jacques put his glasses back on and held up a notebook, in which he had drawn a somewhat accurate recreation of the wolf monster. "This creature is like nothing I've seen before and I'm honestly surprised it didn't kill any of us. We got lucky and I doubt that will happen again."

"We can handle it," Leon said confidently.

"Says the person who fell unconscious," Kaidyn muttered, yawning.

"I'm afraid you're being too optimistic, Leon. If that wolf is any indication, this forest is full of monstrosities and every one of them will pose a threat. We're already weak so I suggest we carefully reconsider our journey into this forest."

"Wait. Reconsider our journey? *All* of us?" Kaidyn frowned.

"*All* of us." Jacques shot him a stern look. "There's still time to turn back. The reason no one's ever made it out of here alive must be due to those monsters. That means we can still survive if we leave now. We've already got plenty of footage. We could still gain fame and fortune on the outside."

Kaidyn continued to scowl, unconvinced. He seemed set on Lili leaving, either to protect her from danger or to avoid letting her slow them down, but he was determined to stay.

"Wait."

All eyes turned on Lili, her hands stretched out in front of Jacques to stop him. She gulped, hating the attention but unwilling to let them give up so easily.

"We can't turn back already," she continued. "I'm not here for fame and fortune like the rest of you. I'm here to find my parents. They might still be alive and need our help." It was selfish of her but she didn't want to do this alone now that she'd seen what they were up against.

"Or they're dead," Jacques countered.

For the first time, Kaidyn's frown disappeared. "I don't want to leave either," he cut in, on her side for once. "Not until I find the bodies of our siblings."

He was actually agreeing with her. Everything in Lili's body told her to keep going. "I understand wanting to go back but even if you guys leave, I'm going to continue on. If I give up on my mother and father now, I'll regret it for the rest of my life."

"So would I," Aidyn added excitedly, joining her and his brother. "We can't leave Max and Minnie behind just because it's dangerous. If anything, it gives us more reasons to find them."

Max and Minnie must be the siblings Kaidyn and Aidyn were searching for.

Jacques sighed and squeezed the bridge of his nose. "I'm trying to save you, you morons. Your families wouldn't want you to die for so little. It's unlikely that your parents—" He pointed at Lili. "—or your siblings—" He pointed at the twins. "—are still alive."

"I don't believe they're dead," Lili interjected. "I can feel it." Even now, she could sense her mother's presence, as though the woman was watching over them from the shadows. The further into this forest they went, the more confident she became that she was going in the right direction.

"Lili," Jacques said calmly. "Kaidyn doesn't think you're fit to continue. He doesn't want to see you die and, frankly, I could say the same for Viktor. Neither of you can defend yourselves."

"I don't care if I die," Viktor commented, looking up from his bag. Something unreadable was in his eyes. "Besides, we've been over this. I'm here to keep you idiots fed. Starvation and food poisoning pose more of a threat than wolves."

"Plus, none of us are professional fighters anyway," Leon backed him up. "The only training the twins have is from their dad and all I know is what I learned in my kendo classes. If you think about it, none of us are fit to be here, including you."

"And I'll do my best to stay out of your way," Lili added quickly. "I'll obey your orders without question."

Jacques sighed. "Kaidyn?" He turned to the twin, who was resting his chin on his fist and staring at the ground. "What's your answer? Does Lili stay?"

Lili sat straighter, hoping he could at least empathize with her motives.

"I don't like it," Kaidyn muttered. "But I guess we have no choice. We all have our reasons to be here and we're stronger as a group." He stood up before anyone could argue and entered the tent he shared with his brother. Once he was out of sight, everyone breathed a sigh of relief.

"Don't mind him." Leon patted Lili on the back. "He gets grumpy when he hasn't had enough sleep."

"He's just looking out for everyone," Aidyn added quietly. "I'll take the first watch, Jacques. You guys can go to bed."

"Very well. If there are no more complaints, I'll be turning in," Jacques said. "We'll wake at sunrise and continue west." Saying goodnight, their leader went to bed and Leon and Viktor left soon after. Only Lili and Aidyn remained in front of the fire, listening to the distant howls of wolves.

"Your last name is Nilson, isn't it?" Aidyn asked her quietly, poking the fire with a stick.

"How did you know?"

"You said your parents disappeared and Nilson was the name of the couple who vanished ten years ago with that hiking group."

"That's right."

"Do you really believe they're still alive after ten years?"

"I do." More than belief, she *knew* they were alive. She had seen her mother with her own eyes, even if the memory was fuzzy. "I just don't know why they never came back."

"Same here. My brother and sister planned to return after two weeks but we never heard from them again. I know they wouldn't stay here unless there was an important reason."

"Or they died," Lili whispered but Aidyn grabbed her arm and shook his head.

"That doesn't make sense. There were several soldiers who entered the walls nine years ago. I'm sure they were well-equipped to fight monsters like these. The likelihood of them dying feels low." He started wiping blood off his sword. "I'm sure there's another reason," he said confidently.

"Maybe there's a trap further in."

He nodded, looking out at the darkness around them. The croaks of frogs and chirps of crickets were unnaturally deep and drawn out. "If there is a trap, at least I'll know they didn't abandon us. I know it sounds dark but I'd rather they died than chose to leave us behind."

"I feel the same." Lili smiled. This was the first time she'd told someone about her loss without feeling pitied. Her uncle never talked about her parents and sometimes acted like they never existed in the first place. He didn't like discussing how he felt about what happened. "Do you want me to stay with you during your watch, Aidyn? I can stay up for a few more hours."

"No, I'm used to this." He gave her a smile and salute, his cheery attitude rubbing off on her. "See you tomorrow, Lili."

Episode 5

"I still have a bad feeling about those statues." Kaidyn's voice cut through Lili's dreams.

"Same here but commenting on it will just worry the others. We shouldn't say anything until we figure out what they are and who put them there."

There was a pause. "What if the same thing could happen to us?"

Lili opened her eyes but remained in her sleeping bag. She could see two shadows on the orange wall of her tent, one taller than the other. It sounded like Kaidyn and Jacques. They were the second watch. It was still dark so she must have only slept for a couple hours.

"I can't be sure," Jacques said. "I don't like the thought of them being real humans."

"They looked too realistic to be anything but," Kaidyn muttered. "And the looks on their faces...I can't understand why someone would intentionally carve them to look like that. They have to be—"

"Let's not worry about it for now. We haven't seen any more of them so it shouldn't be a problem." Jacques sighed. "We have enough things to worry about as it is."

The conversation dropped off for a few minutes, then Kaidyn spoke up again. "I have a feeling walking out of here won't be as easy as we originally thought."

"How so?"

"There must be a reason not a single person exited."

It was horrible to hear her fears confirmed. Growing up, it was easy to assume she'd be different, that she was smarter or luckier than those who came before and would make it out alive, but the reality was that she was just another tally to be marked by her uncle, another tragic loss.

As the pair started discussing supplies, she drifted off to sleep again, dreaming about her mother. She was reliving that day by the wall six years ago, when she saw her mom for the last time. This time, however, instead of leaving without saying a word, her mother opened her mouth to speak. She leaned forward, moving her lips, but no sound came out.

Lili called out to her, telling her she couldn't understand what she was saying, but it only made her mother start shouting instead, still silent. Her mouth was wide open now and the veins on her neck were protruding like vines. Lili wished she could hear her but after one more minute, her mother gave up and returned to the Vanishing Forest just like in the original memory.

By the time Lili jerked out of her sleep, the sun was up and she could hear the others packing their things, ready to get moving again.

"We already ate," Viktor informed her as she exited her tent, her hair messy. He handed her a protein bar before hefting his pack onto his back. "We're leaving in twenty minutes."

"Sorry for not waking you," Leon said. "We were shy about entering a girl's tent so we tried being as loud as possible to wake you up."

"You weren't supposed to tell her that," Viktor hissed. "It makes us look like children."

"Some of us still are, technically," Aidyn said with a laugh.

"Says the youngest in the group," Viktor countered.

Nothing out of the ordinary happened for the first two hours of their journey. They encountered some strange birds with reptilian mouths instead of beaks and Viktor poked some steaming purple apples they found hanging from a tree. They did discover a few strange stone bowls lying on the ground in various spots, resembling shrines or water collectors, but since the bowls were empty and uninteresting, Jacques merely filmed them and moved on.

"I don't think we should eat anything that grows here," Viktor warned them as he sniffed a black apple from a tree, then tossed it over his shoulder. "Unless it's a last resort. Based on the state of that wolf, I don't think it's wise to taste anything here."

There weren't any signs of civilization until they reached what looked like a path, though there weren't any fresh footprints in the dirt. The only reason they knew it was a path was because the trees didn't grow in it and there were some stumps with clear cuts nearby, though Viktor said they looked to have been chopped down years ago.

"Hold on. I see something." Leon stepped in front of everyone and pointed to their right. Lili could vaguely make out what looked like another stone wall through the trees. As they crept closer, she could tell it wasn't smooth like the walls of the forest. This was clearly formed from crudely stacked stones and, judging by the lack of greenery around it, it wasn't built too long ago, just like the cut tree stumps.

"I see an entry through there," Jacques whispered, pointing at a small section of the wall that was open, granting just enough space for a single person to pass through. "This might be the home of our first Vanishing Woods citizens. I'd like to go inside and meet them, though we should exercise caution." Lili could tell he was excited. "It might make for a good interview."

"Aidyn and I will take a look around," Kaidyn said and ran off with his brother before Jacques could respond.

Leon and Viktor hung back while Jacques peered through the entrance, peeking inside. After a few seconds, he nodded at Lili and the other two.

"There's a wooden cottage in there. I'm going to knock on the front door." Jacques paused to rid his clothes of wrinkles and ran a hand through his long hair to flatten any strays. Seeing him do this reminded Lili that Jacques wasn't just an explorer—he was an entertainer. "Leon, watch our backs. Viktor, ready the camera. If something interesting happens, I want it on film."

"And what about her?" Viktor nodded at Lili, looking a little resentful that she was still with them and not pulling her weight. "What's her job?"

"She's coming with me, aren't you Lili?" Jacques flashed her an award-winning smile and pulled her closer. Unlike Viktor, he showed no qualms about being welcoming now. "I tend to intimidate people. She'll help put them at ease."

"You? Intimidating?" Leon laughed, but winked at Lili to show it was all in good fun. "We'll wait for you here. If it's dangerous, give me a shout."

"Don't worry about a thing," Jacques whispered as they walked up to the cottage. It had no windows and the floor was held up on stilts and rocks so it didn't touch the earth below. "I'll do all the talking. I'm just bringing you with me so the others don't start doubting you again." He shot her a smaller, genuine smile, which put her at ease. "Don't worry. We'll look out for you, just like you did for us in the fight. Follow my orders and you'll be fine."

"Thanks," she whispered, clasping her hands together while he knocked on the door. She hoped he was right.

The burly man who opened the door was tall, muscular, and dressed in dirty brown clothes. The outfit looked like something her parents would have worn when they were younger, like they did during their final hiking trip. Lili didn't recognize this man, though.

"Can I help you?" he asked, looking over their shoulders at Leon and Viktor, who were unsuccessfully trying to hide behind the wall. "Are you new?"

"New?" Jacques shot a glance at Lili, then smiled at the stranger. The cottage owner's dirty face and unkept hair made Jacques' cleanliness stand out. "My name is Jacques Abreo and I'm a member of the Rural Rangers. We're a group who makes a living investigating abandoned areas."

"So you decided to come here and film it?" The man chuckled darkly and ran a hand over his mouth. "You never should have come. You won't be leaving now."

"Oh? Mind telling me why that is? You're the first person I've encountered here."

The man hesitated, then looked back into the cabin. As he did, Lili spotted two more people standing inside. The first was a short, brown-haired woman who looked around forty years old, the same age as the man. She was wearing a dress as dirty as his. Clinging to her leg was a small, blond-haired boy burying his face in her skirt. He couldn't be older than five.

"You aren't from the village?" the man asked, suspicious. "I told Kingsley I didn't want anything to do with him. I left for a reason."

"I don't know a Kingsley." Jacques's smile faltered and he laughed nervously, sensing the man's obvious defensiveness. "As I said, we came from the wall and just have a few questions. By the way, is it alright if we film you for our documentary?"

"No point," the man answered. "You won't be taking it back outside." He sighed. "I suppose you can come in but not for long. I won't have you sniffing about my home or family. I don't take kindly to thieves neither."

"Of course. We wouldn't dream of it." Jacques grinned, patted Lili on the back—probably to avert his own nervousness—then motioned for Leon and Viktor to come forward. "I appreciate your hospitality. So it's a no to the camera?"

"No cameras. We came here to spend our final days in peace." The bear-like man looked down on Jacques and narrowed his eyes, making it clear he would have his way. He was even bigger than Leon, so Lili was glad Jacques hadn't pushed his buttons.

The cabin was small with only an entry room and two smaller bedrooms behind it. Lili glanced around the outside of the building before heading in. She noticed an outhouse out back, though it was still within the protection of the walls. There were also some buckets resting atop stilts, holding the rainwater from last night.

"Only a few questions," the man said, leading all four of them inside. As they entered, the woman pulled her child to the corner of the room and stared at them from afar, eyes wide with fear despite Jacques greeting her with a friendly hello.

Inside the main room were several plastic containers of water alongside some buckets of dirt. A few of them contained sprouting plants. There were also long strips of dry meat hanging from the ceiling.

"Honey, why don't you take the plants into the sun?" the man asked as he motioned for the newcomers to take a seat on the floor.

The woman did as he asked. She and her child grabbed the potted plants and scurried outside without saying a word. As they moved past, Lili got a good look at the child and noticed how grey his skin was. He must not get a lot of sunlight inside this windowless home.

"So, when did you arrive?" the man asked gruffly, sitting on the floor in front of Jacques.

"Yesterday," Jacques answered. As he talked, Leon sat next to him like an obedient puppy and Viktor started leaning toward the remaining plants to study them.

"I thought the military prevented new people from entering," the man continued.

"Oh, well, they seem to have slacked off in recent years. We got through without issue. How long have you been here?" She could tell Jacques was changing the subject quickly to avoid mentioning how they broke the law.

"Nine years. We entered right after the place was discovered." He huffed. "You never should have come. You had your whole lives ahead of you. Now you'll never get to live them."

"Tell me more about that," Jacques said, his voice like a news announcer. "Why is it that people can't leave this place? More importantly, why haven't *you* left?"

"Simple. You try to leave? You die." He sniffed and glanced out the open door at his wife, who was now playing with the child outside. "If leaving was that easy, we would have done so long ago."

"How do people die?"

"The forest takes you," he whispered, his words sending a shiver down Lili's spine. "It steals your blood—your body. It takes you as its own and digests you like you're nothing."

"Are you talking about the monsters that roam the forest? The ones eating people? We encountered one, actually, and killed it," Jacques said.

"It wasn't so tough," Leon added.

"The monsters kill some people but they're just a tool." The man's eyes darkened as he stared at the ground. "No matter what you do, don't try to leave the walls. You stand a better chance against the monsters."

Viktor rolled his eyes. "If you're gonna be vague, old man, don't bother answering at all."

"Viktor, don't be rude—" Jacques said but was cut off by Viktor again.

"Can we eat the plants growing outside?" he asked, eyes alight with a need to learn about his favorite subject.

The man shook his head. "Do not eat anything that grows from the ground. It's cursed. You can eat the animals. If you grow plants from seeds that came from the outside world, ensure they never make contact with the ground. The same goes for the water. It's the reason we haven't died."

"What happens if we eat the plants from the forest?" Viktor asked, his excited curiosity almost eerie compared to his typical attitude.

"It will make you sick. I knew a man in the village who ate some berries and later tried to cut them out of him with a knife."

"You keep mentioning a village," Jacques cut in. "Where is that? Who lives there?"

"If you keep following the road," the man pointed outside to the path they had found earlier, "It will take you there, but I advise against it unless you plan to stay there forever. The man who runs it is a madman."

"Kingsley? The man you mentioned?"

"Yes. He won't let you leave his village under pain of death. He's become so afraid of the monsters that it's turned him into a tyrant. I try to warn anyone who comes by, though you're the first I've seen in almost a year."

Lili was still thinking about a man cutting up his own skin because he ate some berries. What would happen to them if they ran out of food? Would it be better to starve? This man seemed to think so.

"I have a question," she said quietly, freezing when his shadowed eyes turned toward her. "Have you seen any of these people before?" She pulled a photo of her parents and their hiking friends from her pocket. It had been taken the night before they disappeared.

The man took the photo and frowned as he studied them, focusing on her mother. Then he shook his head and handed it back. "They're dead," he said. "Have to be."

"When did you last see them alive? This woman was alive at least six years ago."

His frown deepened and she could tell he was studying *her* now instead. Did he know what she'd seen that day in her childhood? Had he seen the same thing?

"Anyone who enters this forest dies eventually. Don't look for anyone, don't go deeper. Just learn to survive and try not to anger the forest."

Lili wanted to say more, to argue, but she could feel Jacques staring at the side of her head and knew he was growing suspicious too, so she backed off.

"I'm surprised a child managed to survive here," Jacques said in a flattering tone. "You must be a great protector."

Instead of responding positively, the man glared at Jacques and got to his feet. "It's time for you to leave. Don't come crawling to us for help if you find yourself in trouble. Everyone has to look out for themselves in here."

"But—"

"Get out!"

Jacques glanced at his friends, thoroughly confused as to what he said wrong, but they all exited without further protest. Lili noticed the little boy watching them from behind his mother's legs as they left. He was staring at them with wide eyes and even smiled a little when she made eye contact. He was cute.

"That was strange," Jacques commented once they were on the other side of the wall. The man shut the cottage door once his family was back inside, dismissing them. "But at least we learned some things. I'm also relieved other people have managed to survive in here. And for nine years, no less."

"But we can't eat the plants," Viktor said glumly. "Way to spoil all my fun."

Lili was glad she had brought her own seeds. Now all she needed was something to grow it in, which might prove difficult since the man said they couldn't grow them in the regular dirt. She still didn't understand why that was so dangerous. Was the ground poisonous?

"I think he's hiding things from us," Jacques whispered as they searched for the twins, who still hadn't returned from their scouting mission. "But I'm not sure what. He didn't explain how people died when they left the walls."

Lili might have an idea. It might be what happened to her mother, morphing her body into something...else.

"Well, let's not risk going back until we get more answers." Viktor shrugged and, spotting the twins behind some bushes, waved them over. "Do we want to go to that village he mentioned? They might have answers."

"But the man claimed the village leader was dangerous," Lili added nervously. "It might not be safe." She didn't want to risk becoming trapped behind another wall. Her uncle had already done that to her for ten years.

"Nothing here is safe," Viktor grumbled. "I think this guy has the right idea, building this place and locking himself inside."

"We can't learn more about this forest if we hide," Jacques warned before pausing to explain everything they'd seen and heard to the twins. Aidyn seemed excited to learn that people could survive within the walls but Kaidyn looked concerned by what the man had said.

"Did you ask him about our siblings?" he asked Jacques and sighed when the answer was no. "Maybe I should ask him myself."

"He *did* tell Lili that her family is likely dead," Leon told the twin. "He'll probably say the same about Max and Minnie."

Kaidyn shot Leon a glare for putting his foot in his mouth. Aidyn looked devastated, his eyes watery.

"Let's head toward the village and study it from afar," Jacques said, swiftly moving their attention away from their siblings. "We'll decide what to do after. I don't think sticking around this cottage is a good idea since the owner's a little hostile. Are we in agreement?" Jacques waited for someone to say no. "In that case, let's press on."

Episode 6

That night, they set up camp again a few miles past the cabin. Leon took the first watch. Since Lili was too nervous to sleep, afraid to dream of her mother's decaying body again, she took a seat next to the large man and chatted with him while the sun went down. He was more than happy to have the company and told her all about his work with the Rural Rangers, as well as what he planned to do after this journey ended.

"I'm from England originally," he told her.

"I'm aware. You still have a bit of the accent." It was actually quite prominent, but she wasn't sure if that was what he wanted to hear.

"Dang. I thought I lost it after moving to America with my father as a teen. My mother's still in England with my sisters." That explained why he and the others traveled between England and America so often. She had assumed it was simply to visit various locations for their documentaries, but it seemed they had other motivations alongside it.

"And what do your parents think about all this?" She waved at the forest around them. As though waiting for the perfect moment, a bird screeched several feet away.

"My father likes the money my occupation brings," he said. "Though it hasn't been enough. I'm hoping to find some valuables here and take them home to pay for my sisters."

"Pay for them?"

"Both my sisters have heart problems," he explained, his cheerful tone countering his words. "And my parents can't afford the surgeries they need, so I'm hoping to take care of it."

"Oh." She was surprised he had a higher motive than simply pursuing fame, as he claimed when they first met. "I haven't heard anything about treasure in this forest."

"That's just because no one's taken it out. I'll be the first." He puffed his chest out, as though he had already accomplished this feat. "And even if there isn't anything to find, I'm hoping the fame will bring in enough money." He sighed before steeling himself. "I refuse to lose faith in this."

"Yeah." But how could one be positive in such a place? Hearing that man in the cottage rant about how no one ever made it out alive had scared her because, in her heart, she believed it to be true. This group wasn't special, even if the men here were famous and moderately good at defending themselves. What made them think they could escape when others hadn't?

Lili was falling into despair when Leon wrapped an arm around her shoulder and pulled her close. She was worried he might be trying to flirt until he shushed her and pointed into the darkness. A second later, she spotted movement behind one of the trees and held her breath. It wasn't a wolf. The eyes reflecting the light were too high.

"I think it's a child," Leon whispered, though he grabbed his axe for good measure.

"Maybe it's the kid from the cottage," she suggested. "Don't hurt him."

"I'm not planning on it. Hey! Boy! Come out in the open where we can see you."

Lili wanted to question Leon's forward way of dealing with the problem but it thankfully worked out, as the child stepped out from behind the tree and crept toward them. When he came into the light of the fire, Lili confirmed that it was indeed the little blond boy from the cabin.

"What are you doing here?" she asked, wary until she saw the innocent look on his face. His nose was scrunched up from trying not to cry and his reddened eyes were wide with fear.

"I got lost," he whispered, cradling his body with his hands. He must be cold. "Can't find Mom and Dad."

"Aww." Leon leaned down and picked up the boy without asking for permission. "We'll take you back. Why did you come all the way out here?"

"I wanted to see you," he said and pointed at Leon. "You're heroes."

Lili raised an eyebrow. The kid must be desperate for attention or any kind of entertainment. Being cooped up in a tiny cottage with monsters outside must be suffocating. "Should we take him back now or wait until daylight?" she asked.

Leon shrugged. "I—"

They all froze when they heard a strange clicking noise from afar, accompanied by the cries of cicadas. "I don't think Jacques wants us to go out at night," Leon continued quietly. "Some of the monsters might have night vision. Plus...I'm a little scared of the dark."

"Okay." Lili considered waking Jacques to ask what they should do since he seemed the most capable of coming up with quick solutions. But Leon's reasoning made sense, so she didn't protest when Leon sat back down and put the child on his lap. It was cute to see him play with the boy, competing in a thumb war and game of rock paper scissors. It was obvious he loved children and was used to entertaining them.

"What's your name?" Lili asked after the boy had settled down and looked ready to fall asleep in Leon's arms.

"Billy," the child said, yawning. "That's what they call me."

She smiled. He was adorable.

By the time the second watch started, the child was asleep, but when Kaidyn stepped out of his tent to take over, he spotted the child immediately and frowned. "How'd he get in here?"

"Wandered in," answered Leon. "Isn't he cute?"

"He belongs with his parents." Kaidyn glared at both of them, then peered out at the trees. It was still dark, though there were a few purple fireflies moving about. "Do his parents know he's gone?"

Both Lili and Leon shrugged.

"Well," Kaidyn continued. "You'll have to—" He paused, eyes still on the surrounding forest to the east. "Did you see that?"

"What?" Lili stood and followed his gaze. After a second, she spotted it too, a light far off in the distance. It swung about like a flashlight. "That might be his parents looking for him."

Kaidyn hesitated, then put his hands to his mouth and shouted. "Hey! We have your kid!"

"Hey!" Leon added, his voice a little louder, though it didn't seem to travel the way it should. It felt like the forest was muffling their voices.

There was no answer and the light moved out of sight.

"I think we should go after them," Kaidyn muttered, crawling back into the tent to grab his weapons. "If they don't come back, we can't return him and it'll delay us. We can't waste time now that we know food is scarce."

"I'll come with you," Lili offered, eager to help and prove herself useful.

"I move faster on my own."

"They haven't met you before so they might not trust you."

"Then Leon should come with me," Kaidyn said. "He has the kid."

Lili bit her lip. They'd already been over this. Leon was afraid to go out there. She shifted her weight from foot to foot, her fingers twitching nervously.

"The kid's sleeping," Leon whispered. "I don't want to wake him."

Kaidyn sighed, then motioned for Lili to follow him. "Hurry up. We don't want to lose them."

"Got it." Glad to be accepted, she took off after the twin into the dark. She brought her knife and flashlight but didn't use them, since the light of the moon and fireflies were enough to help her narrowly avoid the trees. Besides, anything in the distance that could be stalking them was beyond her range of vision.

They kept following the light, but the person carrying it was fast and while Kaidyn kept shouting to the person, they never responded. It was like the trees kept sucking the sound away before it reached the recipient.

Lili and Kaidyn followed them for nearly twenty minutes, never managing to catch up. It felt like the forest was playing with them, slowing their steps like they were in a dream.

After a while, Lili became completely exhausted and could only jog. Even Kaidyn was breathing heavily and finally stopped, bending over and leaning against a tree.

"Do you know how to get back?" Lili asked, hoping they hadn't gotten turned around in the dark.

"Well enough." Kaidyn wiped sweat from his forehead. "You?"

"Yes." She tapped her forehead and felt how wet it was from her own sweat. "I have a pretty good sense of direction. I grew up in the forest." Her uncle moved the trailer to different sections of the wall often, so she had learned to use the sun, moon, and moss locations on trees to guide her. She also had a connection to her mother, which drew her in a constant direction, though she wasn't dumb enough to fully rely on such a thing.

"If you grew up here, you should have realized coming in here was stupid," he muttered, then shook his head. "Sorry. We already settled that."

She got the sense he would never fully accept her but it didn't matter. She didn't need him to like her to work together. "Do you think they're headed for the wall?"

"Maybe, though Jacques said the man warned us not to go there. I don't see why he wouldn't follow his own advice." Kaidyn took a second to stretch, then motioned for her to continue. "Let's keep going. Stay close. I'm gonna run ahead to see if I can catch up to them."

As they took off again, she realized Kaidyn had been holding back for her sake. Whereas before he had been matching her pace, he was now rushing with little effort. After another ten minutes, she saw him stop completely and duck behind a thick tree. When she joined him, she realized why. The married couple from the cabin were several feet away, armed with flashlights and pistols. They were shouting at each other. It would be suicide to step out in the open now.

"Face it, Charles. He's gone. We shouldn't have taken him in the first place," the woman was shouting while waving her gun around. "We should just go back and forget it ever happened."

"And what? Continue wasting our lives away in that cage? Wait for a monster to kill us in the night?" The man's booming voice made his much shorter wife lean away from him. "He was all we had left!"

"He's gone, Charles." Tears streamed down the woman's face, reflecting the light of a passing firefly. "He's gone and there's nothing we can do to fix that."

"Then we should just end it like we planned to years ago." He pointed to the east. "Let's leave."

"You know why we can't do that."

"I would rather end things now than rot away in this place or turn into one of those things. I won't wait here to get killed and become part of this cursed forest! At least if we leave, we know what will happen."

"We don't know what will happen! Not really. For all we know, it could be worse than the alternative."

"We already know what the alternative is and I refuse to let it come to pass. Are you coming with me or not?"

Lili glanced at Kaidyn, who looked just as confused as she was.

"They think their son is dead," he whispered. "Go out there and talk to them."

"Me?"

"They might shoot me if I go."

She glanced at the couple, who were now looking eastward again, toward the wall. Her eyes lingered on the guns in their hands, their fingers on the triggers.

"Fine," the woman said to her husband. "Let's go. Let's leave."

Lili stepped out from behind the tree and opened her mouth to speak but the man suddenly shouted to the sky and she felt her throat constrict.

"We're not playing your game anymore. If you want to kill us, do it now!"

"Lili," Kaidyn hissed. "Call to them."

She was trying to but no sound was coming out. She felt frozen to the ground and couldn't understand why her mouth wasn't working. Was she afraid? No. Rather than afraid, it felt like she'd lost complete control of her body—like an abandoned puppet on a string.

The man taunted the forest again but before he could continue, the soles of his boots suddenly turned a light grey and he stopped moving, his legs cemented to the ground. The same happened to the woman and Lili had to watch, still paralyzed, as the color drained from their hands and faces. Their once-pink skin turned white almost immediately and both of them screamed in pain for a split second before going slack-jawed and freezing in place.

"Get back!" Kaidyn grabbed Lili's arm and yanked her behind the tree but she kept watching as the blood completely drained from their bodies and the grey color continued crawling up their legs to their waists. It was changing the color of their clothes too. Only after the cement-like shade reached their shoulders did she realize they were turning to stone.

"Well, that explains why no one ever makes it out alive," Kaidyn whispered, his mouth right next to her ear but eyes trained on the couple as they turned completely grey. "What were you doing? Why didn't you call out to them?" He shoved her away from him, gently but with loathing. "You could have saved them if you'd just done what I asked."

"I'm sorry. I just...froze up," she whispered, checking the ground to make sure neither of them would turn to stone either. "I'm sorry," she repeated, genuinely upset that her body had disobeyed her mind like that. "I don't know what happened."

Kaidyn swore and clenched his fists.

Lili grimaced, angry at herself and this cursed body. This was just like when she tried to tell her uncle about her mother. "I won't let it happen again...if I can help it." She hadn't willingly done this. Her body had acted on its own, though she knew he wouldn't believe her.

Kaidyn shook his head and pulled a small camera from his pocket. "Stay out of the shot."

"You're going to film them? Isn't that...disrespectful?"

"They're dead. They can't protest." He turned on the camera, glanced at her, then sighed and put it away. "You're right. I was going to show this to the others but they'll have to take our word for it." He grimaced. "I don't know how the boy will react to his parents' death."

"Maybe we shouldn't tell him," she suggested, still speaking as quietly as possible. She was afraid the forest might turn them to stone like it had those two.

"I'll leave that to you. I don't care either way. Just know this, Lili." He sighed, running his hands through his dark hair. "If you freeze up like that again and put my brother in danger..." Instead of finishing the sentence, he left it to her imagination and went back the way they had come, not bothering to match her pace anymore.

Lili felt awful, and the fear of what she'd seen—of the stone creeping up the couple's legs—echoed every time her feet touched the ground.

Episode 7

"What happened?" Jacques asked as soon as they reentered the camp. Everyone was awake and packed when they arrived. The child was riding on Leon's shoulders as though he belonged with them.

Kaidyn shot a look that could kill at Lili, then turned to Jacques with dead eyes. "His parents are dead. They tried to leave and the forest killed them."

"What?" Viktor started shaking like a leaf. "How?"

"They turned to stone," Kaidyn answered with a straight face. "Just like the statues at the door. Those statues we saw were the remains of people trying to escape."

Jacques squinted at him, doubtful, then took off his glasses to clean them. "What exactly triggered this reaction?"

"They started shouting to the sky that they wanted to leave."

"I see." Jacques's expression was unreadable. "Well, now we know what not to do. If they truly are dead, we should return to their cabin and take what we can to survive."

"And the child?" Kaidyn whispered.

"He comes with us. We can drop him off at the village if necessary. If they have sufficient protection from monsters, it will be a better alternative to staying with us."

"But—" Leon looked devastated, like they were asking him to give up one of his sisters. "We could take care of him."

"A child? Be logical, Leon." Jacques turned his attention to Lili, ignoring Leon. "We folded your tent. I hope that's alright. We shouldn't stay here too long. Aidyn found some tracks near our camp, like something was circling us as we slept. It's best to get moving as soon as we can."

So they did. It wasn't difficult to relocate the cabin. While Jacques, Leon, and Viktor went in to investigate the now abandoned home, Lili stayed outside with the twins.

"Should we show her the grave we found?" Aidyn asked Kaidyn quietly as they studied the buckets of water outside the building, which were too large to take with them. "It might be relevant now that the parents are...gone."

"You can if you want. I'm not coming," was all Kaidyn said before turning his back on both of them.

"Okay. Lili, come this way." The friendlier twin smiled at her and motioned for her to follow. "While we circled around the cabin yesterday, we found a grave at the back of the house. Do you want to see?"

Since there was nothing else to do, she said yes. Aidyn seemed eager to show her.

The stone walls had clearly been built with care, held back only by the creator's own limitations and the fact they were most likely built in a hurry. However, the grave Aidyn led Lili to was several feet away and barely resembled a traditional tombstone. Its only identifiers were the remains of a hole in the ground and a round stone beside it with the name WILLIAM crudely scratched in with a knife.

"I wonder what happened to the body," Lili commented as she leaned over the empty grave.

"Probably dragged off by animals." Aidyn shrugged. "Or the forest did something to it."

She didn't like this one bit.

"Do you think we should tell the others about the grave?" Aidyn asked. "Kaidyn didn't think it was important."

Lili didn't know how to answer. It didn't seem important to her either, other than the name. It was expected that there'd be dead people here. Hundreds snuck in after the forest's discovery.

"I guess we should. I'm sure Jacques would like to know. It is strange that the grave has the same name as the son's."

"Not too strange," Aidyn said. "Many people name their children after their grandparents or lost siblings that came before. I was nearly Suzuki Junior."

"We should mention it anyway, just in case." Everything about this forest was odd. Any clue they could find might be valuable.

The only one they told was Jacques, since Viktor was too busy building a cart to transport the potted plants and Leon was taking care of Billy. Jacques immediately started regarding the child with suspicion once he heard the news and his actions made the twins do the same. The boy was currently clinging to Leon, holding onto his arm while Leon tried to collect the boy's extra clothes from the cabin and dress the child in them so he wouldn't get cold.

"Should we be worried?" Lili asked Jacques nervously, her whisper barely audible. They didn't want Leon to hear. He'd become protective of the child in only a few hours.

"No. Not yet. Let's just...keep an eye on the boy. I agree that handing down names is common, especially in a place like this where babies and children are unlikely to last long. William could be an older child they lost."

"And what if it's not?" Kaidyn hissed.

"What would you have me do? Lock the child in a cage just in case he...I don't even know what it is we're suspecting him of." Jacques threw his hands in the air and set to work investigating the cabin bedroom, ending the discussion.

The twins glanced at Lili, then followed Jacques's lead, assisting Viktor with his cart.

Left with nothing else to do, Lili ventured forward to see what Jacques had discovered. She found him reading a book next to the bed. It resembled a diary and when she took a peek at it, she was surprised to find detailed notes about the forest as well as drawings of various monstrous creatures the man must have fought over the years.

"This is the wolf we encountered," Jacques told her when he caught her peering over his shoulder. All distrust of her had passed by this point.

He pointed at the drawing of the monstrosity. It looked smaller than it had in real life, but still made her stomach churn. "And this is just one of many. This bat one interests me the most. It's like a warped cat with wings." Jacques flipped a page, then leaned closer. "Don't tell the others about this." He showed her the eighth page, in which a picture and description showed a giant beetle creature wearing several layers of pink skin atop its hard red shell. Its red arms looked almost human and they were bleeding profusely, leaving a trail behind.

"What's wrong with this one in particular?" she asked, shivering at the sight.

"A few years ago, we had a terrible encounter with insects. We went to sleep in a desert and when we woke, our beds were covered in these horrid beetles. Their bites traumatized Viktor and Leon and the mere mention of this might send them into a panic."

"Got it. I take it I shouldn't mention the strange cicada noises we've been hearing during the night too? They might belong to this creature." She tapped the book and watched the blood drain from his face.

"So you noticed that too, huh?" Jacques shuddered, then took a moment to compose himself. "Yes, don't mention that either. It'll just make them nervous, which means less sleep, and we already have two sleep-deprived members in our troupe." He pointed at her and Kaidyn, the ones who had spent the night trying to reach the boy's parents.

"Is there anything else we can use from the book?" she asked, hoping to find hints about her parents.

"It talks about the village in the center of this forest and how it came to be. The survivor and his wife helped establish the place with this Kingsley person until he tried to murder their child and they left."

"That can't be good."

"Indeed. However, they mention something about a doorway in the village. 'One of many' he says, though the man is very vague about it, implying he doesn't know much. He just talks about it leading to the next level, which I assume means there actually is a way out of this forest that doesn't involve turning to stone."

Lili's heart leapt. "Really?" If that were true, maybe that was how her mother got out. There was an exit after all and her parents found it.

"I'll discuss it with the group, but I think they'll agree that entering the village is our best option right now."

She was glad they had a plan. Even as he spoke, her heart told her this was the right way to go. She was confident it would bring her closer to her mother.

Her mind drifted back to the empty grave behind the cabin, intertwining it with the fuzzy memories of her mother's strange state. She imagined her mom crawling out of the grave herself, her skin peeling and eyes white.

"Do you think this forest has...supernatural properties?" she whispered, eyes trailing over the various sketches of monsters.

"How could it not?" Jacques asked sarcastically. Then he glanced at her and caught her somber expression. He was quick to change his tone. "Are you thinking about the boy again?"

"Something like that."

"If anything happens, Leon will handle it. He's used to protecting his siblings and I can tell he's already formed the same connection with the son. He'll watch over the boy. Don't worry."

That only gave her a little comfort. It was strangely calming to study all the images instead. There was a three-headed beast of black ooze with yellow eyes, a hag-like woman with arms so long they touched the ground, and a beast with a human body but antlers for a head. With each turned page, she felt her heartbeat slow. Seeing monsters they hadn't encountered yet was better than thinking about the ones stalking them...or living among them.

Episode 8

It took a few more days of walking to even get close to the village. To avoid letting paranoia take over, they spent most of their journey documenting new creatures and practicing their aim with bows and throwing knives. Leon and Aidyn helped train Lili and seemed more than happy to do so.

As the group went on, they encountered a few obstacles but it never got too serious. They had to fight more rabid wolves, rabbits that launched themselves from trees, frogs with poisonous skin that left a chemical burn on Viktor's arm, and occasional three-legged beetles that tried to climb up their legs. All of the boys freaked out when they saw the beetles—even Kaidyn—and they resorted to climbing trees to escape even though the beetles didn't pose as much of a threat.

Nothing strange ever happened with Billy, so the group eventually concluded that the grave had been a false alarm. If that assessment turned out to be wrong, Jacques said, then there wasn't much they could do about it anyway. They weren't going to abandon a child just because the cabin was suspicious. There were enough monsters in this forest. No need to add to it with murder.

Their journey led them past a few more remnants of civilization: tents, abandoned cabins that looked over a hundred years old, and plenty of empty graves. The only odd thing was that each grave had a different type of gravestone. Some consisted of rock piles, others were wood or stone crosses. They even found the remains of crudely built coffins on occasion. Most bore fading inscriptions, very few of them written in English.

"I wonder how long these have been here," Jacques commented as they passed another coffin. "A few look decades old." No one knew the answer.

The longer they went without encountering living beings, the more tense everyone became. It only got worse during the night. Lili would sometimes hear the boys' discussions during their watches and it was clear they were genuinely afraid of getting killed. The wolves had been their first taste of genuine danger and now that they'd seen what happened to the couple, they knew they were in over their heads. Wolves were one thing. Turning to stone was an entirely different kind of threat. Without the help of more experienced survivors, they might not last a week.

On the third night, when the twins were on watch together, Lili woke from her sleep to Aidyn shouting.

"Kaidyn," Aidyn hissed, his shadow rising from the log he was seated on. "Look. They're right there. I can see them. I swear."

She watched Kaidyn grab his brother and prevent him from running into the darkness. "Your mind's playing tricks on you."

"No, it's them and we're going to lose sight of them if we don't go now. Hey! Max!"

Lili sat up at the name of the twin's older brother—the one who disappeared a year ago. Could Aidyn really see him? This was just like what happened with her mother.

"I only see shadows, Aidyn. That could be anything," Kaidyn insisted. "We're not leaving this fire until we know it's not a trap."

Lili saw Aidyn's shadow jerk as he yanked free from his brother's grasp. "We came all this way to find them. We're risking our lives to save them and when I finally catch a glimpse, this is what you do? Why are we even here, Kaidyn, if you're going to let them slip away? They might need our help."

Kaidyn faltered, reaching for his brother but no longer holding him back. "I don't want to lose you too."

Aidyn turned back to the forest, then sighed. This was the first time she'd heard him get angry. "They're gone. You let them leave."

"I'm sorry, Aidyn."

"You need to start questioning why we came all this way, Kaidyn. We didn't leave Mom and Dad behind just to—"

The air suddenly filled with deafening clicks, cicada screeches, and a human shriek that made her ears ring. The noise made Lili leap to her feet and grab her pack before she even had time to think. Her entire body told her to run from the noise as soon as possible and, judging by the shouts from the neighboring tents, the others were doing the same.

By the time she exited her tent, the twins had drawn their swords and were staring toward the south, where she saw what looked like a red and brown blob barreling toward them. Once Leon crawled out of his tent with the boy in one arm and his pack in the other, she was awake enough to make out the true form of the creature. It was the giant beetle she had seen in the book, its fleshy skin even more horrific in real life and its cries rising in pitch as it scurried toward them. Crawling all over its body and around its feet were smaller beetles, each of them covered in the creature's blood and leaving red streaks on the grass.

"We can't fight that!" Leon screamed, paling and grabbing the twins' packs, which they hadn't retrieved from the tents yet. They were too busy staring at the oncoming insect with wide eyes and dropped jaws. When fighting the wolves, the boys looked confident and calm. Facing this, they looked ready to faint.

"Let's get out of here," Leon shouted. "To the village!"

Even Kaidyn and Jacques had gone white. They didn't need to be told twice.

Everyone started grabbing their remaining things and leaving the tents behind, too scared to bother packing up. Viktor was the only one unwilling to abandon his plants. He started pulling his makeshift wagon along with him, shrieking at the top of his lungs when it slowed him down. The beetle got closer, its face opening to reveal three sets of pincers lined with human teeth.

"Leave it." Leon grabbed Viktor with his one free arm and pulled him away from the wagon.

"No! We can't leave them behind," Viktor screamed, reaching for the pots. "We'll die without those plants."

"You can't eat them if you're inside that thing's stomach," Jacques shouted back, then led the group in the right direction. Leon was now carrying three packs, a child, and a screaming Viktor. Viktor started to cry when the beetle crawled over the wagon, crushing the contents under its weight.

"Cowards, the lot of you!" Viktor cried but didn't fight against Leon as he was carried away.

The twins would occasionally grab a stone or stick as they ran and throw it at the beetle but nothing had an effect. The attacks only served to make it bleed more. Lili couldn't understand how the thing managed to stay alive while losing so much blood.

"Lili," Jacques shouted.

"What is it?" She stopped staring at the beetle and focused on her leader.

"Are we going the right way? You saw the map in the book, right?"

"Yes."

"Are we heading in the right direction?"

She looked up at the sky, then at the trees whizzing past. Her survival skills were failing her. With no time to stop and get her bearings, she couldn't tell North from South. She'd have to rely on her mother's pull instead. "We need to go a little to the right."

Jacques nodded without question and redirected the group.

She knew they were close to the village but didn't know if Leon could keep going at this pace, especially while carrying so many things. He was already red in the face and grimacing. It was a good thing the camera wasn't on him right now. The fans would be devastated to see him like this.

Even though she didn't know how far they'd have to go, Lili knew she had led them the right way. It wasn't her navigational training that made her confident—it was the connection she felt to her mother. It pulled her forward, tugging on her heart like a string. She wasn't sure if it was their shared blood or her mother's spirit leading her.

The skittery sound the beetles made gave her a headache. As her steps slowed from exhaustion, Lili knew they'd need to either fight or give up. She was about to pull her knife from her pack, her short life flashing before her eyes, when she finally spotted something beyond the trees. It was another wall. This one was built with thick vertical logs that came to a point and formed spikes.

"There it is," she shouted, her steps hurrying with newfound energy. The others did the same.

They could see what looked like a large gate to their right, made of the same wood as the rest, but it was closed and had no handle or indication that it could be opened from the outside. The walls were also too tall to climb. If it weren't for a man patrolling the top of the wall, standing behind the spikes, she might have assumed there wasn't anyone inside to help them. As the group broke through the trees, waving their arms to get the man's attention, Lili felt their chances of survival rise. She couldn't tell how big the village was but judging by this wall's height and its seemingly endless length, it must house a lot of people. Maybe even hundreds. Whoever lived inside could save them.

"Open the gates," Jacques ordered as they ran alongside the wall. The beetle was tailing them, banging against the walls as it swerved to keep up with its prey. "Quick!"

The person atop the wall, a thin male maybe a few years older than Jacques with short brown hair and a spear in his hand, ran toward the gate. "There are survivors outside," he shouted to someone in the village. "The beetle's with them."

Lili could tell he was scared of facing the monster. His voice wobbled when he spoke its name. Would he let them die to protect himself even though they had a child with them?

"Let us in," Kaidyn repeated, throwing a stone at the creature. They were at the gate now but it showed no signs of moving. "You can't let us die here. We have a child with us."

Leon put Viktor and Billy down so he could pull the axe out of his pack. He then stood between them and the beetle protectively. The creature was rolling over itself to reach them faster. Leon's hands were shaking but he didn't cower.

"I don't think they're going to let us in," Jacques hissed and studied the trees near the walls. "Aidyn, can you climb that one?"

Aidyn turned to look at the tall pine his friend had pointed out. "Yeah. Definitely."

"I think we can jump from it onto the wall. Give it a try. Bring the kid with you." Not waiting for an answer, the leader pulled out his bow and shot an arrow at the monster's head. "We'll be right behind you."

Aidyn glanced at his brother nervously, then pulled Billy onto his back, instructing him to hold tight. He then nimbly climbed the tree. Kaidyn chased after him a second later, followed by a screaming Viktor who kept looking over his shoulder at the beast.

"Jacques," Leon warned, now the only thing between the tree and the beetle. "Do we fight it?"

"No." Jacques loosed another arrow. It hit the beetle's fleshy chest but did nothing. It wasn't reacting as that large wolf did. The wolf occasionally slowed when it was harmed but this one didn't seem to feel anything. "I don't know how to kill it."

"I'll cut off its head," Leon said, tightening his grip on the axe, but Jacques grabbed the tree's lowest branch instead. "Fight it if you want but we're so close to the walls. It would be stupid to die when we don't need to."

Lili agreed and joined him. The bark cut her palms as she pulled herself onto the lowest branch. She saw the smaller beetles climbing the base of the trunk. She'd need to move fast if she didn't want to be overtaken.

Leon stayed on the ground, bouncing on the heels of his boots, but after watching Aidyn leap from the tree, past the spikes and onto the inner section of the wall where the guard had been standing, Leon groaned and returned his axe to his pack. "Next time," he shouted at the giant bug before following Lili and Jacques.

Lili felt the entire tree sway as Kaidyn leapt off, followed by Viktor who squealed as he jumped, needing Kaidyn's help to land without falling off the wall. The branches shuddered even more when Leon climbed up, his weight rocking the whole thing.

Her grip on the branches loosened as the tree swung particularly hard, the trunk smacking her knee and drawing blood. She grit her teeth as one hand lost its grip. "Leon," she hissed, making the man pause his upward climb. "Stop moving so much. The tree feels like it's going to break."

The further up she climbed, the thinner the trunk became and the more it weaved back and forth. Her entire body swayed as Jacques pushed himself off toward the wall. Then it was just her, Leon, and the beetles climbing up the branches. She felt one crawl up her ankle, leaving a sticky trail of blood along her skin.

"Jump, Lili," Leon called, breaking off a branch and dropping it on the giant beetle below before looking up at her. "Do you need help?"

She cringed when the tiny beetle bit her skin. The bite made her woozy.

"Lili!" Jacques shouted.

Lili leaned down and ripped the bug off, letting it slip from her fist and fall to the ground. It left two bite marks behind.

"I can do this," she told herself, even as the bitten leg numbed. Would she have the strength to make the jump? She hadn't done something like this before and while the wall had looked close from the ground, it now felt at least thirty feet away and the spikes were too high. She could already imagine her limp body hanging from one, impaled.

"I can throw you," Leon insisted. As he spoke, the beetle monster hurled its entire body against the tree, nearly knocking them off from the impact. "Go now or I'll throw you."

Her mind filled with visions of every conceivable way she could fail this jump. She was tempted to take Leon up on his offer. It would be putting him at risk, though, and they could end up falling together. He was already tired as it was and still had that wound from the wolf.

Feeling her body tense again, Lili looked at the wall. The others had already climbed down, out of sight, and only Kaidyn was waiting for her. Their eyes met and she knew what he expected of her. This was her chance to prove herself—that she wouldn't freeze up as she had before.

"I'm going," she told Leon and pressed the soles of her feet against the trunk. With one final breath, she pushed herself off. The wind whipped through her hair and her brain stopped working as the spikes approached. Then, her feet touched solid wood and Kaidyn caught her, grabbing her shirt to prevent her from falling. As soon as she steadied herself, he released her and shouted for Leon to follow suit.

The beetle slammed against the tree again. Lili watched the trunk start to splinter. It was about to fall and Leon still hadn't reached the top. He had to jump *now*. The alternative was becoming insect food.

"He's not gonna make it," Kaidyn whispered as the tree leaned toward them. "And the tree could crush the wall too." The wall felt strong under her feet but the tree they'd climbed looked heavy. If the wall came down, the beetle could terrorize the entire village.

Lili stepped aside as Kaidyn drew his sword, preparing for disaster.

Leon swung to the top of the tree, panting from the exertion, then he turned toward both of them, ready.

The monster hit the tree again. This time, it swayed away from the wall. Leon had mere seconds to avoid death.

"Jump!" she shouted but Leon was already doing it. As the pine fell away from the wall and crashed into the other trees, the young man flew across the gap and landed beside her and Kaidyn.

He'd made it.

Successful, Leon offered the pair a tired grin, making even Lili smile. But before Kaidyn could grab him, one of Leon's legs slipped and he fell from the wall to the ground below, landing on his side. Lili cringed when he tried to get up, exhaustion making his shoulders shake. At least he fell onto the village side. They were safe for now.

"Well, at least we're all in," Kaidyn whispered as he and Lili watched the beetle creature wander around the base of the tree. Its chittering stopped and she breathed a sigh of relief when it retreated, its prey gone.

Glad they'd survived another encounter, she finally turned to study the village they'd forced their way into. The little boy was helping Leon to his feet below. Jacques and Viktor were standing a few feet in front of them, their feet set apart and hands out defensively. Why were they standing so strangely?

It was then that Lili looked past them and noticed the other members of this city, an entire row of men in black and brown uniforms armed with long spears and pistols. They were pointing their weapons at the group and an older man with grey hair and a well-trimmed beard was walking toward them. He wore a black uniform like the others but had a machine gun hanging from his back. Judging by the sour look on his face, he wasn't impressed by their entrance.

"Well," Jacques said with a nervous laugh, glancing over his shoulder at Kaidyn and Lili, who were still on the wall. "It appears we have left the frying pan and entered the fire." It was a pity they'd turned off the cameras. That bland line would have been perfect for the documentary.

Episode 9

The village was quite beautiful, though Lili didn't have much time to admire it. Aside from the walls, which were formed from thick logs of brown and crimson, the rest of the village was clearly built from stone. There were foundations of rock that looked like they had been built centuries ago. There were even designs reminiscent of ancient Rome and Egypt, though that couldn't be since they were in Canada. Grass and moss grew between the cracks, signs of nature taking over where it could.

Built atop these old foundations were modern homes of wood and steel. Ropes tied most of the buildings together and every window was covered by boards or curtains so Lili couldn't see inside. Each home looked clean and cared for, clearly inhabited. The color patterns were bland, sticking to dark shades. There was only one building that stood out. It was built entirely from stone and had been painted white. It also had a door nearly as thick as the wall she was standing on and a glass ceiling. Whatever was inside must be important.

The people currently threatening her friends looked as dreary as the buildings, wearing old clothes with plenty of patches and holes. Most of their weapons consisted of sharpened rocks or sticks, aside from the occasional gun, and the only clothes resembling armor had been fashioned from wood. The leader of the group was the only person who looked well-prepared for a fight. He wore a black vest over his clothes, likely bulletproof, and clean black boots that nearly matched her own steel-toed ones. It was clear he cared about his hygiene, though the dirty hands and faces of his men proved he only applied that standard to himself.

"Newcomers," the man announced as he stepped toward Jacques. "Welcome to our village. My name is Kingsley and I'm the leader of this sanctuary."

Kingsley. That was the name the man from the cabin mentioned, the one who was tyrannical and had tried to kill their son.

Lili stiffened and saw Kaidyn do the same. He was still holding his sword, but it wouldn't do much good up here.

"Hello, sir," Jacques said politely, straightening from his defensive posture and reaching out for a handshake. "I apologize for our rude entrance but we were being chased."

The man smirked. "That happens often. I apologize for not opening the gate but we can't risk the safety of an entire village for a few strangers."

"Of course," Jacques said. He started introducing himself but the man's eyes drifted toward Leon and Billy. Lili noticed his mouth open slightly in shock when he laid eyes on the boy.

Without skipping a beat, Kingsley turned to his men and pointed at the child. "Seize him."

"What?" Jacques raised his hands in surrender as the men closed in on them, spear tips inches from their faces. "Hold on. We can discuss this without violence."

"Not you," the man cut in and pointed at Billy, who was cowering behind Leon. "We want *him*."

"Why?" Jacques demanded as Leon raised his axe. "He's just a kid."

Kingsley scoffed, then motioned for his men to proceed. "It's for your own protection. You don't want to know. Proceed."

Leon brought his axe down on one of the spears, breaking it in half, then shouted at the men to back off. He was about to shove one of them when Kingsley pointed his machine gun at Leon's chest.

"We don't want any trouble, big man. That child will endanger everyone in this village. Step aside or I'll have to kill you both."

Leon sneered and made himself a shield for the boy. Unfortunately, while he was distracted by the older man, one of the other soldiers grabbed the child and ran off with him. By the time Leon realized, it was too late and he was surrounded by spears pressed against his throat.

"Thank you." Kingsley walked up to the man holding the child, then grabbed him. Billy barely struggled when Kingsley yanked him closer, holding his gun dangerously close to the boy's head. "I know how this looks. Just trust that this is for your own protection as well as mine."

"This is why his parents ran away," Jacques said. "You're a child killer."

The leader backed toward a tall black building, only slightly bigger than an outhouse, and opened the door. "Don't worry. This is not a child."

"What?" Jacques's words were barely out of his mouth before the man tossed the boy into the dark building. They watched as Billy fell through the floor, vanishing just like they had when entering the forest's wall.

Kingsley slammed the door and locked it with a large key hanging from his neck.

"You bastard," Leon screamed and swung his axe around his head, knocking the surrounding spears aside just long enough to jump out of range and kick one of the disoriented men in the face.

"Leon, we don't want to fight them," Jacques shouted. "We're outnumbered."

"They just killed a little boy!" Leon shouted before swinging his axe again. The villagers looked hesitant to fight him. They must be accustomed to fighting monsters, not men. Lili could tell Leon felt the same. The outrage in his eyes was mixed with hesitation.

Lili glanced at Kaidyn to see what he would do but he was helplessly watching the fight, just as Aidyn and Viktor were. They all seemed unsure whether they wanted to fight fellow humans, especially when there were so many of them.

"Tell your companion to back down," Kingsley ordered, watching the fight with an amused smile. "We have no quarrel with you."

"Neither do we," Jacques said, but Leon's fist meeting one of the men's faces proved otherwise. "Leon."

Lili could see tears streaming down Leon's face but he stopped, his axe above his head, about to come down on one of the men's skulls.

"If you wish, we can kick you back out of the city," Kingsley offered. "But I don't think that's what you want."

"We want answers," Jacques answered quietly, his hands stretched out in a calming motion.

With the fight over, Kingsley stepped closer again. "Why don't you and your crew take a breather. You're clearly new here. Find an empty house and settle in. I doubt you'll want to leave once you do."

"I want the answers *now*," Jacques insisted, crossing his arms and peering over his glasses at the man. "We just saw you kill one of our companions. It's the least you could do." Jacques still looked shaken but his voice was level.

"Come back in an hour then," Kingsley said, making it clear this wasn't a request. "Just know that I've been in this cursed forest longer than anyone else. I'm one of the original ten who discovered it. My word means more than anyone else's."

Lili frowned and studied his face. She tried to subtly pull out the photo of her parents and their friends. This Kingsley person wasn't among them. Kaidyn glanced at the photo too and judging by his expression, was thinking the same thing. Kingsley was lying, though they didn't know why.

"He might know where my parents are," she whispered.

"And my siblings," Kaidyn added thoughtfully, then shouted at the others. "Jacques, do as he says."

Jacques glanced at them, confused, but was smiling when he turned back to the village's ruler. "Very well. In an hour then."

Lili and Kaidyn climbed down the wall's inner ladder and joined their friends, who were still surrounded by armed but non-hostile men. Jacques led them toward the houses as instructed. While they walked away, Lili glanced at Kingsley and saw him nod at his men, who began patrolling the streets behind them, some of them making it obvious they were keeping an eye on Lili's group.

"I don't like this," Aidyn whispered as Viktor pulled out some band-aids and handed them to Leon and Lili for their newly acquired cuts and bites. Lili's leg was still numb but the sensation was fading. She hoped it wouldn't get worse later on. If the plants were supposedly poisonous, the beetles might be too.

They passed endless rows of homes, all of them similarly boarded up. Lili spotted a few people peeking through the windows, only to cover them with curtains as soon as she got too close. It made the place feel even more stifling. How could people stand living here?

"Kingsley lied about being the first person to enter the forest," she whispered to the group as they walked. "I have a photo of the original ten. He's not in it."

Kaidyn nodded in agreement. "He's lying. But why?"

"So people respect him, maybe?" Jacques suggested. "I'm glad you told me. It proves we can't trust him. Then again, we knew that already."

Leon was shaking now, both from anger and the fight's waning adrenaline. "He killed Billy."

"We don't know that yet," Jacques warned. "He threw the child into a building."

"It looked like a pit to me," Viktor replied. "Either way, he clearly has ill intentions."

To cement this in their minds, they turned a corner and nearly walked into a tall wooden structure with a large blade hanging from a rope. Lili recognized it immediately as a guillotine. While it didn't have any blood on it, the blade didn't look sharp. It must have had plenty of use over the years.

"Lovely," Jacques muttered, stopping to study it. "I wonder why he has this," he said sarcastically. "His excuse for killing the child was that he wanted to protect everyone, yet he has a guillotine. What a joke."

"We should get our answers, then leave," Kaidyn hissed before kicking open the door of a clearly empty house. Unlike the others, the curtains on the windows weren't drawn. "We can't wait around for him to kill us."

"But where do we go? We don't know any other people or locations in this forest and our rations have a limit," Viktor reminded them as they entered the house and shut the door. Aidyn covered the window so no one could look in, then sat next to it and peeked through the curtains to keep an eye out.

"We're not leaving until we save Billy," Leon demanded, using his one good arm to grab a wooden box from the corner. He sat on it with a huff. "And I wouldn't mind punishing that man for hurting him too."

Jacques sighed and leaned against the wall while Viktor bandaged everyone's wounds. "In that case, maybe I should speak to him alone since taking the rest of you seems like asking for trouble."

"You can't go by yourself," Kaidyn warned. "It's too dangerous."

"I'll take Lili and Viktor with me once we're ready to go. At least *they* won't start attacking people when they're clearly outnumbered," Jacques said, glaring at Leon while his arm was wrapped.

"Lili can't protect you, though." Kaidyn crossed his arms. "I'll come with you instead and the rest can stay here."

"Very well." Jacques sighed and covered his head with his hands, taking several deep breaths. "While we wait, we should take a look around, see if we can find any clues as to what's going on in this village."

"No need."

Everyone shot to their feet and grabbed their weapons when a voice echoed from the rafters. It was feminine and hushed.

"Who said that?" Jacques demanded, his bow already in his hands. Lili looked up. It was so dark that she could barely make out the figure sitting in the rafters.

"I know you," the mysterious woman said. "You're the Rural Rangers, internet celebrities with a stupid name. I used to watch your documentaries before I came here. My husband was a big fan." She hopped down and landed in their midst. It was a young woman, maybe in her thirties, with straight black hair and a gaunt face that may have been pretty before she became dirty and malnourished. She was dressed entirely in black with red on the inside of her leather jacket. "I'm guessing you came here to document this hell hole?"

"That was our original plan," Jacques said. "But it appears leaving is harder than we assumed."

She sighed. "We all come in with big aspirations, thinking we're better than everyone who failed to leave before. We tell ourselves we can overcome the trials that have killed others for years. Yet we all end up in the same place." She spread out her arms so they'd know she wasn't armed. "Tell me, what did Kingsley do to piss you off?"

"He killed our friend," Leon growled. "A child."

She squinted. "I see. He doesn't kill people often, so the child must have done something. What was the crime?"

"Nothing," Leon insisted. "He did absolutely nothing."

"I'm guessing Kingsley didn't behead the child, since the guillotine hasn't been used." She pointed at the window, which would have granted a view of the guillotine if the curtain wasn't covering it. "So, did he drop the kid down the hole?"

"The hole?" Jacques asked.

"The hole to the second level," she answered and tilted her head. "You don't know about that yet? When did you arrive?"

"Less than a week ago," Jacques answered.

"That explains it. Well, since you may be my ticket out of here, I might as well share everything I know if I'm to gain your trust. Right?" She glanced at Kaidyn and Leon, who still looked hostile. "What do you know so far?"

Jacques explained what they discovered about the walls, the statues, and the plants. She didn't seem fazed by any of it.

"That's right. We only drink rainwater here and Kingsley stores all the plants inside that greenhouse by the gate. I assume you already saw it. Big white building, glass roof."

"I did," Lili said.

"Do you think Kingsley plans to kill any of us?" Jacques asked suspiciously.

"No, not unless you threaten him or the village. He's overprotective and if anyone tries to question him, they'll be forced to shut up or leave. That's as close to a death wish as you can get, unless you're good at killing monsters." To emphasize this, she opened one of the windows slightly so the light could flood in. Doing so revealed three long, jagged scars across one of her eyes. They ran all the way to her mouth. It looked almost identical to the cut Leon received from the wolf.

"So, you mentioned wanting to get out," Jacques continued. "Where are you planning to go?"

"To the second level, obviously. There's nothing else here, besides this village and a few stragglers. I've lived here a year and found no other way out. Going down seems like our only option. You lot look like the most capable escorts, considering what I've seen you do on-screen. All except her." She nodded at Lili, who wasn't sure if she should take that as an insult.

"What's in the second level?" Lili asked, getting a nagging feeling that she needed to go there.

"No one knows. Anyone who goes in never comes out. I doubt it's anything good but it's better than waiting around to die of old age." She shrugged, her deep voice permanently hoarse. "If you plan to chase after the kid, I can help you get to the second level. In return, you will protect me and help me figure out how to escape this god-forsaken place. Sound good?"

Jacques narrowed his eyes at her. "How do we know you aren't lying?"

"I have nothing left to lose." She stared him down but Lili got the feeling she was trying to act tough on the surface, concealing her fears.

"You mentioned a husband," Lili said quietly, making the woman's head snap toward her. "Did he come here with you?"

The woman's tough façade dropped for a moment and Lili saw her eye twitch.

"Yes, we came together. We—we were inspired by your videos, actually, but he died not long after we arrived." She pointed at the boys, an unrestrained sneer on her face. "I know it's not your fault that he died but..." Her voice trailed off, unwilling to insult her escort.

"I'm sorry," Lili whispered. "I know how it feels to lose someone you love."

"Doesn't matter now. I just want to leave. Do we have a deal or not, Rangers?"

"Yes," Jacques answered almost immediately. "But first, I want to talk to this Kingsley and hear his side of things."

"Fine with me. Just don't make him suspicious." The woman walked to the corner of the room and leaned against the wall, falling silent.

"What's your name?" Lili asked while the boys huddled to discuss the woman's plan.

"Meriel," she said tersely and took a seat on the floor.

"So," Jacques began as they formed a tight circle. "I think—"

"Let's go with her plan. You and I will talk to Kingsley and get answers," Kaidyn interrupted. "We'll figure out what he knows, including what happened to our families, then we'll find a way into the second level."

"We'll need to get that key off him," Jacques said. "Why don't you three brainstorm with the woman while we meet with him?" He nodded at Leon, Viktor, and Aidyn. "But don't leave this house. I don't want you getting into trouble. Also...keep an eye on her." He nodded at Meriel.

"I can hear you," Meriel grumbled from her corner but Jacques ignored her.

"If anyone has complaints, voice them now," he said. "Otherwise, we'll do this and hopefully be out of here in less than a day. I don't want—" He had to pause to remember the boy's name. "I don't want Billy to wait too long." Lili could tell Leon appreciated the effort.

With the plan decided, the group split into two teams. Jacques and Kaidyn would visit Kingsley while the rest stayed here.

Lili was planning to let them go without her, aware that she hadn't been added to either group, but before he stepped out, Kaidyn stopped at the door and looked back at her. His brow was furrowed, debating his next move. "Lili," he said quietly as Jacques slipped past him. "You want to ask him about your parents, right?"

She nodded. *Desperately.*

The twin raised his chin, then tilted his head, gesturing for her to follow.

Episode 10

Kingsley was sitting outside the large building they now knew was a greenhouse, whittling away at a piece of wood. Some of his men were on the wall thirty feet away and there were a few others patrolling nearby. Lili could feel their eyes on her, waiting for her to endanger their leader.

"Welcome back," Kingsley said, motioning for them to take a seat on the wooden log in front of the building. They chose to remain standing. "You returned earlier than expected."

"We want to get this over with," Jacques said, the picture of composure. Kaidyn, meanwhile, stood like a bodyguard, eyeing their surroundings as though they were on the verge of battle.

"I assume you have many questions. Fire away, though I warn you that I will choose to omit some information when necessary. This knowledge is a curse I do not wish to burden others with."

"And why is that?" Jacques asked.

"If I told everyone what I knew, they would learn to fear the very ground they stand on and mistrust each other. I would rather they hate me alone than live in constant fear. If you remain within the village walls and do as I command, you can live the rest of your lives in peace."

"And if we want to leave?"

"I can't stop you but I strongly discourage it. If you change your mind later and wish to come back, I won't allow it."

"Why?"

The man narrowed his eyes, making it clear this was one of the answers he would not give.

"You said you were one of the original survivors," Lili cut in, knowing Jacques was getting frustrated. "What did you mean by that?" She wanted to catch him in a lie.

"It is as I said. I was one of the ten who entered this forest ten years ago. I have been here the longest and seen the most." He studied her face. She wished she had hidden her distaste a bit better. "I can tell you don't believe me, since age and wounds have changed my appearance, but I assure you, I do not lie."

He was probably hoping anyone who entered hadn't seen the ten before, which would have been unlikely if not for the public photos being small and blurry. Any clear ones had been destroyed by her uncle to preserve the memory of his friends and family. He didn't like seeing his siblings treated like tourist attractions.

"If you're one of the originals, tell me where the others went," she said, holding her breath.

"They died," he told her with a straight face and she felt her heart rebel. It couldn't be true.

"When?"

"A few months into their journey. Those who didn't succumb to monsters died of poison or starvation."

"Then how did you survive?" Kaidyn asked doubtfully.

"I learned from my mistakes and never trusted anyone or anything within this forest. I would advise you to do the same, though now that you're here with me, you won't need to worry about anything ever again. I will take care of you."

"What about these people, then?" Kaidyn asked and held up a photo. On it was a young man and woman, both with black hair and nearly identical faces. "This is my brother and sister. They came here a year ago. Do you recognize them?"

Kingsley took the photo, examined it for a few long seconds, then handed it back. "They came through here," he said, "But didn't stay, despite my warnings."

"Where did they go?"

The man closed himself off again but this time, Kaidyn wasn't having it. He grabbed the front of Kingsley's shirt and shook him before Jacques could prevent it. His movement caught the attention of the nearby guards.

"Tell me where they went, old man. I didn't come all this way to be lied to."

"You would be better off not knowing anything about this forest. Even I have trouble sleeping at night knowing what it does to those who succumb to its power."

"I can take it. Now tell me."

"They went to the second level," Kingsley finally said, raising a hand so the approaching soldiers wouldn't hurt Kaidyn. "And no one who enters has ever returned. You should know as well as I that no one has ever left this forest alive. It is better to remain here, where we can preserve at least a sliver of safety."

"If I wanted to live a safe life, I wouldn't have entered this forest in the first place. They went down that hole, didn't they? Where you threw the kid," Kaidyn shouted.

"Yes. Your siblings were the reason I locked it up. It is better for the temptation to be removed."

"Then that's where we need to go." Kaidyn glanced at Jacques, who didn't say anything.

"I can't let you do that. For your own safety, child, you must remain here."

"Did the original ten go down there too?" Lili asked, sure he was lying about their deaths.

"A few," he admitted.

"Which ones?"

He hesitated. She wasn't sure if he was lying. Although he wasn't one of them, maybe he met the survivors after he entered.

"Kaidyn, let him go. We're trying to have a civil discussion here." Jacques placed a hand on the twin's shoulder and pulled him away. "I have other questions about the forest, like why people turn to stone when they try to leave."

"The forest does not allow anyone to escape," Kingsley answered. "This entire place is a death trap. It enjoys your company but loathes your exit."

Even Lili's patience was wearing thin. She just wanted to know what happened to her parents.

"How do they turn to stone?" Jacques asked.

"Anything within the forest's domain is under its control. It can do as it pleases with us."

"So you don't know." Jacques scoffed.

The man shrugged. "Magic," he said, his voice carrying a heavy level of respect.

"Are there other ways to enter this second level?" Lili asked, desperate to get down there.

The man raised his chin, his eyes narrowing as he debated whether he should tell them more. Lili worried he might lie and be convincing enough to sidetrack them. "There are other holes," he finally admitted, sounding truthful. "Larger ones, in fact, but they have been surrounded by monsters for years. You would need an army of tanks to make your way in." He laughed, as though imagining the group of young adults attempting it. "Now do you see how fruitless it is to resist? There is nowhere to go but here. Stay and you will be safe."

More repetition.

"I think we're done talking," Jacques said quietly. "Let's go."

"We could ask more—" Kaidyn started but Jacques shot him down with a single look.

"There's only so much roundabout talk I can tolerate," Jacques said quietly, even more agitated than Kaidyn usually was. Lili took his statement to mean that if they didn't leave now, he might snap and get them into trouble. That was rare. Leon was usually the one doing that.

"Once again, I remind you that staying within these village walls is your safest option," Kingsley said one last time. "Leaving will only result in your death at the hands of the forest, and it will be a far more painful end than you would meet here."

"Let's go," Jacques whispered. It felt like they had learned very little, though Lili now felt confident that her parents, or at least her mother, had gone down the hole to the second level. That was where she needed to go next. That was why her mother had led her here. It was the next step to reuniting with her family.

"Let me guess," Meriel said when they returned to the house, finding the remaining members of the group playing a card game while they waited. "He didn't tell you anything new."

"He gave us *some* answers but left us feeling just as hopeless as before," Jacques replied glumly as they shut the door and drew the curtains. "He expects us to spend the rest of our lives here while accepting vague answers to our questions."

"He said the same to me. Wouldn't even help me go back and bury my husband," Meriel muttered and got up, stepping between the circle of boys and disrupting their card game. "Are you ready to help me get the key to the second floor?"

"I don't know what else we can do," Jacques said. "The question is, do we want *just* the key or should we overthrow him first so the villagers can be free?"

"If they wanted that, they would have claimed it years ago," Meriel answered. "Most of Kingsley's citizens are cowards who didn't know what they were getting themselves into. They're traumatized by the monsters and are more than happy to obey Kingsley as long as he protects them."

"There must be *some* people willing to stand up to him," Jacques said.

"There were, and they were either killed or banished to the second level. Kingsley isn't afraid to get rid of people if they threaten his sanctuary. He banished his own son a few years back after the guy got caught convincing over twenty people to join him in the second level. He was sent outside the town and eaten alive by beetles. That's when Kingsley made an official law forbidding people from going to the second level unless absolutely necessary. After a few more people disobeyed him, he locked it up for good."

Lili wrinkled her nose. "Does he use the guillotine on his enemies?"

"Not really. No one's rebelled since I came so I've only seen him use it once on a sick old man. He never explained why he did it and I obviously didn't ask." Meriel knelt on the dirty floor and started drawing shapes in the dust. "I'll draw an outline of the town so we can decide how to go about this. I hope you have a plan because fighting isn't my expertise. The most I can do is sneak around for you."

Jacques looked pointedly at Leon and the twins, who grinned. They'd have plenty of ideas.

Episode 11

The stars and the moon shone down on Lili just as they did outside the forest, but it did little to calm her heart as she and Viktor snuck through the dark alleys of the village, trailing after Meriel as she leapt over boxes and around corners like she was being chased. She was faster than both of them and Lili constantly feared being left behind or accidentally running into one of the armed men patrolling the streets. Meriel knew their patterns, but Lili didn't.

Luckily, Viktor's chattering teeth and shaking hands made it clear he was ten times more frightened than she was, and it comforted her a little. It was easier to act brave when someone else was more afraid.

While the fighters proceeded to Kingsley's home, planning to sneak in and steal his key, the weaker ones in the group were going to hide near the shed to the second level. Since they couldn't contribute, their only job was to be ready to leave as soon as that door opened. Plus, Viktor wanted to take a look at the greenhouse before they left, so Meriel agreed to sneak in through the glass windows on the ceiling and unlock the door from the inside. As long as no one spotted them, it should be simple.

Lili and Viktor maneuvered through back alleys without getting caught and eventually reached the side of the greenhouse. The only things blocking their way were empty boxes and suitcases strewn about. The owners must have brought them to the forest like tourists and realized too late how dangerous things were. Now they were used for firewood.

"Can you imagine dragging these things all the way here?" Lili whispered as they leaned against the greenhouse wall, waiting for Meriel to break in. "It must have taken forever."

"Compared to the wagon I made in less than an hour, it's pretty pitiful," Viktor replied glumly, thinking about his lost plants. "The wagon we *left behind*."

Lili wanted to pat him on the back. He looked devastated by the loss of his plants. "At least *we* survived, right?"

"I suppose. I would rather the others be safe than the plants, but it still hurts to lose them." Viktor tapped the greenhouse wall. "Maybe we can take some of these plants instead. We'll need them if we go to the second level. I'm guessing things will be just as inedible down there as they are here."

"I didn't think about that." Lili was so focused on finding her parents that she forgot about general survival. "But it would be stealing if we took these, wouldn't it?"

"That man killed a child. I don't think we need to feel bad about stealing from him," Viktor said, then sighed when he saw the look on her face. "But you're right. We shouldn't steal from the rest of the town. I'm sure they're innocent in this, even if Kingsley isn't. We still have enough food to last a few weeks. This pack of mine isn't for nothing." He patted the giant bag he lugged around all day.

"I'm impressed you manage to carry it all," she admitted.

"Are you implying I look weak?" He narrowed his eyes at her and made her chuckle.

"No. It's just...compared to the others..."

"I know, I know." They both paused when a man walked past their hiding spot. He didn't look their way. Once he was gone, Viktor continued. "I may be unable to wield a sword like the others but I'm still a critical part of the group."

"What was your motive for coming?" He never struck her as the type to enjoy trips like this. "To study the plants?"

"No." He shrugged. "I came because they're the only friends I have."

"Oh. I'm sorry."

"It is what it is. I'm an orphan. I kept to myself until I met Leon in public school. When they let me join their group, I finally had a job, a hobby, and a purpose beyond just existing. If they went into this forest without me and never returned, which we all knew was possible, I would be alone again. I couldn't survive like that." He pursed his lips. The solitude posed more of a threat to him than this forest.

"I'm sure they're glad you're here," Lili said absent-mindedly, listening to the sound of Meriel quietly land on the greenhouse roof and creep across it. "Plus." She lowered her voice. "We may still find a way out."

"Sure," he said, not believing her.

"It's true." She hesitated. "I saw my mother step outside the walls."

Viktor's eyes widened but before he could question her, they heard a knock from inside the building. Lili looked up and found Meriel peeking through one of the windows, gesturing for them to enter through the front.

"Get in here," she hissed, peeking her head around the corner of the building before disappearing through the unlocked door.

Viktor checked the clearing for any men, then slipped inside, pack and all. Lili entered a moment later and shut the door behind them.

The greenhouse was impressive—three times bigger than her uncle's trailer—and every bit of it was covered with plants. The stone floor was lined with wooden boxes filled to the brim with dirt and stems sprouting beans, tomatoes, and squash. Above them were more of the same, though these were on stilts to hold them above the rest. At the top, she could see boxes hanging from the ceiling accompanied by a ladder to reach them. It was impressive how much had been preserved.

The walls were clean, meticulously so compared to the already well-kept buildings in this village, and some of them bore carvings similar to what they'd seen before. There was also a back door they could use to escape if need be.

"The animals reside in two separate areas." Meriel pointed east, then west. "Kingsley set them apart in case some contagious disease spread among them. He relies on rabbits, pigs, and chickens. We're lucky some people were smart enough to bring them. Otherwise, we'd have to hunt the wildlife outside the walls, which risks both the danger of fighting and contamination."

While Viktor was studying the plants, looking ready to grab a few, Meriel headed to the back of the room where the wall was covered in weapons, leather armor, and books. The notebook she picked up was a brown, leather one with several loose leaves jammed between the normal pages. Lili wandered over to see what she was reading. The woman was rushing through the pages, clearly searching for something.

Each page listed a name, date of entry, date of death, and method of death. Many were labeled BEHEADED but some said things like WOLVES, POISON, OLD AGE, and BEETLES. That last person's name, the victim of said beetles, was Stephen Kingsley. The son.

"He keeps track of every single person here," Meriel said, her voice tinged with disgust. Her finger lingered on the person who had been killed by wolves. "But he doesn't bury them unless he's able to put them in a coffin. Anyone else is left to rot."

"Like your husband?" Lili whispered, recalling what Meriel said earlier.

"Yes." Meriel slammed the book shut. "Like my husband."

After Meriel collected some of the weapons and covered her plain black clothes with the leather armor, she handed the rest to Lili and Viktor.

"I do find it strange," Viktor commented as they put the protective layers over their clothes, "how it was so easy to get in here. You'd think he'd have security for such an important building."

"Yes," Lili agreed as she tied the last piece around her chest. She was about to suggest they leave when she heard footsteps above. This time, they didn't belong to Meriel.

Heart racing, Lili looked up to see Kingsley's men racing along the glass toward them, guns aimed at their heads. They'd have to break the glass to shoot but that wouldn't be much of an issue.

Meriel grabbed a knife while Viktor pulled his shield from his pack. Lili considered shoving one of the shelves in front of the door to form a barricade but before she could move, there came a click from the back door. A moment later, someone kicked it open, nearly hitting her in the process.

"Get back," Viktor hissed as two men stepped through, armed with wooden spears. Kingsley came in after them, bearing his machine gun and a satisfied smile as he looked Meriel in the eye.

"You didn't think it would be that easy, did you?" he asked as more men entered, surrounding them. "I knew you'd take advantage of the newcomers to finally break in. You've always struck me as reckless."

Meriel spat in his direction.

Kingsley ignored it. "I can't have you jeopardizing the entire community just so you can chase your end."

"Anything is better than staying here and waiting for you to kill me if I catch a cold," Meriel shouted, stepping toward him despite the guns aimed at her torso.

Catch a cold?

"You can't keep people caged in like animals and expect none of them to rebel," Meriel continued.

"I *did* expect rebellion, which is why I was prepared." He nodded at his soldiers. "Disarm them and tie them up."

"Just let us go to the second level," Viktor intervened. "We won't take any of your plants. We swear."

Kingsley looked down at the armor and weapons they had already stolen, then back at Viktor with a chuckle. "I'm doing this to protect you, boy. I keep constant track of our resources and do what's best for this community. You and your friends will make a fine addition and, if you lead my hunting parties, I'm sure you can make up for the extra mouths to feed."

"We're not here to join you," Lili said quietly. "We're looking for our families. We believe they're on the lower level." If he used to have a son, he should understand the need to protect one's family.

"Trust me, dear. They're all dead. I have seen hundreds die in my time here, including my own child. What makes you think going deeper into this trap will somehow get you out? That doesn't make any sense."

"We have to try," Lili protested. "Besides, I know people can make it out. My mother did."

He shot her a pitying look. "Whatever you saw must have been an illusion, child. No one makes it out except the poisoned remains of those who entered. Your family is dead and you would be wise to stay here and make one of your own."

Of course he didn't believe her. No one would, which was why she never told anyone about her mother. She didn't care what he believed. She knew in her heart that her mother was still alive and calling to her.

While the men yanked the knife from Meriel's hand and tied them up, Lili pleaded one final time. "Keeping us here will only bring more pain to both you and your men. Please, let us go and you can continue living as you wish."

"That or you'll have to behead us in front of your entire village," Meriel sneered. "I wonder how they'll feel about the murder of six young adults for no good reason. It might upset your well-balanced establishment."

"If that ends up being the case, I will finally cave and tell them the truth, explaining why I acted that way. Until that happens, I will continue bearing the burden of knowledge alone so they can sleep well at night. The things I know need not be shared." He turned to his men. "Finish tying them and go get the others."

Lili glanced at Viktor, wondering where the rest were right now. If Kingsley was here, were they still at his house, looking for him?

Episode 12

The sun was coming up by the time Lili and her two friends were escorted out of the greenhouse, back into the courtyard where they'd first entered. The building housing the second level, where little Billy had been thrown, was a mere ten feet away and Kingsley, walking alongside them, had the key to it swinging from his neck. She wanted to grab the key, open the door, and jump in hoping for the best but knew it would only get her and the other two killed. She had to think of something else or wait for the others to act.

"Keep them in the center of the courtyard," Kingsley instructed three of the men. "We'll use them as bait. The rest of you spread out and prepare for their arrival. I doubt they'll be as weak as these three. Not if the rumors are true."

Rumors? Lili glanced at Meriel, who shook her head. "I described your group to him when I first arrived. It was what inspired my husband to come, remember? Everything Kingsley knows about the outside world, he learns from the people who come in."

Lili gasped as the butt of a gun hit the back of her legs, knocking her to her knees. When she fell, her palms sinking into the dirt, she could almost feel her mother's presence beneath her. She had to get down there.

The three of them waited and watched as several of Kingsley's men stood guard while the others dispersed, disappearing into the shadows of nearby buildings. Kingsley was the only one who remained, standing by the door to the greenhouse.

"This fight won't end well," Viktor whispered.

Lili spotted movement in the shadows.

"I don't think the others will be able to handle fighting people. The most we've had to protect ourselves from are animals," Viktor continued. "I don't know how my friends will react if they accidentally kill someone. None of us expected to harm our fellow humans when we came in here."

There was a shout from one of Kingsley's men, then Lili saw one of them fall from the roof he'd been standing on, an arrow in his shoulder.

"They're here," Kingsley shouted. "Remember, do not kill them. I want them alive." He planned to use them as hunters, more pawns to order around.

Lili watched as Leon's huge figure barreled down one of the alleys and shoved the two guards in it against the wall, knocking them out of the way on his path to Kingsley. While he ran, screaming, the twins appeared at the other end of the courtyard. Completely silent, they threw nets over the men on their side, then yanked them up so they dangled from the roof.

"Get yourselves untied," Meriel hissed, already attempting to use a stone from the ground to cut her ropes. She was unsuccessful. Lili tried to wriggle out of her restraints too but kept her eyes trained on the fight.

The twins leapt from their hiding spots, armed with tasers, and attacked the remaining men. Their weapons sent the guards to the ground, bodies twitching from the pain. She cringed when one of the twins—she was pretty confident it was Aidyn—got punched in the face and fell to the ground, hitting his head on the wall of a building when he landed.

"It looks like they found the hidden weapons in my room," Kingsley commented aloud while watching the three fighters take down his soldiers, his hands reaching for his gun but not touching it yet.

Lili froze, noticing movement behind Kingsley. The rising sun reflected off a head of long blond hair.

"Your armory was barely hidden," Jacques retorted, sneaking up behind the old man and pressing an arrow against his throat. Kingsley tensed. "It took us less than a minute to find it and realize where you were."

Kingsley's eyes shifted toward Jacques but he didn't grab his weapon. "It seems I've gone soft," he said quietly as Jacques stepped into the light. "This is why I need new leaders in this village, recruits for when I'm gone."

"We don't want to stay here. Just hand me that key and you won't get hurt." Jacques nodded at his necklace, then turned to the guards standing nearby. All of them were prepared to spear him but afraid to risk their master's safety. "Lower your weapons and release my friends or I'll kill him."

Lili didn't move. Two of the men bent down to untie her. A few feet away, Leon tied up the men he'd attacked in the alley, ensuring they couldn't retaliate. Kaidyn helped his brother to his feet. The back of Aidyn's head was slick with blood.

"You don't want to kill me," Kingsley warned Jacques. "Believe me. It will give the forest exactly what it wants."

Jacques rolled his eyes. "Give me the key. My patience is wearing thin."

"If you knew what I knew about this forest, you wouldn't risk dying down there."

"Then tell me." Jacques pressed the arrow's tip against the man's skin. "Stop hiding things and tell us what we want to know."

Kingsley leaned away, then nodded. Lili tried to listen as Kingsley spoke to Jacques in hushed tones but the young man's reaction was all she got. By the time Kingsley finished speaking, Jacques's eyes were wide. He lowered the arrow slightly before bringing it back up.

"We're still going down there."

"You're a fool."

"If we succeed in our quest, we might be able to save you too, Kingsley."

Lili and her friends were untied and standing by this point. Leon reached Kingsley and yanked the key from the man's neck. Jacques didn't try to stop him.

"Hurry up and deal with him, Jacques. Billy's been down there for too long," Leon said angrily, shoving Kingsley aside as he headed for the locked building.

"Well, Jacques?" Kingsley stared their leader down. "What are you going to do? I won't kill you, as you now know, and I won't stop you either. You've hurt enough of my men already. Your lives aren't worth those of my people."

Lili knew Kingsley's men could have killed them by this point and wanted to know why they hadn't. He knew they wouldn't join him, yet he still let them live. She'd have to ask Jacques what he learned once this was over.

"Meriel," Jacques said, not taking his eyes off Kingsley. "You've been here longer than I. What should we do with him?"

Meriel shrugged. "Tie him and his men up, then leave their fate to the villagers. If they want Kingsley to stay in charge, they can set him free." She raised her voice as she spoke so whoever was within earshot in the nearby homes could hear. "But if they're tired of his control, they can banish him as he did his son."

"I'm almost mad they didn't put up more of a fight," Kaidyn muttered as he followed Leon, Aidyn stumbling along behind him. Viktor was quick to pull out a white cloth and press it against the twin's head.

Meriel took part in tying up the others alongside Jacques. Lili, meanwhile, knelt next to the restrained leader of the village and pulled out the photo of her parents again. "This is my mother and father," she told him, pointing at them. "Why did you lie about being part of this group?"

Kingsley looked at the photo, then at her. "I knew a few of those members before they died. I...considered myself one of them after we fought together." He sighed, shooting her a sympathetic look. "After they died, no one took me seriously until I claimed I was part of their group. Word had already spread about their journey to the second level so I knew if I said I was the only remaining member, they would feel motivated to stay and build a life rather than descend to their deaths."

"So my parents *did* go down?"

"I don't know. They weren't the ones I met. If they *were* here, they either died or left before I arrived. It's been so long that I no longer remember. I didn't keep every name in the ledger back then."

She began to understand him at that moment. He kept track of everyone's names and deaths so he wouldn't forget them. She would have done the same in his position.

"Before you go down there, I need to warn you. If you do find your parents, they are likely an illusion. Do not trust your eyes. The forest is a master of deception." He studied her, squinting as though *she* might be the illusion. "Not all monsters from the forest look like animals."

Lili leaned away from him. She was almost as annoyed as Jacques by the man's cryptic talk. He seemed to enjoy avoiding specifics and keeping everyone in the dark.

"You'll understand what I mean when you get down there," Kingsley said as she stepped away. Jacques and Meriel were almost done tying everyone up. She didn't have much time. Lili looked back at Kingsley once more, wondering if she should ask him anything else.

"Kingsley," she whispered. If they were going to leave him behind anyway, she might as well be up front. "I know my mother came back. She left the walls."

His eyes widened. "...What?"

"Tell me how—" Before she could say another word, a strange rush of anxiety overtook her. For a moment, her feet felt glued to the ground again. It must be the tense situation paralyzing her, just like when Billy's parents turned to stone. Her mind was going fuzzy.

She opened her mouth to speak but before she could, Kingsley's face turned white. She frowned as he scrambled away from her, fearful.

"Don't come near me!" Kingsley shouted, looking at her like one would a monster.

"Lili, let's go." Jacques led her toward the door. The others were already on their way into the shed.

"Wait." Kingsley jerked out of his slouched position, then pointed at Jacques. "Don't go yet!"

"What's his problem?" Meriel asked as they stepped into the building containing the hole.

"He's trying to slow us down," Jacques said, ushering Lili forward, though he was twisting his head sideways to listen, still curious.

The shack they entered was small, barely the size of her camper bedroom, and the wood was painted black on both the interior and exterior. On the floor was a large circle with nothing but blackness within. They couldn't see what lay beneath. The only indicator that it was a hole was the hook in the floor and the rope attached to it, which disappeared into the circle.

"Thanks for the help," Meriel said to both Jacques and Lili before grabbing the rope and swinging down without hesitation. She disappeared just like they had when entering the wall. Lili was next and as she lowered herself down, she once again felt that tug from her mother, drawing her in.

"Wait!" Kingsley shouted, crawling toward her. "Jacques! She is—"

Jacques slammed the door closed to block out the man's voice. "Hurry, Lili. It sounds like he wants to stop us after all. I'm not letting him throw us back out to those beetles. Let's go."

Lili nodded and stuck her foot in the hole. It was difficult to hold her body up with just her arms, since she'd never slid down a rope before and could feel the fibers digging into her skin, but she managed. As soon as she felt herself slipping below the barrier of blackness, the air around her became frigid and took on a damp smell, like rotting leaves after a spring thaw. She wanted to look down and see what lay below but was too focused on keeping her arms and legs moving. The light of the surface had been replaced by a blue and green glow.

She was so busy staring at her hands and begging them to remain strong that she didn't notice the water beneath her until her boots touched it and she lost her grip, falling in with a splash. The cold liquid sent a chill up her arms and legs, weighing down her clothes. Kicking her legs and making for the surface, she opened her eyes to figure out which way was up. As soon as she saw what lay at the bottom of the pool, she screamed.

Episode 13

T he pool was fairly shallow, barely ten feet deep, and lying at the bottom were several humans—or what used to be. Their grey skin was frozen, as were their clothes, and many of them had their hands intertwined like they'd been climbing the rope when they turned to stone.

Terrified by sharing a pool with dead bodies, she swam toward the surface and away from the rope so Jacques wouldn't land on her. The last of her air left her lungs before she reached the surface and it made her racing heart nearly stop beating. In her mind, she could see the statues coming to life and dragging her down with them.

The visions of death left her mind as she broke the surface, the air far colder than it was a minute ago. The others were already resting on the shore, squeezing the water out of their clothes. By the time she reached them, Jacques had fallen in too.

"Did you see what was in there?" Viktor asked, pointing at the pool while she joined them. "The bodies?"

Lili nodded and tried to wring out her shirt, shivering from the recent memory. "I guess that means we won't be going back," she said quietly.

"But we already knew that," Kaidyn replied somberly as he bandaged Aidyn's head.

Viktor was grumbling about his pack getting wet when Jacques finally surfaced, struggling to doggy paddle. It was strange to see the most competent of them have trouble with something as simple as swimming. Once he was on the shore, he quickly composed himself and instructed everyone to take a breather. The fight had taken a lot out of them.

While everyone tried to dry off in the cold air, Lili examined this new area they'd entered. The pool they had landed in was right next to a massive wall, which was composed entirely of dark brown earth, though there were a few black roots running through it like veins. It was too dark to see most of their surroundings but it was easy to estimate the size of the area they had entered. They'd landed in an underground location. The dirt walls weren't as tall as the stone ones they'd passed through before but were still unnaturally large.

They all knew the walls surrounding the forest above were two hundred miles across. She had driven across the entire wall several times in her uncle's trailer and she'd even ridden over it once in a helicopter. When she flew, there had been no village in the center of the forest. It was hidden by whatever magical force kept everything concealed from the outside.

This new level looked considerably smaller, at least half the size, and even though it was hard to see the entire place, the walls curved around like the interior of a snow globe, locking them in. The only outside sunlight came from the holes in the ceiling. At the other end of the level was the biggest one, offering a thick stream of light. The only other sources of illumination were the plants and wildlife. The trees, unlike the tall pines on the surface, were thick and short. Their bark was lined with veins that glowed bright green, blue, and purple. The leaves were a matching color and were mesmerizing to look at. Lili spotted a few rabbits hopping by, the spots on their backs emitting that same colorful glow. Their eyes were in a similar state, shining and pupilless. She nearly jumped when one of them looked in her direction with bright yellow orbs.

The ground itself was damp and muddy and the entire place gave her constant chills. It felt like a living creature, ready to eat her. It was so different from the first level, which had been relatively normal.

"I don't like this place," Kaidyn whispered, glaring at the ominous trees. "The ground looks like it'll suck you in."

"Well, if that does happen, make sure to film it," Jacques said, holding out the camera to capture this darker but prettier forest. "Good thing Viktor thought to pack waterproof bags, right?"

"Very funny, Jacques." Kaidyn started sorting through the new weapons he had found in Kingsley's armory. They'd procured some tasers, batteries, and a sniper rifle. Kaidyn mulled over the weapons with a serious face, unlike Aidyn who was grinning at the passing bunnies instead, back to his cheery self despite his head injury.

"Can any of you see Billy?" Leon asked, making Lili feel guilty for nearly forgetting the boy.

"No. I checked from the top of that rope and didn't see him or anyone else," Jacques answered, ending his recording. "But I did spot a manmade structure in that direction." He pointed northwest, near the biggest hole in the ceiling. "That's where we need to go. If we want any chance of surviving down here, asking those with experience is the best way to go about it."

"Give me a few more minutes to patch up Aidyn," Kaidyn protested.

Since they had time, Lili took the chance to finally ask a question that had been nagging her.

"Jacques, what did Kingsley tell you before we came down?" she asked, making him tense.

"Right. I nearly forgot." Meriel leaned toward him too, wringing out her hair. "Spill it. What did he tell you about the forest?"

Now all eyes were on their unofficial leader who looked strangely nervous, his now empty hands struggling to find something to fiddle with. "Well...he told me what to do if any of us died."

Kaidyn and Viktor stopped bandaging Aidyn.

"And?" Meriel waited, arms crossed.

"He said to cut off the person's head," Jacques answered quietly, making Lili cringe.

"Did he say why?" Kaidyn asked.

"Yes but...I agree with him that not everyone needs to know about it. It might make killing the monsters here even harder, and we're struggling enough as it is."

Both Kaidyn and Meriel rolled their eyes. Jacques was turning into Kingsley.

"Harder? Seriously, Jacques. If you keep it from us, you're just as bad as him," Kaidyn protested but Aidyn cut his brother off.

"Jacques is only trying to protect us. If we needed to know, he would tell us," Aidyn said. "We know *what* to do so the *why* doesn't matter."

"It matters to me," Meriel hissed. "I lost my husband in those woods and didn't cut off his head. I want to know why I should have."

Jacques stared at her, his eyes glassy, then turned away. "Like Kingsley said, you'll find out the reason soon enough. We should focus on our progress before it gets dark, if it even gets darker down here." The light was already dim. "I'm not sure how the day and night cycles work underground."

"Well, the lights from above will go out at night," Viktor said, heaving as he pulled on his pack again. It had gotten wet in the fall, increasing its weight. "But I don't know if those glowing lights will change."

"So, you've never seen anything like them before?" Jacques asked.

Their resident plant expert shrugged. "There are bioluminescent plants and animals like that on Earth, though they don't look quite like this. I've never seen plants and animals this ominous, at least on land."

Lili recalled the anglerfish of the ocean and how it used a yellow light to lure in its prey. Were these trees similar, trying to attract victims with pretty colors so they could consume them?

When they stepped closer to the woods, their boots started sticking in the ground, not pulling them in like quicksand but slowing their pace. She kept her eyes on the trees while they entered their perimeter. The plants looked more cartoonish than anything she'd seen in real life. The knots and branches on their thick, lumpy trunks resembled faces with open mouths and empty eyes. A chill ran up her spine every time she made "eye contact" with one of them. The yellow-eyed rabbits darting past didn't help either.

The only consolation was that as the sun started descending—made obvious by the light from the ceiling disappearing—some colorful fireflies of blue, green, and yellow started flitting about. One landed on her finger and looked cuter than the real fireflies, resembling a bumblebee.

"Be careful," Viktor warned in a panicked whisper as she let the insect fly off her hand. "They might be poisonous."

She shrugged. It was too late to stop it now. "It didn't hurt me."

Viktor shrugged back angrily, mocking her nonchalance. "Can't be too careful."

They continued their walk silently but talking to her must have reminded Viktor about their earlier discussion because he broke the silence by saying, "Lili said she saw her mother leave the wall."

Lili stopped in her tracks and waited for the others to turn toward her, every one of them shooting her a doubtful look. Only Jacques seemed to believe her. She wished she'd kept her mouth shut. This was not the time to bring up her secret. They might stop trusting her if they knew she'd withheld important information.

"Tell us what you saw," Jacques said calmly, like a schoolteacher. "Every detail."

She did. It only took a few minutes, since it was a short story to tell. She described the way her mother looked—her lifeless skin and the moss or rot growing on her body. The more she talked about it, the more insane it sounded. Clearly the others thought the same but they listened without interruption, not surprised by anything anymore.

"We'll have to give this information to the folks we find down here, if there are any," Jacques said. "She just went back inside after looking at you? Nothing more?"

"Nothing more."

"That seems strange." The group formed a huddle to discuss Lili amongst themselves, congregating in a clearing between the thick trees.

While Lili waited for them to debate her questionable childhood memories and how they connected to the forest, she felt a stabbing pain in the back of her head. It felt like she had missed something while recounting that memory. It was just out of reach and on the tip of her tongue. Had she really seen her mother that day? Or had she forgotten something crucial during the six-year gap?

No, she dreamed of it and recalled it a hundred times over. She couldn't be mistaken. The memory was crystal clear in her mind's eye.

"Well," Jacques finally concluded after the group finished their discussion in hushed whispers, "If what you say is true, it means it is possible to leave the walls, though I don't like the implication your mother's strange body creates." He sighed. "Until we figure out how exactly your mother left, we can't risk following in her footsteps. You two saw that couple turn to stone with your own eyes, so unless there's some secret down here that explains how your mother got into her...zombie-like state, we'll have to assume we're no different from all the escapees who fell into that pool."

Lili nodded in agreement.

"Why did your mother go back into the forest?" Kaidyn asked, breaking her train of thought. "Why didn't she get help instead?"

Lili had asked herself the same question and never found a definitive answer. "I assumed it had to do with how...plant-like her body had become." A few of her companions shivered, no doubt picturing their own bodies becoming that way if they stayed here too long.

"Let's keep going," Meriel interrupted and continued marching through the mud. "If you have more to say, you can talk while we walk."

The rest were quick to follow.

Leon asked the group if he could have permission to shout Billy's name and everyone but Kaidyn consented, since they had yet to encounter anything dangerous. A second later, Leon's voice echoed through the forest and caused a flock of glowing birds to flutter from the tops of trees. When the animals ascended, Lili saw the tree next to her shift slightly, like it had been disturbed. She could tell Aidyn noticed it too and they shared a frightened look. Only after the tree stopped did they decide it was nothing more than the wind...though there was no wind down here.

The further they went into this closed-in forest, the more lifelike the trees became. Trunks started resembling heads and roots running through the mud looked like fingers, lifeless and long.

"I think something's following us like that beetle did on the surface," Kaidyn eventually said after several hours of traversing the land. "Be on guard."

Lili started checking over her shoulder as they proceeded but saw nothing. She almost hoped she would. At least that way she'd know what they were up against.

The group eventually reached a point where the mud became water, turning into a waist-high swamp that soaked their clothes and made them even more miserable. The only consolations were some new discoveries they found ahead.

Unlike the surface, which only had the well-fortified village and a few graves, this area was littered with the remains of stone buildings, all of them mossy and ruined. It became common to stumble into bricks hidden under the murky waters and cut one's leg, which made Lili paranoid about every step. When they passed by what looked like old chimneys and stone foundations—even a few floating hammocks and beds in disrepair—her sense of wonder increased. Just like the statues and village foundation, there were remnants of countless ages and cultures in the architecture.

"Thousands of people must have lived down here at some point," Jacques whispered. When they looked to either side, they could see the remains of hundreds of buildings. It was a shame so much of it was hidden by the gnarled trees and muddy waters. Some of the buildings bore English and French carvings on the walls.

"It's a warning," Jacques said, pronouncing the French words aloud as the group passed another set of nearly identical marks. "They say: Do not die alone. Stay away from the trees. Beg the forest for protection." He frowned. "Those sound contradictory."

Lili assumed they had reached the middle of the ruins when the ground was starting to rise, becoming dry again and giving them a brief respite from their soggy shoes and muddy legs. Past this high area, the land dipped back into the water again. In the middle of this dry patch was a tall tree and this one was unmistakably carved to look like a human. It had glowing red and orange branches, the only one like it they'd encountered on this level. Below the branches was a round, misshapen head of brown wood and bark. It had empty eyes and a pointed nose. Its face was angled downwards, staring at its open-palmed hands, which were holding a round basin of smooth stone.

"This looks like an offering bowl," Viktor whispered, stepping onto the dry land and examining the basin. It had carvings along the outside but the inside was empty. "I wonder what they put in here."

Leon looked into the basin. "Plants, maybe? Fertilizer?"

Lili saw Kaidyn focusing on the crimson leaves. Following his gaze, she spotted some red veins traveling from the base of the tree to the branches. They looked similar to the walls of the level they were standing in.

"Maybe they used to sacrifice people," Kaidyn suggested. "This writing looks ancient, like everything else here. People used to sacrifice their own back then. This might be no different."

"Let's not assume the worst," Jacques countered, looking beyond the tree to the rest of the swamp. It would take hours to reach the end of it and nightfall was approaching. "Do we want to camp here?"

Lili looked up at the mysterious tree, recalling the movement they saw from the others and envisioned it coming alive while they slept. She didn't protest as the others set up tents—voicing those fears might sound paranoid—but she knew she'd have trouble sleeping tonight. She wasn't the only one who looked frightened. Aidyn did too. When she noticed his quivering hands, she made a suggestion.

"Since there's seven of us now, we can have two or three people take watch. Whatever is stalking us might try to attack while we're asleep, so we should have multiple people up and ready to defend us at any moment."

Jacques raised an eyebrow but didn't shut her suggestion down. "Good idea. We have to be on guard now, more than ever. I'll have to finish teaching you how to use a bow then." He turned toward the rest, who were still examining the strange basin. "Do we want to set up a fire and make our presence known?"

"We won't need the light," Kaidyn commented, gesturing to the glowing plants and insects around them. "Though it is colder down here."

"Very well. I will take the first watch with someone," Jacques offered and Meriel agreed to stay up with him. Viktor and Leon offered to take the second watch and the remaining three made up the third.

When Lili went to sleep, sharing her tent with Meriel, she could feel vibrations in the ground beneath her head. She could also hear the moan of branches moving in the nonexistent wind. The noises gave her nightmares—visions of trees wandering around their camp, using their branches to trap her in makeshift cages. Then the trees in her dream shifted until they resembled her mother.

There was another feeling that remained present while she lay on the ground. Just like before, she could feel a tug urging her to go below the earth. As her dreams continued, allowing her to once again relive that fateful day outside the walls where she saw her mother, she realized her mom wasn't here, on this level. She was still beneath them.

There must be another level below and it was where her mother was waiting.

Episode 14

Once Lili's shift with Aidyn and Kaidyn began, she was able to fully appreciate the beauty of the forest in the peace and quiet. The trees loomed over them but the glowing bugs in their branches made them feel like guardians instead of ominous threats. The fresh scent of grass and moss felt a little less suffocating now that her body had adjusted to it.

At the start of their shift, Kaidyn sat with his brother and said nothing, but after a while, he got bored and started studying the offering bowl again. Aidyn sat by the campfire, constantly peering over his shoulder, as though anticipating eyes in the shadows. Lili knew who he was hoping to find.

"Hey, Lili," Aidyn called to her from across the fire. "I'm glad you mentioned seeing your mother. It makes me feel a little less crazy, since I've been seeing my siblings too."

She smiled at him. "I don't think you're crazy." She wasn't sure if he was *actually* seeing them or was only seeing what he wanted to. However, if she thought of Aidyn that way, she'd have to admit perhaps her twelve-year-old mind had done the same thing, and that was something she'd never do. They'd come too far to give up on their families now.

"Let's not rule out the possibility that you might have dreamed it or had hallucinations," Kaidyn cut in, ruining their positive mood. He tapped the bottom of the offering bowl, then wiped his finger along its surface. It came up clean. "Sometimes you think about something so much that your mind starts visualizing things that aren't there."

"I know what I saw," Aidyn huffed and turned away from Kaidyn, facing the darkness.

Lili wanted to agree with Aidyn but felt the two brothers should sort things out on their own.

The conversation over, Kaidyn marched into his tent and returned a minute later with some food and tools. Not a word was said as he placed each item in the bowl one at a time, waiting for a few seconds while looking up at the nearly human tree, then taking the object out and putting in something else.

"What are you doing?" Lili whispered, stepping closer.

"Testing to see what kind of offerings people put in here," he answered, removing a wrinkled apple and placing grass inside instead.

"Are you expecting something to happen if you put the right thing in?" she asked.

He shrugged. "Nothing in this forest makes sense so—I was starting to wonder if the right offering will make the tree reveal a doorway or protect us or something." He tried a leaf next but nothing worked. "They built this thing for a reason. I want to figure out what they knew."

"Maybe we need to add some kind of liquid. It is a bowl, after all," Lili suggested.

Kaidyn glanced at her, looking ready to call her stupid, then he nodded instead and left to retrieve some water from the bog.

"Kaidyn," Aidyn said, staring at the forest. "I think I can see them again."

All three of them paused what they were doing. Lili looked where he was pointing but couldn't see anything.

"Just stay put. If whatever monster it is comes closer, warn me then," Kaidyn ordered in a tired monotone. He poured the water into the bowl and looked up at the tree again.

"I don't see anything, Aidyn," Lili said. She squinted at the forest. It was so dark and the tree's shadows were eerie enough on their own, but she couldn't spot anything out of the ordinary.

"This isn't working," Kaidyn said to himself. Lili glanced at him and saw him pull out a knife.

"Kaidyn!" Aidyn shouted, jumping to his feet. "It's them! It's Max and Minnie! I swear!"

"Don't move," Kaidyn commanded again. He held his hand over the bowl and raised his knife. "Maybe it takes blood."

"Kaidyn, we should at least take a look," Lili said, reaching for him. "Aidyn, I still don't see anyone." There were movements among the shadows but they didn't strike her as friendly. "We should stay here until we confirm what it is."

But as Kaidyn started cutting his hand, Aidyn drew his sword and stepped into the water, away from their tents.

"I can't lose them again," Aidyn whispered. Before Lili could stop him, he ran into the trees. For a split second, she thought she could see two humanoid figures among the shadows in the direction he was running, but then she blinked and they looked like normal trees again.

"Kaidyn!" she shouted, grabbing the twin's arm before he could drip his blood into the offering. He finally turned, noticed his brother running away, and growled.

"That idiot. Lili, wake the others. Aidyn!" He yanked his hand from her grasp and dashed after his brother, drawing his sword.

When the twins ran through the muddy swamp, Lili noticed some ripples in the water. There was something under their feet, stalking them.

"Watch out!" she shouted. "There's something in the water."

Breathing heavily, she ran to Leon's tent and yanked it open, shouting to wake everybody up.

In moments, everyone was awake and leaping out of their tents, grabbing their weapons. Lili pulled her own knife from her pack and ran to the edge of the dry land.

The twins were still trudging toward where the shadows had been but while Leon leapt into the water and Jacques followed after with his bow at the ready, Lili spotted several human-shaped shadows leaping from the water and toward the twins. They must have swam along the bottom, waiting to strike.

The first creature was tall and lanky with arms long enough to reach its feet. It had snow-white skin and long, knotted black hair. Its legs and arms were covered in black hairs that weren't thick enough to be fur but too long to be human. The worst part was its mouth, stretched so wide it could swallow Aidyn's head whole. It was about to do so to Kaidyn when the twin turned and sliced its jaw off with his sword.

The second creature trying to kill the twins wasn't as tall as the first. It didn't have fully formed limbs either. Instead, its arms and legs came to a point like blades of flesh. Just like the first, it was snow white but its face was completely wrapped in flat skin, devoid of hair and facial features. Its long limbs tried to slice Kaidyn in two but Jacques managed to shoot the back of its head with an arrow and sent it back into the water.

Leon charged toward the twins and roared, grabbing the now jaw-less creature with his hands. Lili cringed as he sent it crashing into one of the trees, its head hitting a trunk with a sickening crunch. By the time Leon joined Aidyn and Kaidyn, a third creature had emerged from the woods and was towering over the trio. This third beast reminded Lili of a human, an insect, and a tree morphed into one with numerous limbs tied together to form two arms and legs. Its neck stretched far above its shoulders, casting shadows on the three fighters. Its head was a round, featureless circle of rotting flesh, dripping blood into the water.

"That thing is huge," Jacques whispered as he loosed another arrow at the creature, hitting it in the shoulder. "And the other two aren't dead. I think it's best if we flee."

"I don't think we can outrun those things," Meriel warned, stepping out of the tent with a taser and staring at the creatures with wide eyes. "We're dead."

"Don't talk like that," Viktor shouted with a shaky voice, quivering behind his shield. "I'm scared enough as it is."

Leon and the twins tried to cut off the giant creature's head while the other two monsters circled around them. They were attempting to flank the fighters and were barely delayed by Jacque's arrows.

Lili felt her legs shake. She wanted to help but knew she'd get in their way. Looking over her shoulder at the tree, she wondered if dripping blood in the offering bowl would protect them. Maybe Kaidyn had the right idea. The French words on the houses said to ask the forest for help. What if offering a sacrifice was how they went about that? Sacrifices were common throughout history.

"We're not prepared for this," Jacques said, grimacing. "If we distract the monsters, maybe you three can escape without getting caught." He flinched when Leon was shoved underwater by the biggest creature. Jacques stuck an arrow in the monster's arm and Aidyn cut off the other, freeing Leon, but he came up sputtering and out of breath.

"There could be more of them." Meriel started toward the water. "We need to fight together or they'll pick us off one by one."

Lili backed up to the bowl, peering down at it. She could feel invisible eyes watching her from above.

There was still water in the bowl from when Kaidyn filled it but nothing had changed. Looking down at her knife, she wondered if she had the guts to cut herself hard enough to draw blood.

"You three get back here," Jacques shouted at Leon, Kaidyn, and Aidyn. The twins were bleeding, dying the water beneath their feet.

They were still alive and fighting but were out of breath and Leon was being pushed underwater again. They wouldn't last much longer.

"Please protect my friends," she whispered to the tree and slit the bottom of her palm. A sharp pain shot through her arm, then immediately dulled. She heard more cries behind her but ignored them, watching the drops of blood touch the water and swirl in a circle. The blood and water spun to the bottom of the bowl and vanished, as though it had a funnel at the bottom that she couldn't see.

It had worked. Would her wish come true now?

She turned back to the fight and managed to catch Aidyn slicing off the head of the black-haired, long-armed beast. Kaidyn gave the giant the same treatment, forcing it to release Leon.

They'd done it. They were going to be okay.

Lili was about to breathe a sigh of relief, glad they hadn't needed the sacrifice after all, when the faceless creature with its pointed limbs dove under the water and started swimming toward the dry land where the rest of them were standing. Its limbs rose and spread, imitating a perfect breaststroke.

Jacques shot another arrow at it but missed. Once it was close enough, Meriel tried to hit it with her taser, but it had other plans. Regardless of how many arrows were now sticking out of its arms and skull, it wouldn't stop.

Lili ran toward her friends, as did the three fighters, but before she could do anything, the beast leapt into the air, its arms stretched in front of it. Everyone shouted as it dug its pointed limbs into Jacques's chest. Viktor screamed. Everyone froze, paralyzed, as Jacques fell with the monster on top of him.

"No!" Viktor continued to scream while Lili charged toward it, her bloodied blade still in hand. She shouted to energize herself, then jumped on top of the thing, shoving her blade into its skull. The monster went limp.

Lili tried to yank out her knife, knowing she'd need to behead it to kill it, but screaming Viktor got to it first. He drove the edge of his shield against the creature's neck, cutting off its head and knocking it off Jacques in the process. Lili tumbled to the ground, her hands shaking so badly she nearly dropped her weapon.

"Jacques." Viktor leaned over their leader's body. There were two holes on both sides of his chest, narrowly avoiding any vitals. He was already bleeding profusely and was fading in and out of consciousness.

Meriel leapt to Jacques's side and pressed both hands against the wound on the right, shouting for Lili to do the same on the left. After recovering from his shock, Viktor jumped back into his tent and came out with bandages, needles, string, and bottles of unlabeled liquids. As Lili pressed both hands on Jacques' left side, his skin uncomfortably delicate and squishy beneath her blood-soaked palms, she watched Viktor clean and bandage the wounds. Jacques tried to tell them something but each word was cut off by his mouth clenching shut from pain and exhaustion.

"If...I die...cut....my head..." Jacques eventually whispered, emphasizing the words as though this was the most important order he could possibly give. "Don't...let me...turn..."

The twins finally reached them, bleeding from fresh cuts on their arms and legs. A soaking Leon followed after, breathing heavily and clutching his throat. He had fresh red bruises on it from the monster trying to drown him.

"Finish patching him up," Kaidyn told Viktor, assuming the role of leadership in Jacques's absence. "Then Leon can carry him. Let's hope we can find some help before...you know."

Viktor nodded.

Satisfied, Kaidyn turned on his brother, who was gripping his bleeding arm and staring at Jacques in shock. "If you *ever* go out there again, I will kill you myself, Aidyn. Do you hear me?"

Aidyn nodded meekly, well aware of his mistake.

Kaidyn clenched his fists, then addressed the others. "Pack up the camp and stop trying to get yourselves killed. We're leaving in two minutes."

Everyone flinched when he spoke, his deep voice sending chills down Lili's spine. He sounded ready to murder them if they made the wrong move. She knew it was his way of showing concern but it made her nervous regardless.

Once Viktor had finished bandaging their leader, Leon picked up Jacques and carried him as gently as possible. He asked Lili which direction Jacques told them to go. With Jacques incapacitated, Lili was in charge of directions now. After Lili told him, Leon started charging through the water, not caring if he left them behind. Jacques's life depended on his speed.

"What happened back there?" Meriel asked as they ran, the water soaking their clothes and slowing them down. They'd had to leave some heavier items behind. "Why were you in the water in the first place?"

"Worry about that later," Kaidyn said, pulling a small flare gun from his pack and aiming it upwards. Lili covered her ears as he fired a shot at the air, launching a small red light into the sky. Once it was empty, he threw the gun over his shoulder. They must have only brought one flare. "If they see this, maybe they can find us."

"He might already be dead," Viktor said, tears springing to his eyes as they followed the trail of blood Leon and Jacques left behind. "What will we do if he dies? He's the only one who actually knows what he's doing." Viktor was crying again and his panicked questions were making the group even more nervous. If this continued, they would all lose hope and give up completely. Lili had to encourage them somehow. She couldn't allow them to abandon their quest. Her parents' lives depended on it.

"Jacques wouldn't want you guys to give up, even if he died," she told them.

Kaidyn nodded in agreement. "She's right. His mother sent him here to document the forest and show it to the world. He wouldn't want us to give in. Even if he dies, we need to continue forward," he said confidently.

Lili hadn't heard anything about Jacques' parents or his true motivation for coming, other than wanting to learn the secrets of the forest. Now she understood him a little better. In the end, all of them were here to protect or follow their family, even Viktor, who treated these young men like his brothers.

"His heartbeat is slowing!" Leon shouted back to them, still running. He was nearly twenty-five feet ahead of them. "Viktor. What do I do?"

Viktor stopped crying for a second, struggling to keep pace, then he closed his eyes and called back. "Keep running. There's nothing more I can do." He sounded ready to kill himself for being so useless.

"You did what you could," Kaidyn reminded Viktor as they ran, light beginning to stream through the two openings in the ceiling again. It was morning. "You helped kill the monster."

Viktor looked at him with a tear-streaked face and child-like fear.

"He's right," Meriel said. "Even I can acknowledge that."

"I barely did anything," Viktor sobbed. "I should have trained in combat before we came instead of studying at home."

"This isn't helping, Viktor," Kaidyn warned but Meriel cut him off.

"If you feel bad about your weakness, work to improve it instead of wallowing in self-pity," Meriel said to Viktor, panting from their sprinting. It felt like she'd told herself the same thing several times. "I waited around for a whole year after my husband died and look where that got me. Stop crying and start improving so the rest of us don't have to die."

After breaking free of the forest and reaching a clearing, they finally found the large stone building they'd been searching for this entire time. It was closer than they'd assumed and Lili could already see several men running toward them, dressed in black vests and armed with guns. The only exception was a woman wearing a white doctor's uniform. She was running toward Jacques with a bag of tools in hand.

They might be able to save him after all.

Episode 15

Just as the village on the upper level was built on top of old buildings and foundations, this one was built on the remains of a stone castle with high walls and a moat surrounding a bridge, which led them to two large stone doors. In the moat was a river, which flowed from the hole in the ceiling. That water was likely the only thing they could drink that wasn't poisoned by the forest.

On top of the ancient stone walls, which were lined with sharp points to prevent anyone or anything from getting in, Lili saw modern buildings of concrete mixed with the older stone and wood. It looked like the cement walls had been brought here intentionally from the outside world and placed here by machines. There were also modern turrets and trebuchets lining the walls, pointed at the surrounding forest. Judging by the ropes hanging from the massive hole in the ceiling, they must have carried everything down. That, or they dropped it and hoped for the best. Lili remembered seeing machines and troops head in when she was young, never to return. Now she finally got to see the result.

The sunlight pouring through the hole above helped Lili spot the men and women charging toward them. It was clear from their attire that they were soldiers, with the exception of the doctor. They wore black armor—a mix between a modern soldier and historical knight—and black plates guarded their shoulders and chests. Their helmets concealed everything except their eyes. Like Kingsley, every one of them bore a machine gun, though these were thankfully aimed at the forest instead of the newcomers.

The doctor, on the other hand, was wearing completely modern clothes, including the round glasses covering her grey eyes. Her blonde hair was darkening, likely from the lack of sunlight, and her voice was croaky as she shouted at Leon.

"Let me have a look at him," she ordered while the soldiers surrounded them. It took less than a second to see the damage done to Jacques's chest. "Bring him inside. Hurry."

The rest didn't have time to react as Leon followed the woman across the moat and into the castle without thinking to look back. He was so panicked that he didn't realize he'd left them behind.

"Are you being followed?" One of the men stepped forward and removed his helmet, revealing the scarred cheeks and square jaw of a middle-aged man. Lili and her friends froze in front of him, the men's guns scaring them into silence. Realizing he had frightened them, the soldier lowered his weapon and looked past them. "I don't see anything behind you but some of you are injured. What attacked you?"

Lili glanced at Kaidyn, unsure if they could trust these people. They might be just as bad as Kingsley.

"We were attacked by three creatures," Kaidyn answered slowly. "But we killed them."

There were murmurs as the soldiers reacted to their success.

"What did they look like?" the man continued.

Kaidyn described them. When he mentioned the one that stabbed Jacques, Lili noticed one of the soldiers gasp and turn away, lowering her gun.

"I see. That must have been Cody," the man said somberly, glancing sympathetically at the soldier, then turning back to Kaidyn. "How did you kill them?"

"We cut off their heads," he answered without hesitation.

"Good. That's the only way to end their torment." The man's smile, a mix between a proud father and stern soldier, made Lili feel inclined to trust him. "If you want to live, follow us inside the castle. We'll protect you. I can talk more inside."

Everyone but Kaidyn was eager to obey. They didn't want to see anyone else die and the dry castle looked far better than the swamp-filled forest full of monsters and crumbling ruins.

"Better in there than out here," Viktor told Kaidyn quietly, gesturing to the dark trees they had just escaped. Even now, the plants looked alive, like miserable old men eternally trapped in rotting bark.

Kaidyn nodded. "We'll come with you, as long as you help Jacques and answer all our questions."

"Of course." The man gestured for his soldiers to step aside, then led everyone across the moat, the water barely flowing beneath their feet.

"What are your names?" the man in charge asked as they went. The soldiers' kept their backs to them, focusing on surveying the forest.

After Kaidyn listed their names, Meriel added how long each of them had been there and the reputation of the Rural Rangers.

"You were foolish to come here," the leader told them after they explained their reasons for coming. "But so were we. My name is Diego and we were sent here nine years ago after the initial discovery of the forest and its walls."

Meriel didn't look surprised. "You're one of the reasons my husband was confident about entering. He figured if the military was stationed inside, you could protect us."

Diego shook his head, leading them past the walls. "When we realized there was another level in this forest, we stationed some of our people above and the rest of us went down, confident our weaponry and machinery would protect us. Most of it broke on impact..." He pointed at the hole, far above both them and the castle. This one was huge compared to the hole under Kingsley's village. "But I'm glad we brought them since the monsters down here are far more dangerous than the ones above."

Lili immediately felt safer once they were past the walls and the bridge raised behind them. The inside of the walls felt empty and sterile, holding only white boxes and grey benches alongside a few tanks that looked like they hadn't moved in years. The wheels had no tracks. The interior of the building was the same with torches and lanterns lining the smooth grey walls and polished floors. Every door they passed was closed.

The soldiers remained outside. Only Diego stayed with the newcomers, leading them forward. The only indication that they were going the right way was the trail of bloody footprints Leon had left on the floor.

"I'm glad it's possible to live here for nine years," Lili said. If these soldiers had survived, her mother could too.

"Anna and I are the only survivors. The rest of the soldiers were sent in five years ago," Diego said, leading them into a large room with a window pointed toward the hole in the ceiling. The walls were lined with weapons and armor, similar to the back of Kingsley's greenhouse but cleaner and more organized. There were a few people inside the room cleaning weapons. Only one of them paid the newcomers any mind. All he offered was a sympathetic nod, seemingly saddened by the sight of them.

"I remember the day the soldiers were sent in," Lili said, the memory flowing back. "My uncle warned them not to go."

"Who's your uncle?" Diego asked and when she told him, he nodded. "I remember him. He was right, though I don't think he knew how right he was. We were sent here to discover the forest's secrets and bring them back to the government without the public's knowledge."

"And what have you found?" Kaidyn asked as they proceeded down another hallway.

"Not as much as I would like," the soldier said, sighing. "But we know enough to survive and that's more than most get. Now that you've increased our numbers, we'll be able to continue exploring again."

"How many people live here now?" Lili asked, knowing the man expected them to stay here permanently, just like Kingsley. He'd be disappointed when they left.

"Currently? Forty, excluding you and your friends." The man smiled at them. "You're the youngest I've seen in years. Most children die within days of entering. All of them, actually." His voice quieted and his brow furrowed, as though recalling such an instance.

"Speaking of children," Kaidyn cut in. "We came down here because Kingsley threw a child down one of the holes. We haven't been able to find him. Have you seen him?"

"Or have you seen two people who look like me and my brother?" Aidyn asked excitedly. "A boy and a girl."

"I haven't seen a child," Diego began slowly, thinking it over and coming out unsure of the true answer. "Not for a few years, at least. Regarding the second question, do you know when those two arrived?"

Both twins stopped walking, their faces filling with hope for the first time. "You *have* seen them?"

"Maybe." Diego scratched the scruff on his chin. "But we'll discuss that after checking on your friend, since you may not like the answer and it will take a long time to explain."

"Just like Kingsley," Kaidyn muttered, making the soldier chuckle.

"So you met Kingsley? I'm not surprised. He seemed intent on taking over after we left."

"He did."

Diego nodded. "Kingsley withholds information because he believes himself stronger than everyone else, at least mentally. I don't believe that. I won't hold anything back. I just want to wait for a better time."

Neither the twins nor Meriel looked happy with that answer but followed along anyway, passing through more halls. The west wing of the castle contained a large room converted into a terrarium. It was filled to the brim with plants, far bigger and more vibrant than Kingsley had in his greenhouse. The sun was shining straight into the room from the hole above.

"I need to take a look at that greenhouse later," Viktor told Diego. Even though Viktor's face was still stained red from tears and his eyes were pink to match, he'd regained some of his spark after discovering the terrarium.

At the end of the main hall, they finally found a white lab twice as big as her uncle's camper. The inside contained a mix of tools from the overworld and homemade devices, most of them made from metal, stone, and redwood from the forest's trees. It was encouraging to know that these people were smart enough to build their own tools. There were several smooth stone tables in the center, all but one covered in bottles, syringes, and assorted papers.

The center table was the only one Lili cared about. Jacques was lying on it, no longer bleeding but paler than she'd ever seen him. Leon was standing behind the table, leaning over his friend with a worried grimace. The blonde doctor was doing the same, using a knife to cut through Jacques' clothes. She didn't acknowledge the others when they arrived.

"How's he looking, Anna?" Diego asked. They moved closer but were too afraid to get in the doctor's way.

There was a long silence as the woman finished removing Jacques' clothes and bandages so they could see the full extent of his wounds. "Without my full arsenal, I'm not sure if I can save him," she told Diego, studying everyone's faces before turning back to Jacques, who was still unconscious. "I might be able to delay his death but...you know how risky that is."

The soldier nodded, though Lili didn't understand what she meant.

"There's nothing you can do?" Kaidyn insisted, anger creeping back into his tone. "Nothing at all? The wounds can't be that bad." Lili could tell he didn't believe his own words but refused to accept Jacques' fate.

The doctor gestured to the two grave wounds Jacques had sustained. As she spoke, she pulled out a thread and needle and started sewing the cuts closed. "It's risky to keep him in here. If he dies inside the castle, it will put everyone at risk."

"Because of infection?" Kaidyn asked and the doctor shook her head.

"You don't know what happens after death?" she finally asked after closing the first wound and covering it with fresh bandages. The doctor had wiped the rest of the blood away but the bitter scent lingered. "Diego, you need to tell them everything." She set to sewing the next hole shut.

"Right." Diego gestured for everyone to gather around him. "Let's leave the doctor to her work and talk in the greenhouse." As he spoke, a few more soldiers entered the room and stood around the operation table with their weapons drawn. Their presence, which made Lili feel safe before, now made her uncomfortable because they were glaring at Jacques so intently.

The group followed Diego into the terrarium. Tall vines lined the walls and potted vegetables hung from pots on the ceiling. They took a seat on some benches in the center. Viktor and Leon immediately started exploring the place, barely listening when Diego spoke. Kaidyn chose to stare out the glass window overlooking the castle walls and forest beyond it.

"Before I explain, ask any questions you might have. I suspect what I'm about to tell you will interfere with any further discussion," Diego told them, resting his helmet on the stone bench and focusing on Aidyn, Lili, and Meriel since they were the only ones who bothered to join him.

"You said you came here nine years ago," Lili began. "Did you find the original ten who came here a year before?"

"Yes," he said immediately. "Five came down with us and three continued into the third level."

"Who? Which ones?" She leaned forward, her loud voice making Kaidyn turn from the window to listen.

"The ones who stayed with us were Stepan Clostrum and Christine Solstice. They both died in their third years on a journey from the castle to our southern base."

Not her parents, though she recognized the names. She'd memorized all ten.

"So there *is* a third layer," Meriel said thoughtfully. "I wonder how many levels there are in total."

"None of us know," the soldier continued. "The three people I mentioned descended eight years ago with our team of researchers to continue excavating. Their names were Grant Brin, Dennis Nilson, and Cynthia Nilson."

The sound of her parents' names made her chest tighten. She had nearly forgotten how this felt, to visualize their faces as best she could and once again sense the gnawing hole their absence had left behind. Her mind recalled them playing with her in the backyard, helping her build sandcastles. Then the image transitioned to their imagined deaths within this cursed mousetrap.

"And you never saw them again?" Lili clarified, wanting to mention seeing her mother outside the walls but unsure if Diego would react positively.

"That's correct, though the fate of your other friends is different," he added, referring to Aidyn and the siblings he was searching for. "I'm sorry."

"Just tell us where they are," Kaidyn cut in. For the first time in Lili's acquaintance with him, his voice was filled with concern. "And confirm their names before you do so."

"Of course." Diego turned his attention to Kaidyn. "Their names were Max and Minnie Myers and they came down here less than a year ago."

Aidyn grinned, excited to finally find some answers. Lili felt bad for him because she could tell the next part wouldn't be positive.

"They lived in our second lab in the south but a few months ago, it was overrun by monsters and they were killed." The man sighed and Aidyn's smile faded. Kaidyn turned away. "I am sorry," Diego repeated.

"No!" Aidyn said suddenly, making Lili jump. "It's not true. I saw them today. They're not dead. They must have survived the attack and you didn't bother to look for them."

"Believe me, we did. We don't like leaving others behind, just as we wouldn't want to be abandoned. Besides..." Diego sighed again, deeper this time. "We've seen their bodies and what they turned into."

"Turned into?" Kaidyn crossed his arms and glared at the man. "Explain. What happens to people after they die? Kingsley wouldn't tell us what he knew."

"This forest is cursed, as I'm sure you know, and if you die here, whether it be of natural or unnatural causes, the forest turns your body into something that serves it better. The monsters you see here used to be people like us, normal humans until the forest twisted them into something else."

Lili's entire body went cold. Nobody moved except for Meriel, who looked down at her hands and ground her teeth. Kaidyn noticed her reaction and pointed at her. "You knew, didn't you?"

Meriel looked up at him slowly, her eyes empty. "I always suspected my husband turned into the wolf that ate him."

"...We killed a giant wolf," Kaidyn whispered, realizing the monster's true origins. "It was your husband, wasn't it? You knew. You knew the monsters were human yet you never told us." He had the blood of innocent people on his hands now.

"They're not people." She leapt to her feet and raised a fist to hit him. "They're not human anymore. That wolf wasn't my husband!" Her face turned red, making the scars across her face stand out. "Once they die, they turn into animals like everything else."

Lili grabbed her arm before she could slap Kaidyn across the face. She could tell Meriel was still trying to rationalize the death of her husband.

"So every time I see Max and Minnie, it's just the monstrous remains of their bodies?" Aidyn whispered, tears springing to his eyes. "I've been following their corpses?"

"I'm afraid so, son," Diego answered.

Kaidyn looked down, nodding with realization. "If Jacques dies, he'll turn into a monster too. That's why you don't want him in this castle when he does. He might kill more people."

"That's correct. If he dies, one of our soldiers will cut off his head. That's the only way to permanently kill someone so the forest can't take them."

"But what's the point of the forest turning them into beasts?" Meriel asked, clenching her fists but barely struggling against Lili. "Why did it turn my husband into that thing?"

"I don't know." Diego shook his head. "We've tried to understand this place for years, to bring logic into it, but the process cannot be explained. The same can be said for why people turn to stone when they try to leave. I doubt even the greatest minds in the world could unravel why this forest acts as it does. Anna's conclusion is that the forest is playing with us, like a child watching us suffer for its own entertainment. It has its own made-up rules."

Lili felt the air in the room change as everyone, even Viktor and Leon who had been listening from afar, stopped what they were doing to focus on the real enemy: the forest.

"If this forest is alive, perhaps there's a way to kill it," Lili said what everyone else was thinking. "If we do, we can avenge our families and Jacques...that is, if the doctor can't save him."

"I may have a way to save him." The doctor's voice interrupted their conversation from the doorway.

Everyone turned to see her standing in the doorway, her sterile gloves removed and hair loose. "The medicine I have here isn't enough but there are some tools and drugs I could use that might change that. The only problem is, they were in our southern lab when it was overrun. We don't have enough people willing to go there to retrieve it, but if you go with them, you'll have enough numbers to not only retrieve our tools but take the lab back."

"No." Diego got to his feet and spoke over her. "We can't send them. Especially not...those two." He glanced nervously at Kaidyn and Aidyn. "They're too young. They're not soldiers."

Doctor Anna followed his gaze and seemed to understand his hidden meaning but didn't stop. "Our former companions in that lab were all turned so it will be a tough fight. But if you were able to kill three of them on your own as Leon said, you might stand a chance."

"*All* of them turned, huh?" Kaidyn growled, understanding why Diego was hesitant to let them go. "That includes our brother and sister. We'll have to kill our own family if we want to save Jacques." They came here to protect their siblings. Now they'd have to stain their hands with their blood.

"I can't promise it will save your friend but it's better than nothing," the doctor continued. "We wanted to retake the labs eventually but with a population of forty and less than thirty with combat experience, it's too much of a risk."

"So you plan to send in inexperienced civilians instead." Kaidyn said, unimpressed.

"Alongside ten of our men." Dr. Anna added, ready to leave. She didn't seem to care what their answer was. "Think on it and let Diego know. If not, I'll leave the fate of your friend's death up to you. You can either behead him or let him turn."

"There's really no other way?" Lili asked, worrying about the state she'd find her mother in. If she was injured, would she turn too? This doctor had to at least know something.

"If he dies and turns, there's nothing we can do but behead him. We've tried burning the monster's bodies and cutting off limbs but as long as the head is connected, it can live for a long time in perpetual pain. Whatever the forest does to them seems to grant increased healing, which is why the darn things keep fighting even after we cut off their limbs. If you choose to let him die from his wounds, I'll study him in my lab and behead him once I've found what I can. His death won't be in vain."

Lili gasped and looked at the others, who had all gone still as statues. Leon and Viktor were both shaking. Even Kaidyn's lip was quivering.

They had three options. Try to save Jacques and potentially die in the forest, behead him so he could die in peace, or let him turn into a monster and rot in a cell forever.

"I don't recommend the second option," Diego told them once the doctor was gone. "We have no way of knowing if the victims are able to think and feel in their monstrous forms. They could be in immense pain and we'd have no way of knowing. We've only had three people volunteer to turn after getting wounded." He paused. "I don't want to see any more people suffer as they did."

"Where are they now? Those three people?" Kaidyn stepped forward, already recovering from the shock. With Jacques gone, he had forced himself to become the group's voice of reason. "I want to see them."

"We killed them after learning what we could," Diego answered. "I didn't want them to suffer any longer than necessary."

"…I would do the same," Kaidyn muttered, looking pointedly at his terrified brother. "Even if the doctor's plans don't work, I still want to go to this lab and put our siblings to rest. If they're being tortured by this forest, I want to end their suffering. This hellhole doesn't need any more playthings."

Episode 16

When Lili entered the castle a few hours ago, she had been outfitted with only her normal clothes and a few leather pieces tied over her chest from Kingsley's greenhouse. Now, as she reentered the forest with her friends and ten escorts, her entire body was protected by a black bulletproof shirt and a thick pair of pants, as well as a lightweight helmet and chest piece similar to that of the soldiers. Her clothes were lighter than the rest, since Diego said most of them wouldn't be able to move properly in the heavy armor. She'd also been given two pistols, which were attached to her belt, and her knife from back home now sat in a holster on her leg, making it easier to reach.

The others wore similar outfits, though Leon had been equipped with swords rather than his single axe, and the twins had crossbows and guns. They looked grateful for the extra protection and offensive tools but the new weapons were making Lili nervous. If they were being outfitted like this, it meant the area they were entering would be far more dangerous than anything they'd encountered before. That trio of monsters in the swamp had nearly killed one of them. Soon they'd be going up against an entire lab full of monstrous soldiers.

"You don't have to come," Diego told her before they headed out. He had spent an hour training her, Viktor, and Meriel but Lili felt just as unprepared as before.

"No. I have a feeling I need to be there," she told him honestly. "That lab is where the hole to the next level is, right?"

Diego hesitated. "It's the closest one. How did you know that?"

"Just a hunch," she lied. Even if he hid it from them, her body kept pulling her toward the entrance, which happened to be near or directly under the lab.

Diego gave her a strange look when she answered but didn't question her again.

Diego was part of their sixteen-person group and Anna saw them off, promising to lock up Jacques' body if he turned so they could make the final decision upon their return. They had yet to choose an option and most of them didn't want to think about it, so the choice had been delayed.

"If none of you make it out alive," Dr. Anna told them, stone-faced, "I will find what I can about the forest from his body, then behead him as we did to the rest."

"Jacques would want his body to be used for research," Kaidyn assured her. "But we'll be back before he dies."

"I dearly hope so," the doctor said, speaking more to Diego than the rest of them.

Their decisions made, the groups parted. The doctor reentered the building while the rest of them approached the forest. The soldiers went first, some of them discussing what type of creatures might be encountered, while others walked like robots, stiff with fear.

Lili's group had the same rigid tension. While Kaidyn, Meriel, and Leon walked with purpose, unafraid, Aidyn and Viktor trembled, their eyes darting about the trees. She could tell Viktor simply feared for his life but Aidyn was searching for his siblings, desperate for proof that they weren't dead. He eventually took out his camera and started filming to calm himself. They'd forgotten to document everything after Jacques got hurt.

"The trip will take a full day," Diego informed them a few minutes into their journey, following an overgrown path that used to be a brick road. The grass was peeking through gaps in the grey squares and Lili could feel her mother's call beneath it. "During that time, I will instruct you on our plan of attack and what to do."

Lili tried to listen while he explained how they would surround the lab, sticking together to lure the monsters out one by one, but she spent most of her time watching her friends and the other soldiers. Despite the helmets concealing their faces, the men and women's body language gave her enough information to understand how most of them felt. Some of the men looked bloodthirsty, ready to kill and avenge their allies, while a few looked terrified like Viktor. One woman had removed her helmet and bore the same fright in her eyes as Aidyn. After Diego's lecture, Lili sought her out to ask some questions.

"Did you have friends or family in the lab when it was overtaken?" she asked the woman, feeling small next to the soldier's six-foot height and thick metal armor.

"Most of us did," the woman answered, her voice deep but full of emotion. "My husband was stationed there on the day it fell. I...want to ensure I behead him so the forest can't abuse him any longer."

Lili noticed the twins listening in on their conversation. "And you're sure he can't be saved?"

"If he could, I would have done it years ago." The woman sounded insulted by the question but wasn't willing to lecture a teenager. "Doctor Anna has been trying to find a cure for nine years. If *she* can't do it, none of us can. If a solution does exist, we won't find it here."

"Do you think it could be below us, in the next level?" Perhaps there was a cure. Her mother could have found it and used it to leave, though the way she looked back then implied more of an adaptation than a cure, allowing her to keep her humanity intact but make her body inhuman enough to trick the forest into letting her go.

"Maybe, but I wouldn't bet on it. Some of our best went down there and never returned."

Lili knew the woman had to be right but her stubbornness told her there had to be more to this forest. Everything had a solution, right?

Thanking the woman for the conversation, she slowed her steps so she could fall in line with Aidyn and Kaidyn. Neither of them looked happy.

"What will you do if you find your siblings?" she asked quietly.

"Behead them," Kaidyn said. At the same time, Aidyn answered, "Try to save them."

"Perhaps we can lock them up," Lili suggested, planning to do so with her parents, and Aidyn nodded vigorously.

"Right. We can find a way to fix this, like a zombie movie. We don't need to kill them." Aidyn looked to his brother. "They might still be alive in there, like a possession or something."

Lili smiled encouragingly but Kaidyn didn't look convinced.

"If they are still alive and able to think, that gives me even more reason to end their suffering. This isn't up for discussion, Aidyn." Kaidyn moved to a different part of the group so he wouldn't have to talk to them anymore.

The trip felt longer than their journey to the castle. They encountered five separate monsters during the day, though the soldiers made short work of them. The creatures didn't stand a chance when they were so greatly outnumbered by armored soldiers with huge swords.

Now that Lili knew the monsters used to be human, parts of their original bodies hidden within the new ones became obvious. Now that she knew what to look for, it was easy to figure out what had killed them or been nearby when they died. Two of the five creatures had bark and twigs covering their skin, making them blend in with their surroundings. Two others were a mix of insects, fur, and human flesh combined into horrible, two-legged monstrosities that Lili knew would haunt her nightmares. The final creature attacked them near nightfall and was the biggest of the five. It was simply a human body hanging from the mouth of a giant, six-legged mutant. It was a mix between a six-eyed spider and a squirrel. The soldiers struggled to kill that one, as they had to first cut off the spider head, then the human head locked inside its jaw. The thing bled so much that, by the end of that encounter, they had to spend an hour cleaning themselves before proceeding.

"We'll make camp here," Diego announced as the light from the ceiling faded. "It'll take two more hours to reach the lab but the monsters are more docile during the day, so we'll wait until morning to strike." Diego instructed the soldiers to guard their camp, set in the remains of a stone house. It, like the swamp, had a humanoid tree sitting over an empty stone bowl. As Leon and the twins set up their tents. Lili asked Diego if he knew what the offering bowl's purpose was.

"I have no idea. Anna had some theories but most of us chalked it up to being the remnants of some ancient religion. A lot of people were trapped here before your parents came along. They had to believe in something."

She reached down and touched the bottom of it, wondering how old it was. More importantly, how did it work? Had her blood offering actually done anything?

When she heard Kaidyn approaching, she yanked her hand back.

"I put blood in it," she admitted to Kaidyn when he stopped next to her. "And it disappeared when I did."

Kaidyn pursed his lips. "When did you do it?" he asked.

"Right before Jacques got hurt," she admitted. She initially expected him to frown as he always did but instead, the only expression she saw on his face was curiosity.

"Do you think it changed the result of the fight?" he whispered.

She shrugged. Jacques still got hurt, so it certainly hadn't helped. "Should we try it again?" she asked.

He nodded. Before she could even reach for her knife, Kaidyn grabbed one of his own and slit one of his fingers.

"You shouldn't be injuring yourself before a fight," Diego warned.

"Too late." Kaidyn released three drops into the bowl. Just like before, Lili saw the blood swirl into the bottom and vanish.

"Amazing," Diego whispered. "I don't know what to make of it. I'll need to tell Anna." He patted both Lili and Kaidyn on the back. "Now I feel like a fool for not trying it sooner." Shaking his head, he left, but not before warning them to stop cutting themselves.

Both Kaidyn and Lili waited for something to happen but just like before, nothing did. The blood sacrifice had no effect.

"It might do nothing at all." Kaidyn conceded and walked away, though he was no longer smiling when he left.

After the camp was ready—consisting of two large brown tents for the soldiers and a campfire where they heated canned food for dinner—everyone turned in with the exception of the five soldiers assigned to the first watch.

Lili slept next to Meriel. She could hear her crying into her pillow before falling asleep.

After drifting off, Lili saw endless visions of her mother and father playing like a movie in her mind. She watched her father get sucked into a bog, then he rose out of it, reborn as a brown creature of mud and stone. Next, she watched his body get buried by a tree, sucked into its roots like a snake smothering its prey. A moment later, his face emerged from the bark of the trunk, his eyes turned to knots and his limbs into branches.

The visuals made Lili want to squeeze her eyes shut and dig out her eyeballs but even when she did, his cries continued to echo in her head without end. He screamed her name, uttering curses for leaving him to die. The cries were only silenced when the dream shifted once more, returning her to that fateful day when she saw her mother. The dreams always ended this way, never letting her forget her purpose.

She was once again trapped in her younger body, sitting on that stupid tree branch and watching her broken mother exit the wall. However, instead of walking away as she had before and leaving Lili alone on that branch, the series of events changed.

This time, Lili's small body jumped from the tree and ran toward her mother, arms outstretched to hug her.

Lili tried to stop herself but her dream form moved on its own, driven by the mind of a child desperate to be in her mother's arms.

When Lili reached her mother and felt her hands wrap around her back—her skin cold and prickly like Velcro—Lili awoke with a start and nearly shrieked when she felt a cold hand on her arm. It made the dream feel real. She looked over and saw Kaidyn sitting above her, gently shaking her awake.

"I want you to practice using your gun," he told her quietly without so much as a good morning or apology for waking her. He paused when Meriel rolled over behind him and stayed quiet until he was sure she was still asleep. Then he continued speaking. "Viktor refused to let me do it with him."

"Diego already helped me practice."

"I want to make sure you know what you're doing," he said. She could tell this was about more than distrust or a lack of experience. His brother's life was still on the line, as was hers. He wanted to ensure she and Viktor didn't get themselves killed.

Lili didn't want to stand up and embrace reality just yet, but the dreams about her parents turning into monsters motivated her to follow him out of the tent. Sleep could wait.

The amount of light outside hadn't changed, but the soldiers' shifts had. They were sitting on top of the stone ruins now, watching for intruders. One of them had binoculars and was looking to the south, staring at their destination. He was frowning, not too happy about entering the lab.

Kaidyn didn't lead Lili toward the soldiers. He took her to the edge of the ruins instead, still within range of their escort but away from the tents so they couldn't be overheard. Once they reached the far wall, he handed her one of his pistols and waited for her to become accustomed to its weight.

"Are you concerned about my safety?" she asked to fill the silence, pointing the gun at the nearest tree.

"No, but your inexperience will endanger Aidyn. He might hurt himself while trying to protect you," Kaidyn answered, his voice cold and tired. There was also a hint of dishonesty, as though he was worried about her too.

"So, what are you planning to teach me?" she asked, gripping the weapon with both hands.

After studying her form and raising an eyebrow, only a little surprised by her use of the gun, he tapped her shoulders and commented on how she should strengthen them. Then he leaned against the wall and looked back at the tents, as though he'd already given up on training her.

"If you encountered the monsters that used to be your parents," he said softly. "Would you kill them?" His voice was raw, unveiling his true feelings for perhaps the first time.

Lili lowered the gun and gave it some thought. She knew this was the real reason he had brought her here. "If I had to protect myself and the others who were still alive? Yes, without question. If I thought there was a chance to save them or lock them up, like Aidyn suggested, I might try to find another way."

"I don't think we have that option," he replied hopelessly.

"Then I would kill them," she clarified. "My parents would rather die than have my blood on their hands. I know it."

"How well did you know them?" he asked, catching her off guard.

"...Not as well as I would have liked. They left when I was a kid but, if they're anything like my uncle, I know they would want to protect me."

"If that were the case, why would your mother gesture for you to enter the forest?" He crossed his arms and studied her face, as though he was asking himself the same question.

"Because..." She paused and took a deep breath, wanting to explain her reasoning properly. "I think my mother found a way to end all this suffering and destroy this forest, but she couldn't do it alone. That's why she wanted me to come...And my guess is, you were summoned the same way. It can't be a coincidence that I encountered your group on the very day I entered the walls."

He tilted his head. "Wishful thinking," he muttered but didn't sound as doubtful as before. "You might be right. Perhaps God sent us to save everyone, not just the ones we love." He glanced at her. "So that's why you're continuing? You want to be a hero?"

He said it like a statement rather than a question, but she answered him anyway. "My mother brought me here for a reason and I know we're headed in the right direction. Our destination is the third level. She's leading me there."

"And if it's a trap?"

"Then at least I tried my best." She jutted her chin out to show she meant it and he smiled briefly.

By the time they returned to camp, everyone was awake and Leon was asking the soldiers if they'd seen Billy during the night. None of them had.

Lili noticed the impact her conversation had on Kaidyn. Before, he had been unsure about his motives but now he seemed focused. His steps had been slow on the way to their "training" session, but now he walked with purpose and spoke confidently to the soldiers as they prepared for the upcoming battle.

She was glad they had talked. After seeing those dreams, she'd doubted whether continuing was the smartest decision. This had changed that. Now she was sure her goal—to save the people trapped here—was right. Her nerves had calmed and her connection to her mother was stronger than ever. This was their fate. Their destiny. There were too many coincidences happening to mean anything else.

Episode 17

After a quick meal of dried greens and chicken from the castle, they continued through the forest with eight of the soldiers ahead and two behind. They never left the road despite Meriel mentioning how exposed it left them. Diego explained that some of the trees were monsters in disguise, so the road was the safest option. Meriel didn't question him again after that. Once they reached the lab, no one bothered to speak at all.

The lab was much smaller than the castle but made up for its size in weaponry and security. It was completely modern, not built on the remnants of a collapsed society like the other buildings. Thick walls surrounded the lab, just like the wooden ones around Kingsley's village, and there were cannons atop them. The lab entrance had circular handles like a safe, but the door was sitting ajar now. There looked to be the remains of a chicken coop in the far corner but the only animals there now were black rats with long teeth. They were chasing beetles along the concrete.

On either side of the opened door were two huge trees, their branches and green leaves nearly tall enough to reach the top of the building. Their roots spread over the ground. It would be difficult to walk in there without tripping over them.

Lili crept to the edge of the wall, next to the large gate. The doors had been ripped off their hinges by some monstrous creature. She tried to peer into the lab but it was too dark inside to see. The trees cast shadows on its interior.

"Don't bother," Diego whispered in her ear as she squinted. "The monsters won't reveal themselves until we get close. They're probably waiting inside, loitering around uselessly as they always do." He gave her a fatherly pat on the back, then stepped away to join his fellow soldiers.

Lili had been instructed to climb the surrounding walls, using ladders carved into the stone. Then she would wait up there with Viktor and the soldier that had lost her husband. They would shoot at any approaching monsters and draw them away from the infiltration group.

The walls were taller than the lab building and Lili prayed the monsters didn't know how to climb them. Otherwise, she'd be more vulnerable than the people who stayed below.

Lili reached the ladder and caught Viktor staring up at it with shaky breaths. "Are you scared of heights too?" she whispered.

He nodded fearfully, then motioned for her to climb. "Ladies first."

"What *aren't* you scared of?" she asked, meaning for it to be a joke but realizing it sounded cruel once it came out of her mouth.

Viktor just scrunched up his nose and waited for her to go, not offended. "I'm not afraid of *plants*," he defended, "including the poisonous ones." As though that was something to be proud of. "Can you hurry up, please?"

"I'll go first." The widowed soldier shoved both of them aside and climbed up with quick strides.

By the time Lili followed her and reached the top, crouching beside her with a gun ready, the twins had snuck past the walls and were hiding behind the remains of the chicken coops. Two soldiers were with them, shorter ones who moved faster than the rest.

Leon and Meriel stayed with Diego and the others, waiting at the front gate and focusing on the trees guarding the building. After the twins were in position, Diego and one other soldier pulled oil-tipped arrows from their packs and loosed them at both trees. Lili knew why they were doing it but it was still strange to see the trees start shifting as soon as the arrows set their roots aflame. The plants weren't normal. They moved intelligently, like a human frantically swinging their arms after waking. They had looked normal when Lili walked up but as soon as they turned around, reacting to the fire, she saw two human bodies trapped beneath the bark. They were squirming about like babies, struggling to escape their cages, but their eyes were dead and emotionless.

"There they are," Diego shouted at Leon and one of the other soldiers. "Now!"

Just as instructed, Leon and the soldier raced toward the trees, both wielding axes. Lili smiled as Leon leapt into the air, shouting like a child, but her cheer vanished when he dug the axe into the throat of the bark-covered person inside. Blood spewed from its body and the tree stopped moving when the head disconnected from its neck.

Lili knew the people controlling those trees were no more than corpses now, but it still hurt to know Leon had just killed a fellow human.

The second soldier struggled to cut through the bark to reach the person inside and when one of the roots rose off the ground, wrapping itself around his legs, Lili aimed her gun and fired, hoping the bullet would at least slow it down. She missed, but luckily it didn't matter. With another swing, the soldier succeeded in beheading the second tree's body.

"Now get back here," Diego ordered as soon as the pair of trees died. "Before—"

Lili spotted movement in the lab's doorway. The creatures inside had been alerted to their presence and were coming out. It was too late for Leon to make a run for it.

What happened next was utter chaos.

Diego and his fellow soldiers charged forward to help Leon and his companion, while the twins and their two soldiers stayed put. Lili saw more roots emerge from the doorway, wrapping around the walls like tentacles. Two trees crawled out, the knots on their trunks similar to pupilless eyes and screaming mouths. Alongside them came more meaty white creatures with swords stuck in their hands and elbows. They jumped toward Leon, then the tree roots covered the entrance like an ocean. The fight only became more confusing as Diego and the other five soldiers dove in with axes and swords to help.

Lili kept her gun pointed at the battle but didn't know where to fire. Everything was moving too fast to keep up.

The original plan had been to kill the two trees on the outside, then lure the rest away from the building. Once the monsters were out far enough, the twins and their group would leap out from the chicken coops and attack from behind so the monsters were surrounded. However, the trees had moved faster than Diego predicted and had yet to leave the safety of the door. Leon's shout hadn't helped either. Now the humans were trapped within the walls, together with the monsters.

"What do we do?" Viktor asked the female soldier. She shook her head. "We need to draw them away. Fire at the ones on the left and lure them over here." She pointed at the far wall where she wanted them to go. "If that doesn't work, we'll have to jump down and draw the monsters toward the exit. If we get all of them out of the lab, we can barricade ourselves in and regroup. It'll be easier to defend if we get access to the cannons on the lab's roof." She said all of this so quickly that Lili had to repeat it in her head to understand.

Lili's ears rang when she fired at the pale monsters but they were so distracted by the soldiers that they didn't seem to hear or feel the bullets. She stopped when she heard Viktor scream Leon's name. Lili searched for him, worried he'd been killed, then eventually spotted him on the ground near the lab's door, his legs restrained by some roots. He was chopping at them ferociously, his face red and teeth grinding as he screamed a battle cry. None of his swings cut through.

He was going to die if she didn't draw those monsters away.

"I'm going down." Lili could feel her mother's presence nearby and it encouraged her to face her fears. She climbed down the inside of the wall, all too aware of the monsters less than ten feet away. The soldier tried to prevent her from going alone but wasn't fast enough to grab her. Once Lili's feet touched the ground, she fired her gun at the nearest tree creature and attempted to taunt it.

"Get over here! Kill me!"

The tree turned to face her, human ribs mixed in among the branches. Its appearance nearly made her freeze up, its form so eerie and uncanny it triggered her fight or flight. The numbness in her body took a few seconds to fade. After regaining control of her legs, she scrambled toward the gate. "Come and get me!"

Once she started waving her arms above her head, the tree finally gave up on Leon, who had chopped up several of the roots by this point. It released its prey and leapt toward her, gaining traction by digging into the dirt. It pulled the ground up in clumps, leaving its version of footprints in its wake. It was faster than her and even though she was fleeing, she knew it would be upon her in another second. She could already visualize it wrapping its roots around her throat and squeezing the air from her lungs.

I refuse to die until I find my mother.

"Lili!" Kaidyn's voice met her ears. "Drop!"

She obeyed, falling to the ground and feeling the damp roots whip past her head, yanking some of her hair but missing her body.

Gasping from the adrenaline, she looked up in time to watch Aidyn bring his sword down on the tree's roots, cutting the human inside. Once its host was dead, the tree went limp.

Her chest aching from the fall, Lili sat up and saw Kaidyn dig his blade into what looked like the mouth of the tree. The scent of blood filled her nostrils as it poured from the mouth. The rest of the roots collapsed. It was dead. She was safe.

The others weren't, though. Leon and the soldiers were still being overrun by the lab's trees and monsters. There was blood everywhere and many of the men were trapped beneath the branches and roots.

"Aidyn. Kaidyn." Lili leapt to her feet, mud clinging to her clothes. "Can you two climb the lab walls?" She pointed at the square building in the middle of the base. A cannon rested on the edge of the building, pointed at the monsters.

Clearly this full-on attack plan wasn't working. The soldiers were still alive for now, but the monsters were bigger than Diego had described and the final tree had two soldiers in its grasp, squeezing their bodies between its limbs. Lili gasped when one soldier's body suddenly twisted and turned unnaturally. His torso swung entirely around, breaking his back. Its target now dead, the tree tossed the man to the ground like a forgotten toy. In a few more minutes, everyone here would meet the same fate.

Kaidyn looked up at the lab's roof, then at his brother. "Probably, but I doubt those cannons are loaded."

Lili couldn't remember what Diego had said about them but regardless, it was their best shot. Those guns would be able to remove the monster's heads with ease. "We'll have to pray they are. Can you reach them?"

"We can," Aidyn said, huffing with confidence even though Kaidyn was shaking his head. They'd have to run past the creatures to reach the lab roof. "It's our best option, Kaidyn," Aidyn added.

Lili pointed at the protective walls surrounding the lab. "You can run across the walls to avoid the monsters, then climb up the side of the lab to reach the top."

It was a waste of time to discuss it any longer, so the twins sped up the ladder on the nearest wall and ran across it before Lili could even reach the front gate. She tried to lure more creatures away from the fight with her gun, but two of their soldiers were already lying dead on the ground. To her horror, one of the remaining soldiers brought his own sword down on both of his fallen companion's necks, beheading them. He was destroying their corpses so they wouldn't turn.

Since her attempts to distract the monsters weren't working, she scanned the area to see if anyone else needed help. Leon and the others were still struggling and Viktor was still trying to lure the monsters from his perch on the wall. Meriel was the only one not fighting. She had remained behind the chicken coops. The original plan was for her to fight alongside the twins. During the journey here, she'd held a fierce bloodlust for killing monsters, but now that she was staring them down, her mouth was slightly ajar and her eyes red. She was crouching, hiding from the beasts.

Lili couldn't understand why Meriel was paralyzed like this. What had changed since yesterday? Then she watched Leon bring his axe down on one of the more human-looking monsters and understood. Meriel saw the humanity in those beasts, just like when she looked at the wolf that used to be her husband. She couldn't fight these things. It was the equivalent of murdering her own family.

A new monster exited the lab's doorway, snarling and bleeding on the tangled roots covering the ground. It had the body of a wolf but the eyes of a human. When it leapt toward one of the soldiers and took hold of the woman's leg with its teeth, it reminded Lili of the wolf they had fought on the first day. She could tell Meriel thought the same.

At least Meriel was hiding, not making herself vulnerable and putting anyone else in danger. Lili should do the same. She continued shouting at the monsters but it wasn't doing any good. Leon and a few others were still standing but some of them had their arms or hands restrained. One person had even lost an arm, bitten off by the white monstrosities.

Even if the twins reached the cannons, they might still lose.

Lili jerked to attention when Diego retreated and joined her at the gate. He patted her on the back, then shouted for every survivor to retreat. After he spoke, he pulled a small explosive from his pack. "I didn't want to risk using this and destroying the lab but we've got no choice. Everyone get down!"

The soldiers dove out of the way. Once they were safe, Diego pressed a button on the explosive and threw it. It took out the remaining smaller creatures, including the wolf, and sent blood and flesh flying. The entrance nearly caved in on itself but thankfully remained intact. Now only the trees remained. It would be easy to take them down with axes now that they were outnumbered.

The twins had reached the far side of the wall by this point and were climbing down so they could reach the lab and start climbing that instead, but there was little point now. All of the monsters were dead and they had won...or so they thought.

Episode 18

All the soldiers who had fought the creatures head-on climbed out from the broken roots. Dead bodies from both sides littered the ground. Lili smiled with relief when Leon came out alive with only a few bites and bruises on his body. Viktor was alive too, shaken but okay and maybe even a little ecstatic from joining in on the battle.

When Lili looked to her right, she could see Meriel still hiding. Her pale hands were wrapped around her head and she was rocking back and forth, like a child comforting itself. The twins had reached the lab building and were raising an intact wooden ladder, granting access to the roof. Kaidyn started climbing first but before Aidyn could grab the rungs, everyone heard a voice within the lab.

"Are they gone? Did you finally kill them?" It was a female voice, similar to Meriel's but a little sweeter. It came from inside the lab's darkened doorway.

Diego immediately grabbed a grenade and the soldiers pointed their guns at the lab. Lili saw the twins freeze halfway up the ladder and Aidyn's eyes widened, nearly sparkling. They recognized the voice.

"Hello?" The voice echoed.

"Stay back," Diego ordered, holding one arm in front of his soldiers. "Don't trust your eyes."

Kaidyn climbed down the ladder again, so quickly he nearly slipped. Aidyn peeked around the corner of the building to see the speaker.

Everyone watched as the young woman around Meriel's age stepped out of the lab. She had fair skin, bags under her eyes, and long black hair that needed a good combing. As soon as she spotted Aidyn, she smiled, then started to cry, stumbling toward him. "Aidyn! You came!"

"Minnie," Aidyn replied, tears in his eyes.

Kaidyn reached for his brother, trying to stop him before he could reach her.

"Aidyn!" Diego shouted, preparing to throw the grenade. "Stop right there! Don't go near her!"

Aidyn stopped, torn between reaching for the sister he spent a year searching for and obeying everyone else. The girl did the same, looking toward Diego with what looked like genuine fear in her eyes.

"They're the ones who abandoned us," Minnie suddenly told the twins, her lower lip wobbling. "When we were attacked, we had to lock ourselves in. They didn't come to save us." She pointed accusingly at Diego and the other soldiers by his side. "They abandoned us and they'll do the same to you!"

While she accused them, a second person emerged from the building. This one was the twin's height and had a similar but older face, though he had those same bags under his eyes and pale skin like his sister. His arms and legs were also eerily thin from malnourishment.

"Minnie, get back!" this other person, Max, yelled at his sister. Then he gasped when he noticed his younger siblings.

Lili was conflicted. "Didn't you say they died?" she whispered to Diego, who nodded.

"No one survived the attack, not even them. Boys! This is your last warning. Get away from them or you'll get caught in the blast." Diego's fingers twitched, still gripping the grenade but hesitating.

"Aidyn, get back," Kaidyn said, grabbing his twin's shirt and tugging, but Minnie reached for Aidyn at the same time.

"You can't trust those soldiers, Aidyn!" Minnie screamed, her voice hoarse from crying. "They care about nothing but their research! We barely survived on rations and they never checked on us. Please, don't go with them. They'll kill you."

The brother Max ran toward them, shouting the same thing. "They experiment on people, Kaidyn. You have to come with us."

Kaidyn struggled, wrinkles forming on his forehead. He continued pulling Aidyn's arm. He didn't know who to believe and Diego couldn't throw the grenade without hurting all four of them.

Lili held her breath, trying to figure out who was lying. She asked her mother in her head, begging for an answer or at least a tug in the right direction, but she felt nothing besides fear for the twins' safety.

As Max and Minnie continued approaching the boys, Kaidyn finally lowered his head and forcefully grabbed his brother. "Come on, Aidyn. Something's not right about this."

"Kaidyn, it's us. I promise!" Max sobbed. "We can prove it. Ask us anything. Your birthday is March third and our parents' names are—"

Kaidyn pulled a gun on both of them and Aidyn screamed, trying to place himself between the barrel and his sister. "Kaidyn! It's them! What are you doing?"

"Diego has no reason to lie to us," Kaidyn told him, then turned on the siblings. "Back away! If you really were our siblings, you'd be okay with backing up until we figured this out. You were never this impatient before."

Minnie gasped, tears streaming down her cheeks. She started whimpering, betrayed, but Lili noticed her fists clenching.

"Kaidyn," Lili warned. "Watch out." She pulled out her own gun and pointed it at Minnie, no longer believing her.

The sister turned toward her, eyes wide and bloodshot. When she did, Lili realized Minnie's skin wasn't pale because she'd been trapped in the lab without sunlight. It looked identical to the white skin of the monsters that attacked Jacques. She had turned.

Kaidyn clearly thought the same, but when he tried to pull Aidyn toward the chicken coops, his twin freed himself and stumbled toward Max and Minnie.

"Kaidyn, we came all this way to find them. We went through hell to get here and now you won't believe them," Aidyn said, straining to speak as he looked between his twin and Max, who was smiling and reaching for him. Kaidyn wasn't falling for it. He pointed the end of his pistol at Max's head.

"They're dead, Aidyn. We should have accepted it a year ago when they never came back." He sighed and reached out a hand to Aidyn one more time. "The forest took them. They're gone. We can't let it take us too."

Aidyn was frozen. Lili could tell he believed Kaidyn but didn't want to lose his family.

"*I'm* real, Aidyn. Come here!" Kaidyn shouted, no longer waiting for his brother to think things through. His finger was searching for the trigger.

Max and Minnie stepped toward Aidyn, trying to grab his back. "Aidyn."

"They're family," Aidyn whispered at the same moment both siblings leapt toward him, jumping higher than should be possible.

The soldiers shot at Max and Minnie but the bullets had little effect. As the shots cut through their flesh and drew blood, their human forms shifted. Max and Minnie grabbed each other's hands and, in mere moments, they morphed into a single being. They became a mesh of clothes, flesh, and black hair, like playdough figures melting together. Their necks stretched and turned black like the branches of a tree. Their arms sharpened into points.

Lili screamed as the arms cut through Aidyn's chest, the monster that used to be Max and Minnie raising his body into the air and drawing him closer. Kaidyn stared at his brother, the blood draining from his face. Then he screamed and finally fired his pistol at the beast. Tears streamed from his face when he ran out of ammo, threw his gun at it, and climbed up the lab's ladder to reach the cannon.

"Now!" Diego shouted and finally threw his grenade, as did two other soldiers. However, now that the monster's heads had been stretched high into the air, the explosions only took out chunks of the body and didn't manage to cut off the neck. With an intact head, damaging the limbs only served to slow them. They didn't react to pain the same way humans did.

Lili watched, paralyzed, as the monster took Aidyn's body and pressed him against its chest. His skin and clothes were absorbed. Kaidyn screamed as a third head sprouted from the torso like a tree. It had Aidyn's face with empty white eyes and an open, unmoving mouth. He was part of them now, dead and lifeless like the other two.

"You kids get back," Diego yelled, shoving Lili away from the gate. "I was a selfish fool to bring you with me. Leon, grab your friends and get back on that road until we have this under control."

Leon nodded and grabbed Viktor, who was crying, but Lili dodged his arms and started climbing the wall surrounding the lab. If Kaidyn was going to use those cannons, he'd need help.

Part of her body wanted to shut down, unable to comprehend what had just happened, but by looking away from what remained of Aidyn, she was able to keep her legs moving. There were more shouts and screams as the monster tried and failed to grab Kaidyn's legs. Kaidyn managed to leap over three rungs and avoid it. The beast looked like it was going to try again, but then it turned toward the others standing at the gate instead and lumbered after them, the three heads twitching sporadically, their necks jerking at unnatural angles.

Lili was glad the monster didn't notice her as she charged across the wall, avoiding moss growing on the stone surface. Once she reached the far left corner, she started climbing down the ladder. This tall wall was the only safe place, too high for the monsters to reach—but if she wanted to help Kaidyn, she'd have to force herself down into danger.

When her feet touched the ground, she heard Viktor screaming and knew the monster had nearly reached them.

"Kaidyn?" she whispered as she circled around the lab and found the ladder. She saw the monster wrap its long neck around one of the soldiers, squeezing his body like a boa constrictor.

Kaidyn was on top of the roof and moving the large, black cannon, pointing it at the monster that used to be his family. The cannon was a mix of modern and old technology. Luckily, Kaidyn looked confident when it came to the mechanics. The only things that held him back were the tears in his eyes and the grinding of his teeth. He was avoiding looking at Aidyn's remains. Kaidyn barely acknowledged Lili as she pulled herself onto the roof. Her hand slipped on the water and mud but she wiped it off on her pants, eager to help.

"What can I do?" she asked. The glare he shot her sent a shiver down her spine but she knew it was targeted toward the forest and what it had done to his family, not at her.

"Come here and hold the cannon steady," he ordered, grabbing her hand and placing it on top of the device. It was cold under her fingers and wobbled on the uneven concrete, the roof full of cracks from the fight that had killed Kaidyn's siblings a year ago.

"I've got it," she told him, ensuring the cannon's barrel was pointed at the abomination. She'd have to do the aiming for him.

They heard a screech from below. The monster had killed the soldier by squeezing him to death and was reaching for another. Leon and Viktor were far enough away to avoid it, but Diego was its next target. He was firing his gun at the beast but its bullets only soaked him in its blood.

"Good." Kaidyn grabbed one of the balls next to the cannon and opened a slot so the ammo could be inserted. He then grabbed the back of the weapon and wrapped his finger around what looked like the trigger. "Look over here you bastard!" he screamed at the monster, his voice making all three heads swivel toward him. "You missed one of us!"

Then he pulled the trigger and the power of the blast knocked the cannon against Lili's chest, nearly forcing her shoulder from its socket. She screamed in pain but held fast so he could reload. The cannon had hit one of the creature's legs. It only made Kaidyn angrier that he had missed.

"Stop wearing my sister's face!" Kaidyn shouted again. This time, his shot hit Minnie's neck, cutting out a chunk and nearly severing it. The head flopped over but didn't fall. The cannon shoved Lili back again but she was more prepared this time. The creature was charging toward them now and she had to strain her arms to move the cannon so it wouldn't lose sight of the beast.

Kaidyn didn't say anything as he reloaded and fired again, this time taking off the head of his older brother. It didn't halt the monster's charge. Until all three heads were gone, the body could still move. It began digging its dagger-like fingers into the wall of the lab and climbing toward them. Aidyn's face still held no expression. It didn't feel like him anymore. Aidyn was truly dead. That made it easier for Lili to point the cannon at his neck.

Kaidyn nearly lost his grip on the slippery ball when loading it into the cannon, but he caught it just in time. Unfortunately, when he looked up and saw the monster's neck shoot up right in front of him and Lili, the twin froze, his finger on the trigger. He was staring at Aidyn's face and Lili saw his chin wobble.

It must have been easier to kill the other two, since he'd accepted their deaths a year ago. Aidyn was different. Kaidyn couldn't just kill his brother and best friend when they had been fighting alongside each other less than ten minutes ago. There was still color in Aidyn's cheeks, unlike the other two heads lying on the ground. Lili could even hear a slight groan from Aidyn's mouth, the final remnants of his voice.

Lili gulped, then let go of the cannon just long enough to touch Kaidyn's arm. "You can do this," she whispered. "We can't save him. It's too late. You promised to end their torment."

"I know," he whispered, a tear sliding down his cheek.

The head of their stolen friend sped toward them, aiming for Lili's throat. Perhaps the final fraction of Aidyn's humanity made him try to behead her so she wouldn't meet the same fate.

"I'm sorry, Aidyn," Kaidyn told his brother. "I couldn't protect you."

Then he pulled the trigger.

The cannonball cut straight through Aidyn's throat. Blood splattered Lili's face. His head landed at their feet. There was a loud crash as the body's arms lost their grip on the lab walls and fell to the ground.

The battle was over. They had won, though it didn't feel like it.

"I'm sorry, Kaidyn." Lili wiped the warm blood from her face with one hand and took off her coat with the other, using it to cover Aidyn's head. Once the head was hidden, she looked up at Kaidyn to see if he was unharmed. His eyes were squeezed shut like a child, leaning away. His hands were still clutching the cannon's trigger and his other hand was clenched in a fist so tight that his nails were drawing blood from his palm.

"It's not your fault," she assured him, pulling his cold hands away from the weapon. She felt tears fall from his chin to her hands. A moment later, his head came to rest on her shoulder, soaking her sleeves. She bit her lip. His shoulders shook with sobs. It was so strange to see the normally stoic Kaidyn break down like this, but she knew she'd be doing the same if she was forced to kill her mother or father.

Remaining silent, she stepped in front of him so the others couldn't see him cry. There were groans from below as the soldiers pulled the wounded out from under the dead trees and tended to them.

"Lili! Kaidyn!" Leon shouted from below. "Are you okay?"

"We're alive!" she called back, feeling Kaidyn tense against her.

"I'm coming up!" Leon shouted. A second later, she heard both him and Viktor climb the ladder.

Kaidyn stood up straight again and wiped away his tears before the others could see him. He looked different now, just as determined to accomplish their goal but with a hardened expression, no longer sad or angry. He'd lost all traces of emotion. His eyes were empty now.

Lili didn't know what to say. She simply waited for his friends to come and comfort him. They did so as soon as they reached the top, wrapping Kaidyn into a group hug.

"You did your best," Leon assured him while Viktor stayed silent, his entire body shivering.

"I have to check on Meriel," Lili whispered, afraid to interrupt the reunion, and moved toward the ladder. As she put her leg on the first rung, she looked back at the group and saw Kaidyn staring at her. He gave her the briefest nod, like he was saying thank you, then she stepped down and the group disappeared from sight. Her heart felt full—full of sorrow for Aidyn, but glad Kaidyn retained his determination. If he gave up, they might lose him too.

Meriel was still behind the chicken coop, in the same position she'd been in during the fight. She was muttering to herself when Lili approached, saying words like "promised", "alone", and "monsters". Her rambling didn't end until Lili crouched beside her.

"Meriel? Are you okay?" She tapped the woman's arm but Meriel slapped her arm, shoving her away.

"I can't do this," Meriel whispered, staring at the ground with red eyes. "I thought I could, but I can't fight these things. All I see is...him."

"It's okay." Lili hesitated, then wrapped both arms around the woman's shoulders. Meriel was quivering beneath her. "I understand and everyone else does too, Meriel. No one expects you to fight."

"But if I don't fight, what good am I?"

Lili had asked herself the same thing, especially after Kaidyn confronted her at the beginning of their journey.

"Fighting isn't the only thing that makes someone useful. You have plenty you're good at. These soldiers need people to make food and collect water while they fight. You can help them do that. Plus, even if you weren't able to cook or collect, you still hold value as a person. You helped all of us get down here, remember? That means something."

Meriel lowered her hands, no longer crying. The fight was gone from her eyes. She had given up. "Let's just go. I don't want to stay here any longer."

"We'll leave as soon as we get the medicine for Jacques." Lili helped Meriel to her feet and led her to a corner, just in case there were more monsters in the forest outside the gate. Once she knew Meriel would be okay by herself, she went to find Diego.

It pained her to step around the headless bodies of people who had escorted them here. By the time she reached Diego, her boots were soaked with blood. Diego was peering into the lab's dark doorway and standing over the warped body of Kaidyn's siblings.

"It's always a shame to see someone so young fall victim to this," Diego told her as she joined him. "I should have thought twice before bringing you here."

Lili studied Minnie's face. The neck was still long but her head looked normal again, albeit too thin and white to be natural. "I've never seen such a human-looking monster before," she whispered.

"It's rare but happens. We've had a few occasions when we lost a companion to the forest, then they would return a few days later looking like these two, perfectly intact and human but...off. It makes you paranoid. You start doubting the person sleeping next to you." He tightened the grip on his gun and shined a flashlight inside the building.

That must explain why Kingsley was so secretive. Maybe he assumed Billy was the same way because he was so pale from living inside a cottage all his life. That wasn't an excuse to throw the child to his death without evidence, but it explained his reasoning. Lili had to ensure she never reached the same level of fear.

The first floor of the lab wasn't large. It was the same size as the greenhouse. The inside had been trashed. There were knocked-over steel tables, broken bottles, and smashed cans of food littering the floor. The coast was clear, so Diego went inside and headed straight for the stairs leading to the second floor.

"The medicine is up there," Diego told her as two more soldiers joined him. "And we should collect the rations that weren't destroyed if any remain. I'd appreciate the help, if you're able."

Lili followed them, wanting to do what she could just like she told Meriel a moment ago. When she reached the fifth step, she heard her three friends catch up to her.

Glancing over her shoulder, she found an expressionless Kaidyn on the first step with Leon and Viktor behind him. When Kaidyn's eyes met hers, her knees buckled with concern. He looked ready to give up, as Meriel had, but his weariness was mixed with a stubborn vengeance. If the opportunity arose, she was confident he would do anything—even throw away his own life—to destroy this forest. Without Aidyn to soften him, only the hardened hatred remained.

Lili steeled herself and finished ascending the steps, her mind hopping between worry for her friends and curiosity about the lab.

The second floor looked the same as the first, though there were some extra rooms with closed doors to explore. Diego had a master key for each room and when he opened them, the shelves Lili found inside were full of bottles and cans of medicine, alcohol, and vinegar. Diego smiled when he found a particularly large, green bottle. It must be what they needed to save Jacques.

Kaidyn, Viktor, and one of the soldiers went inside the storage rooms to collect the items. While they worked, Lili leaned against the wall and spoke to Leon. "Do you think he'll be okay?" she whispered, nodding at Kaidyn's back. "He just watched his brother die."

"Kaidyn's strong," Leon said slowly, stripping off his shirt and squeezing blood out of it before wrapping it around his wounds. Lili avoided looking at his bruised, shirtless chest. "But without Aidyn, I don't know if he'll try to..."

His voice trailed off but she knew what he meant. Kaidyn might do something violent or enter the forest alone to die fighting monsters, killing himself in his grief.

"Then I need to remind him why we're here," she said, recalling their conversation that morning. "We're not just here to find our families. We're here to put an end to all these deaths for good." She had to remind herself too sometimes.

"You really think we can?" Leon asked. When she nodded, he forced a smile and held out his fist for her to bump it. "Right. I'm with you. Let's get Jacques and Billy back, then burn this forest to the ground."

Episode 19

As soon as the group—or what remained of it—reached the castle, the soldiers carried in the supplies while Lili and her friends ran down the hall to check on Jacques. Dr. Anna encountered them at the halfway point and raised her hand to wave but before she could even speak, they brushed past her.

"Is Jacques okay?" Lili asked as she trailed after the boys, who were in too much of a hurry to address the doctor.

The woman hesitated. "Barely. His condition is worse than I initially thought. Even with the scavenged supplies, it will take months for him and recover and he may never walk again. You found the tools and medicine I requested?"

"Yes," Lili replied. "...But it had a price." One they could never take back.

Jacques was still unconscious on the operating table. The doctor had covered the table with straw and blankets so he could sleep without getting cold. There were still two soldiers next to him with swords hanging from their belts. They were ready to cut off his head as soon as he took his last breath.

The group surrounded him while Viktor checked for a pulse. The doctor reentered the room while they scrutinized Jacques. Diego trailed after her with a pile of bottles and tools in his arms.

"He's burning up," Kaidyn commented, glaring at the doctor. He was glaring at everyone now, even Leon and Viktor. "Will your medicine work? We gave up a lot to get it."

"I can't make any promises." The doctor took Diego's items and set them on a nearby table. "Have you decided what to do with him if he passes?" Her words were so straightforward that even Lili felt her chest burn with rage. It was especially hard to hear about Jacques's death immediately after losing Aidyn.

"Yes," Kaidyn answered without hesitation. "We'll behead him."

"Now wait a minute—" Viktor started but the twin cut him off.

"We've seen what happens to people who die down here. No one deserves that," Kaidyn continued, gripping Jacques's arm. "Plus, Jacques told us to behead him before he fell unconscious. He wouldn't want to hurt us."

Both Leon and Viktor looked horrified. It was up to Lili to speak before a fight broke out. "I agree. It's what Jacques wanted."

"But that was before we found the doctor," Viktor continued. "He would have wanted his body to be used in research ...right? We went over that before we came here."

"Things have changed," Kaidyn said, nearly shouting.

Viktor backed away and looked to the others for support. Leon kept shaking his head, unsure what to do. It was Meriel who finally raised her hand.

"I agree with him," she said, pointing at Kaidyn. "I don't want to see more people turn into beasts. The forest has stolen enough."

"Then that settles it," Dr. Anna said with little emotion. "Now get out of here so I can do my job. Diego wants to discuss your future anyway. We have plenty of spare rooms and always need more hands. You'll make a fine addition to our fortress."

"We're not staying," Kaidyn said, once again drawing a gasp from Viktor. "We're going to the level below to figure out what controls this forest and how to destroy it."

"Now hold on, there." Diego placed a hand on his shoulder. "I already let you kids go to a dangerous place once and I won't be doing it again. We've had scientists, soldiers, and even tanks go down there and it didn't change a thing. If you so much as set foot in the next level, you'll die."

"You think I care?" Kaidyn growled.

Dr. Anna stepped between Kaidyn and the soldier. "Get out of my lab before I lose my temper, all of you. You're getting on my nerves."

"Sorry." Diego pulled all five of them from the room and only spoke again once he'd shut the door behind them. They were now standing in the hallway with Meriel leaning her head against the wall, Leon and Viktor cautiously staring at Kaidyn, and Lili studying the entire group. She agreed with Kaidyn about going to the third level but he wasn't going about this the right way.

"I know you want to avenge your brother," Diego began. "I do too. But going down there is suicide."

"So you want us to waste away up here until we die of old age?" Kaidyn asked. "That's all you people have done and it hasn't changed a thing."

"Then what do you plan to do?" Diego asked, pressing an accusing finger against Kaidyn's chest. "What can you do differently from everyone else? Do you really think you and your young friends are more capable than all the soldiers I worked with?"

"I don't know, but I can't just sit here." Kaidyn shut his eyes and turned away, pressing his fists against his face. He was breaking down again.

"I..." Lili felt a lump in her throat but pushed through it, stepping between Kaidyn and Diego. "I have to go down there too. I need to find my mother. I know she's still alive and needs my help."

"Yeah, and Billy might be down there too," Leon added.

Viktor sighed. "Jacques wouldn't want us to give up," he muttered and glanced at Kaidyn. "And Aidyn wouldn't either."

"So you're just going to leave your friend up here?" Diego asked, grasping for anything that might prevent them from going.

"Jacques won't recover for months," Meriel cut in. "There's no point waiting for him."

"Then you'll—"

"I'll stay with him," Meriel cut in before Diego could continue arguing. Her words surprised everyone, even Lili. "I can't keep doing this. I thought I was strong and angry enough to keep going but for now, I'm done. Maybe with enough time, I can follow in your footsteps but..." She looked back at the door to the doctor's lab. "I can keep an eye on your friend. If he wakes and decides to follow you guys, I'll go with him."

Lili smiled, glad Meriel hadn't given up completely. Diego didn't look pleased.

"None of you are leaving without my say-so, got it?" He sighed and massaged his forehead. Lili noticed his fingers shaking. "I won't be responsible for the deaths of any more people. Plus, Leon needs to recover from his wounds." He pointed at the fresh bandages over Leon's cuts and bites. "Promise me you'll at least stay the night."

Everyone shared a glance, then Kaidyn nodded. "One night."

Episode 20

It felt strange to sleep in a room larger than three feet across and in a real bed. The last time she had a bedroom this large was before her parents died...before the forest tore her life apart.

Lili fell asleep to Meriel's breathing from the neighboring bed. As Lili once again drifted off, dreaming of the day she met her mother, she didn't feel afraid anymore. Instead, she was eager to see what would happen next. Would things be the same as they were in her memories or would she see more, like she had last time?

There was her mother, in the doorway. Her skin was grey and green sprouts crawled through cuts in her skin. Her flesh wasn't the same white color as Kaidyn's siblings. Her eyes still had that spark of life too. She didn't look dead. Not yet.

Lili leapt off the branch, like last time, and ran toward her mom, arms outstretched.

Her mother reached down, her fingers aimed at Lili's chest.

While Lili ran forward, she heard her uncle calling for her from behind. His voice made Lili freeze and turn away from her mother, worried she was about to get caught. He'd forbidden going near the walls.

"Lili!" he was screaming, panicked. "Get away from that wall!" She saw him running toward her, waving his arms and wearing an expression of pure fear. She'd never seen him so scared. He was too far away to do anything. She doubted he could even see her mother from that distance.

Then Lili heard another familiar voice behind her, calling out to her. It didn't belong to her mom. "Lili, wake up. We're leaving."

"No. I need to see what happens next," she whispered, willing her younger self to turn back to her mother, just to see.

Unfortunately, before anything else occurred, her vision blurred. "No! Wait. I can't leave yet."

A hand pressed harshly against her chest and her eyes opened. She was back in the real world, eighteen again and lying in the soft castle bed. Meriel was shaking her.

"The boys are waiting for you," Meriel hissed, focusing on something behind Lili. "You need to go before the guards come back."

Lili still felt like she was in a dream but sat up anyway.

Kaidyn, Leon, and Viktor were standing behind her, next to one of the glass-free windows. They'd retrieved their packs, plus the armor and weapons the soldiers had given them.

"Diego gave me a tour of the castle," Kaidyn explained quietly as they handed her a pack. "And Leon asked the guards how often they'd check our rooms, so we know how to avoid running into them."

"I'm sure they figured Leon was too dumb to plan an escape, so they answered all his questions without suspicion," Viktor added, looking a little more positive about their situation. He held up a small bowl filled to the brim with dirt. A green stem sprouted from the top. "And I stole one of their plants to bring with us. We'll need it down there, though I don't know if the sun will even reach the third level."

"...What about Jacques?" Lili whispered.

"We told him goodbye," Kaidyn said. "And Meriel will keep an eye on him. He should be fine without us. Besides, research was always his goal, so studying with Dr. Anna will make him happier than continuing down."

She nodded, knowing he was right, but now she was a little scared of entering the lower level without any adults. Leon was the oldest and he was only twenty.

"Why don't we ask Diego to come with us?" she ventured. "I'm sure there are some soldiers who wouldn't mind—"

"I already asked and he said no. They've made it clear they're too afraid to go. Don't tell me you're backing out on us now." Kaidyn paused. "Maybe you should stay here after all."

"No. I'm going. My mother's down there." She frowned at him and Kaidyn looked away. She could tell he was only speaking out of concern now, his tone the same as when he used to speak to Aidyn.

"Sorry, I shouldn't have said it like that. You have as much right to go as any of us. Are you ready?"

"Sure." It wasn't like there was anything else she could do to prepare. She hoped this would be their final descent.

Before leaving, she gave Meriel a stiff hug, then turned toward the others, smiling. For the first time since she lost her parents, Lili felt like she had a family again. She'd forgotten how nice it felt to be part of a team. Even if it only lasted for a few more days, she was glad she'd been able to feel this one more time.

"Okay," Kaidyn said when Meriel motioned for them to hurry. "We're going. Thank you for everything, Meriel."

Lili caught Meriel smiling before she waved goodbye. "If you find a way to destroy this forest, even if it means the rest of us will burn with it, do it. Do it for me and Daniel and Aidyn. Save anyone else who might get caught in this trap one day."

The four of them nodded and climbed out the window together.

Lili hoped she'd see Meriel again. If they failed, she would have to eventually finish the job on her own.

Episode 21

The trip back to the lab took a little longer than planned, since they had to defend themselves against a few small tree monsters trying to grow over the road, but the repetition helped them figure out a pattern and settle things fairly quickly.

It became apparent by the time they reached the lab that they likely *would* survive if they stayed up here, since they were capable enough to defend themselves. Plus, Viktor was proficient when it came to food and water. However, proceeding downward would likely end up killing them. The danger was unknown and it would be ten times harder to find sustenance, according to Viktor. A lack of sunlight was a death wish.

But none of them particularly cared anymore. They knew this was a suicide mission and were willing to risk it. Aidyn's death would mean nothing if they gave up now.

"So," Viktor said when they reached the lab, slouching from the exhausting day's walk. "Are we going to have a nap before we continue? We've been walking all day and it's almost nightfall."

Leon shrugged. Both he and Lili looked to Kaidyn for an answer. He in turn looked back the way they'd come and shook his head.

"They've definitely noticed our disappearance by now and will try to stop us. If they manage to bring us back, they'll keep a better eye on us. We'll never get another chance to escape," he said.

Leon nodded. "If we wait any longer, Billy will definitely get hurt," he added.

Viktor sighed. "Hate to break it to you, Leon, but if the boy isn't here and actually found his way down there, which is unlikely since it's supposed to be under the monster-infested lab, then he's probably dead," Viktor told him, glaring at the now empty building. The bodies had been buried and the blood was gone, though the soldiers hadn't cleaned it. The earth must have sucked it up like the offering bowls.

"I don't believe that," Leon answered, looking down at his friend. "If Lili believes her mother is still alive, I can believe Billy is too. He's...he's a kid. It's our job to look out for him. If he was one of my siblings..."

Lili tried to smile encouragingly but wanted to agree with Viktor—though agreeing with him meant her own mother might be dead too and she couldn't bear to admit that.

"Let's have this discussion *after* we get down there," Kaidyn cut in, ending the conversation before it got out of hand. "Leon, where did the soldiers say the entrance to the next level was?"

Leon studied the lab, then pointed at the ground floor. "They said it was in the basement but I didn't see one when we went in earlier."

"Maybe there's a door we didn't notice?" Kaidyn suggested.

"Or it's hidden under a carpet," Leon added.

"It's a lab. There aren't any carpets," Viktor said grumpily. "Maybe they lied to throw you off."

As the boys wandered into the building and began their search for the door, walking past fallen tables and gingerly stepping over broken glass, she heard a faint sound behind her and turned to see what it was. When she peered down the long, brick road they had traveled on, she spotted dark figures approaching in the distance.

"Guys, I think the soldiers caught up with us," she warned, running into the lab and scanning the room for any kind of door or hole. As soon as the others heard her, they did the same, tossing things aside and kicking furniture out of the way. They couldn't get caught after coming all this way. They had to get to the third level.

"Mother," she whispered, walking to the back of the room and crouching under one of the desks. "Please tell me where it is." She searched her heart, trying to sense the familiar tug that had led her here in the first place. "How do I reach you?"

"If we don't find it," Leon asked, "are we going to fight the soldiers?"

"Of course not," Kaidyn said, pushing over a locker to look at the wall behind it. "We're not murderers. Besides, they don't plan to hurt us. They're trying to protect us because we're kids...most of us, at least."

Lili couldn't feel anything besides the rumbling of footsteps. Diego was nearly here. Why wouldn't her mother answer?

Finally, while the boys threw entire tables about and shouted at each other, she felt it, like gravity shifting her toward a certain spot on the floor.

"Wait," she said, stomping her foot on the ground where she felt the tug. It sounded hollow, like it was made of wood rather than concrete. "Maybe there is no basement. Maybe after the others went to the third level and never came back, the soldiers covered the hole so no one could go down again."

Kaidyn nodded, understanding her immediately, and shouted at Leon. "We don't have time to search for any other entrances. Leon, use your axe."

"I can't believe they would willingly live right above the hole," Viktor muttered as Leon drove his weapon into the wooden floor. The floorboards splintered under his blade. "Weren't they afraid the lab would fall through?"

"They did it to protect everyone else," Kaidyn said, peering at the dark red boards blocking their way. After a few more chops, Leon uncovered a hole the size of a fist. Below it was the same eerie blackness from the last doorway in Kingsley's village. "Leon, do you need help?"

"Nope. Besides, you don't have an axe. I've almost...got it." Leon started to bellow with each swing, as though his voice would somehow make the impact greater. Soon, the hole was large enough to fit a human, though they'd have to go feet first.

"Okay." Kaidyn tied a rope to one of the doorknobs and a second to a hook hanging from the wall. Once he was done, he threw the bottom into the hole. "Who wants to go first?"

Viktor shook his head vigorously and glanced at Lili, who sighed and conceded. They didn't have time to argue. She could hear Diego's voice now, shouting orders to his men as he pursued them. Judging by the rise in his tone, Diego had caught sight of Lili and her friends.

"All done." Leon stepped back from the hole he'd created and tied his axe to his pack so he wouldn't drop it during the climb. "Did you guys decide who's going first—"

Before he could finish his question, Lili grabbed the rope and stepped in. If she gave herself time to doubt, she might never go. They made their choice hours ago when they left Jacques and Meriel behind.

The last time she entered the new level, she hurried down because she was afraid of being chased. This time, she knew it was best to study the new level from as high as possible. They wouldn't have a second chance to climb back up, since the forest might take that as a sign of escape and turn them to stone. As soon as her entire body passed the barrier, she spared a moment to survey this new third area.

The temperature dropped yet again, as it had on the second level, but it wasn't as drastic. It wasn't humid or moist at all. On the contrary, everything felt dry and...dead.

The light down here was grey. None of it originated from the sun. Instead, the ground and walls glowed. The level's walls weren't an earthy brown anymore. They were a dark grey, nearly black. The only bright colors were crimson roots running across them like veins. There was no hiding the fact that this level was clearly alive. The very walls were feeding off something red from the level above, most likely blood based on everything they'd seen. The liquid was being pumped into the ground. She could hear the faintest heartbeat beneath her feet.

On the ground, which didn't extend nearly as far as the first two levels, everything was grey. The tall pine trees had next to no leaves and the bark was black, like it had been burnt and charred but never fell. Any animals running beneath the pines were a variation of black, grey, or white with eyes to match. She saw only rabbits, birds, and foxes.

It felt like she'd just entered a black-and-white film.

There were three clearings where the woods didn't extend. The one to her right was the biggest and contained the ruins of a town carved from stone. It was filled with empty shrines and broken foundations. Just like the last two settlements, this one was also surrounded by thick, manmade walls.

To the left was another clearing but this one consisted of stone and dirt hills, devoid of wildlife. Beside those hills was a waterfall, which roared into a stream that ran along the edge of the hills.

The final clearing was at the far end of the level, past the forests. The ground rose, forming a slight hill. Lili wanted to study that final clearing more, since she could see the faintest hint of pink there, but she didn't have time.

"I see ruins," she told the others as she continued climbing down, referring to the town on the right. "Do you think anyone still lives there?" She knew it was unlikely. Without sunlight, even the most resourceful human wouldn't last long...unless the supernatural occurred and kept them alive, which didn't seem out of the question in a place like this.

"We'll worry about that later," Viktor called from the top of the rope. He had entered next. "Keep moving before I accidentally kick you."

"I'm going." Lili slid down the rope, glad the soldiers had given her gloves to protect from rope burn. She landed on the hard ground and accidentally kicked up some black dirt, which left dust on her shoes...or maybe it was ash.

Unlike the second level, which had a pond at the end of the rope, this one was dry. There were more human statues, though. Some of them had clearly fallen and shattered on the ground but others were climbing on top of each other, attempting to reach the top before they froze.

"There's another one of those shrines," she commented, noticing another bowl nearby. This one was held in the arms of a stone statue. The bowl was empty and she didn't want to put more blood into it, even if she knew it would be accepted. They had no way of knowing who or what was receiving it.

"This place is definitely the worst of the three," Viktor whispered shakily as he landed beside her. He paused to study the landscape stretching before them. Far away, maybe a five or six hour walking distance, they could see a thirty-foot tall creature lumbering among the tall pine trees. It looked humanoid but was too shrouded in shadow to confirm. "I hope there aren't any more levels. Anything beyond this would be straight-up hell."

Kaidyn and Leon looked just as nervous when they landed. Once they were off the rope, they looked up to see if anyone had followed them down. It quickly became clear no one would. The soldiers weren't willing to risk entering this place, even for them. Looking out at this dark and dreary land, Lili was glad they hadn't. No one else should become trapped down here if they could help it. Lili didn't want to be here either. She'd be very upset if she came all this way and couldn't find her mother.

"Part of me was hoping the reason no one returned from this place was because it was so beautiful that they chose to stay," Viktor grumbled, crossing his arms and staring at the barren trees. "There might be some caves in those hills. Should we go there to find shelter and sleep?"

Kaidyn shook his head. "Seems risky."

"Well, everything down here looks risky," Leon replied, filming the place with their remaining camera. Lili wondered how many batteries they had left.

"He's right but the hills offer no protection." Kaidyn turned to their alternative on the right: the abandoned village and its high walls. "I think heading into those ruins is our best bet."

"That didn't go well last time," Leon reminded him, referring to Kingsley.

"But the people here are more likely to be soldiers or scientists," Lili pointed out. "Not random stragglers like Kingsley."

The others took her response into consideration but, in the end, they looked to Kaidyn for guidance. He was hesitant, his eyes lingering on the giant creature plodding about miles away. "We'll head to the village. If there's any sign of danger, we'll go to the hills instead. It looks like that giant's headed our way so I'd rather be behind those walls than out in the open."

"Village it is then." Viktor sighed and trudged down the dirt path toward it.

There was what used to be a wooden gate at the front of the village wall but it had been torn off its hinges and left to rot.

The village interior, while in similar disrepair, was clearly built with care. It wasn't like Kingsley's hastily built homes. The stones here were placed carefully and there were even carvings above the household doorways, written in letters Lili couldn't read. Fabrics hung over windows—the torn remnants of curtains—and she found a few piles of clothing strewn about too, though they were so old that any color had faded.

A wide street ran down the middle of the village, starting at the gate they'd entered and ending at a second gate on the other side. Several smaller alleys ran between each house, filled with broken barrels and ash. Next to each home—most of them missing doors or glass—were small pens and cages that must have held animals at one point. There were none now, obviously. The animals must have died around the same time the humans did.

"It's a ghost town," Viktor muttered as they followed the main street.

"Unless the people are hiding from that giant," Leon added, his head twisting this way and that, searching for the boy the rest of them had given up on. "Let's check some of the houses. Billy might be hiding in one of them."

Kaidyn sighed. "Let's hurry." He drew his sword and entered the nearest house. It was stuffy, just like every other part of this level, and they found rotting tables and chairs inside. There were no people, though, or even remains.

"This architecture is old," Lili commented as they crept around the two-room house. "It looks like something from medieval Europe." She hadn't been particularly interested in history, but anyone who went to school would recognize the woodwork beams and arched rooftops. Whoever built this must have lived here for years and had a lot of helping hands.

"Let's check the next one." Kaidyn continued on.

Each house was the same. Old. Rotting. Abandoned. Some homes held little beds, which made Lili pity the children who had to grow up without sunlight and color.

The fifth house was where they finally found something. It must have belonged to a scholar. The home had a makeshift bookshelf leaning against the wall and books of bound paper, accompanied by thinly cut wood once the paper ran out. While the writing was filled with familiar Latin letters, it looked like gibberish to Lili.

"It's German," Kaidyn commented, removing one of the paper books from the top shelf. He held it out to Viktor, who grinned and immediately poured over the words.

"Why would there be Germans in Canada?" Leon asked.

Viktor gave him a judgmental look. "Who do you think emigrated here?" he asked, rolling his eyes and returning to his reading. "The first pages outline the man's journey into the forest, but it's marked over a hundred and fifty years ago. He came here because he and his fellow pioneers heard rumors that this forest would make a good settlement. By the time he realized it was a trap, it was too late. He kept descending until he reached this place."

"A hundred and fifty years ago," Lili whispered. How long had this forest existed and how had none of them heard about it before?

Viktor flipped through the pages, his eyes whipping back and forth to spare them the minute details. "The giant we saw is described here, said to have existed longer than the villagers. There were other monsters—hundreds, he says—but the townspeople were able to kill a lot of them over time and even ate some. The bigger ones were avoided, like the giant." He paused to pick up one of the wooden books. "The people sacrificed blood to the altars around the city in the hopes of appeasing some fallen angel they claimed kept the giant at bay. Then the writer began doubting it a few months later...He says some of the citizens left to destroy the angel's tree."

"Tree?" Kaidyn frowned, as confused as the rest of them.

"It says," Viktor paused to quote it, "My neighbors are sure the tree is the source of the angel's power. They don't believe the forest is a god but know it watches over them, spying on their every move. So many people have died by now that they no longer believe the blood sacrifices are effective. They think we are feeding a monster with an endless thirst. It does not protect us or our children."

Lili recalled the little empty beds. How many parents had outlived their children?

Viktor stopped quoting it directly. "The next week, his friends failed to return from the tree after trying to destroy it. He thinks they were killed by the giant or something else he refers to as the Hunter."

"That doesn't sound good," Leon commented.

"December twelfth. The hunter has arrived. The Samurai. He must have followed the path of our dead comrades and is here to take vengeance. I know hiding will only result in death but what more can I do? I can only pray he will behead me when he finds me. I do not want to turn into one of those things." He closed the book. "It stops there. He must have died."

"Hunter." Kaidyn looked out the door of the household. Lili noted scratch marks on the inside of the wall. "While Germans living here isn't out of the question, a samurai feels a little stranger. It's not unheard of but..."

"I don't think a man with a sword could have made marks like that," Lili commented, pointing at the scratches on the wall. They were thick and dug in deep. "Not unless the person had inhuman strength."

"After all we've seen, I wouldn't be surprised." Viktor closed the book and respectfully placed it back on the shelf with the others. "Should we keep searching the houses or set up camp?"

"That might be risky," Leon warned. "If there's an intelligent monster out there able to track people, lighting a fire would definitely alert it to our presence."

"Good point." Kaidyn sighed. "If the people who lived here couldn't protect themselves, we're at an even greater risk. Let's keep searching for a safer place." Kaidyn looked ready to move out but before they could, they heard a low moan outside and froze. It came from the main street and sounded like a bear attempting to imitate a human. Lili felt the floor shake and heard the scrape of something dragging along the ground.

Viktor glanced at the rest of them and mouthed the word, "Hunter."

Kaidyn motioned for everyone to crawl toward the back of the house while he moved to the front windows to take a look. Whatever he saw made him gasp and immediately sneak back.

"What is it?" Lili whispered as their new leader pushed the back door open with a slight creak. Leon exited first.

"Whatever it is, it's huge," Kaidyn hissed, pushing the back of her shoulder lightly to get her moving. "It's just a...blob. A mass of flesh. Like someone took all the people and animals living here and mushed them together."

Episode 22

Lili's mind became flooded with visions of human playdough as she crawled from the scholar's house. A new scent of copper filled her nose. They had reached another section of the village wall. It would take at least five minutes to locate the entrance they'd used to enter.

"Can we fight it?" Leon asked, already reaching for his axe.

Kaidyn shook his head. "It's as big as three houses and nearly as tall too. I doubt an axe will do anything." It might take hours to cut off all the heads and by that point, they would all be dead. "We need to run."

"And go where?" Viktor hissed, tugging on Kaidyn's shoulder as he peeked around the corner of the nearest house.

"To the hills, like you suggested," Kaidyn answered. "Was there any mention of the hills in the books, Viktor? Anything dangerous we should know about?"

"The rocky hills? No. There's just the giant and some angelic tree further in, though I don't know what an angelic tree is supposed to look like. I wouldn't let my guard down outside this village. They did mention other monsters. We—"

"Then the hills are our only option. We'll head there and risk facing the giant. It looked slow so we might be able to avoid it."

"But it might be slow because it has nothing to hunt," Leon whispered as they crept along the wall, grey dirt and ash crunching under their boots. The moans were still behind them, keeping pace, but they hadn't gotten louder.

"That's a risk we'll have to take," Kaidyn replied.

They were halfway to the exit when Lili turned and looked down an alley, hoping to catch a glimpse of the thing following them.

Instead of seeing the empty street that cut through the village, she found a face looking back at her, buried within a pink and bloody mass of flesh. Just as Kaidyn described, it looked like someone had mashed up some humans and pressed them together like dough. The mass was sliding through the alley toward them, the moans coming from numerous deformed mouths. As soon as she made eye contact with one of the faces, it screamed.

"I guess we know what happened to the villagers," Viktor commented, starting to jog. "But they have to be over a hundred years old. How are they still alive?"

"Don't worry about that right now." Kaidyn sprinted, loosing a flurry of dirt behind him. The need to stay quiet was gone.

Lili took a deep breath, then did the same, feeling her ankle twist uncomfortably when she changed speeds.

While the four of them ran, it became frighteningly apparent that Viktor and Lili would have trouble keeping up. They were shorter and not as fit as the other two.

Lili resisted the urge to look back as her lungs burned. She could hear the squelch of the blob pursuing them. At first, it tried to squeeze its thick form through the tight alleys to reach them, then it sped down the street instead, rolling like a ball. She could hear all its teeth chattering, like the faces were itching to eat them. Viktor was sobbing now, and Lili felt the urge to do the same.

The blob was gaining on them and the voices were shouting now. The ground was vibrating so much that her legs were going numb. "We're almost there, Viktor," she assured him. She could differentiate between the many voices. There were a few children crying among all the adult ones, boys and girls forever trapped at a young, tortured age.

The gate was right in front of them, still open and inviting. It was smaller than the monster. If they managed to pass it, she doubted the thing could chase after them.

Kaidyn and Leon were a few feet ahead. Kaidyn was the first to reach the gate. When he turned around, Lili saw his eyes widen in fear. A moment later, she heard Viktor shout and realized why. Her red-haired friend had tripped and fallen on his face behind her.

"Leon! Grab him!" Kaidyn drew his swords. Lili joined him, finally reaching the security of the doorway.

Leon scooped up Viktor with little effort but the blob was a foot away from him now and the monster was rising, preparing to fall down on top of them and absorb them into the mass.

"Jump!" Kaidyn shouted. Leon did so, diving away from the blob and flying through the air. He landed next to Lili, shielding Viktor from the ground. The blob shrieked, angered by the loss of its prey, and Lili took two steps back as it leapt after them.

She reached for her knife, joining Kaidyn on the defensive. They were behind the gate now. If the blob made it through the entrance, they were dead. If it failed, they'd have nothing to worry about.

Lilli squinted, wanting to close her eyes completely as the blob reached the doorway. If it succeeded and killed them, she'd rather not witness it.

The blob of human dough pressed itself against the doorframe, the faces turning red, but it couldn't squeeze through. Just as she'd hoped, the mass wasn't flexible enough to change its size. It certainly tried, though, and even cut itself against the edges, covering the floor in crimson pools. No matter what it did, it couldn't reach them.

"I don't want to wait around and see if it makes its way out," Kaidyn said while Leon and Viktor got to their feet, a little bruised but otherwise okay. "Let's head for the hills."

Lili looked in the direction of the giant, who was slightly closer than before. Then she looked back at the faces, arms, and legs sticking out of the lump. She could see the body of a baby inside, so small and innocent.

"We have next to zero chance of killing that thing," Leon replied, shaking his head. He cringed when the children screamed. They must sound similar to his little sisters. "We can't behead every person in there. It's impossible."

No one protested as they ventured toward the rocks, hoping for shelter. However, when they neared the towering hills, the lumbering giant in the trees continued its approach. Now that it was within range, Lili could see it in complete detail.

The tall monster had human skin, though it was so old and bloodless that it had turned a deep grey. The skin had been stretched for so long that it hung over the bone and muscle to the point where it looked like the outer layer might fall off at any second. It was missing its jaw, bearing only a row of top teeth sharpened to points, and there were two empty holes where its eyes should be. The thing's hairless head was angled upward, as though yearning for the sky it would never see again.

"I don't think that thing used to be human," Viktor commented thoughtfully when they reached the first hill. "If it were, it would have to be formed from a bunch of people, strung together like the blob, right? The giant's clearly just one person, albeit a very tall one."

"Maybe it used to be a real giant?" Leon ventured, which sounded ridiculous until Lili recalled the theories that giants used to exist thousands of years ago. "I used to study them growing up, since people used to make fun of me for my height," Leon added sheepishly.

"Whatever it was doesn't matter. What we should be focusing on is what it's carrying," Kaidyn said, prompting Lili to look at its long, skinny arms. Kaidyn was right. It had two giant metal cleavers—one in each hand—and they were being dragged along the ground. Its arms looked too thin and weak to raise them.

"We need to hide," Lili whispered, scanning the stone hills for any openings or at least an overhang. They needed shelter. All she could see were more shrines, most of them built into the roots of trees or atop stone statues. "Do you guys see anything?" The behemoth would reach them in a few more minutes at this rate.

The quick shake of their heads made her skin crawl. The monster's footsteps were giving her a headache.

Viktor squeaked in panic and rushed through the hills, leaving the rest behind to catch up. No one rolled their eyes or called Viktor's name as they darted after him, dodging lone pines and nearly tripping over the uneven ground. There was no time to utter a sound. The giant's footsteps were directly behind them now and Lili could hear its raspy groans. The scent of blood was intensifying too. She snuck a glance over her shoulder and saw blood dripping from its jawless mouth. She'd seen enough blood in the last month to fill a pool.

"This thing's gonna kill us if we don't find a cave *now*," Kaidyn hissed, catching up to Viktor and leading them around a corner so they'd be out of the giant's view for a moment. He paused, eyes darting around. They were nearing an open part of the level that would leave them exposed and cornered if they didn't redirect and find a hiding spot.

"Guys." Leon pulled them all close and hugged them, breathing heavily and stinking of sweat. He squeezed them awkwardly before opening his mouth. "I'll distract the giant. You three go ahead." His fingers reached for the hilt of his axe, tears in his eyes, but Kaidyn grabbed his hand before he could do anything rash.

"I think there's a cave right there," he said and pointed behind them. Sure enough, in this hill they'd hidden behind, there were some rocks that looked intentionally piled atop each other, forming a makeshift wall at the bottom of the hill. In the middle of this wall was a crack big enough to fit a single person. "We can hide in there. Let's go."

Kaidyn went through the crack first, sword in hand. Lili followed. The groaning was right above them now. In just seconds, the giant would be upon them.

The cave was cold but surprisingly well-lit. It wasn't small either. The space was almost as big as her uncle's trailer and had clearly been created by a human. The walls were lined with shelves, which held dry plants, rabbit furs, and dirty clay pots. On the floor lay a thick blanket sewn from straw and in the corner of the room sat a filthy, middle-aged man in a dirty jacket and jeans, crouching against the wall and covering his eyes with his hands.

"Who's that?" Leon asked as he and Viktor climbed inside. Leon had drawn his axe and Viktor did the same with his shield.

"No idea." Kaidyn pushed them away from the door and motioned for everyone to stay quiet. A moment later, the colossal giant's legs came into view, pacing in front of the cave. Lili could hear it sniffling and held her breath, staring at its massive feet. A second later, its blade moved past, grinding against the stone ground and making her ears numb.

Everyone—even the filthy man in the corner—froze as the creature stopped in front of their cave. It wheezed, lingering, then continued west until it was out of sight. The silence was finally cut off by everyone's sighs of relief. They were safe, at least for now.

"Okay, now that it's gone..." Kaidyn turned toward the stranger. The person was still hiding from them. He had scrabbly brown hair that ran to his shoulders and no shoes on his dirty feet.

Despite his filthy appearance, Lili felt like she'd seen him before.

"Who are you?" Kaidyn asked the man. "How long have you lived here?"

"And *how* have you been living here?" Viktor added. "There's no sunlight to grow plants."

"There is water," the man said suddenly, his voice so deep and raspy that it made Lili jump. "By the wall, lots of water. From above, maybe. Don't know." He was talking so fast that it was hard to understand him, plus his hands were still covering his face so they muffled his words. "Eat the rabbits. Reproduce often, very nutritious. Eat the plants too, not healthy but keep alive."

"He eats the plants?" Viktor frowned. "But we were told they were poisonous."

"Usually are," the man said, finally lowering his fingers and staring at them with bloodshot eyes. "But forest won't kill me, keeps me around. Only survivor. Keep it entertained, maybe. My own theory. Will you replace me?"

"No." Kaidyn glanced at the others and shrugged. "Maybe the plants don't poison people but turn them insane instead."

"Aha!" Lili pointed at the man. "I *do* know you." She'd finally remembered him from the photo.

The man squinted at her. "No. Don't know you. Wait, yes I do! Cynthia. No. Too young. Cynthia's ghost? No. No ghosts here. Forest must have made you to trick me. Won't be deceived."

Kaidyn and the other two turned to her. "You know him?"

Lili pulled out the photo of the first ten hikers and pointed at the man standing beside her parents. "Grant Brin. He was one of the first to enter the forest and I think Diego said he came down here with my parents." She gasped and walked up to the man, no longer afraid of him. "Do you know what happened to my parents? Cynthia and Dennis Nilson?"

All three boys had their weapons pointed at the man now, just in case he jumped at her, but they didn't interfere.

"Yes. Came with me. Went with soldiers. Investigate city. Kill monsters. Many monsters. Killed many. Lost many. Dennis died. Killed by giant."

"Oh." Lili's heart dropped and tears welled up in her eyes. "Was he...beheaded?" She hoped he at least had a merciful death.

"All were. Giant's method. Merciful? Maybe." The man counted down a few more soldiers by name but Lili didn't recognize any of them. Then he continued to explain her mother's fate while Lili recovered from the acknowledgment that her father was well and truly gone. "Cynthia go. Talk to tree. I not go. Too afraid. Would die to hunter. Didn't join her. One week, alone. Then, she comes back. Changed. Wrong. Like doppelgangers, but different. Still has eyes." He pointed at his own eyes to emphasize this.

"Still has eyes? What do you mean?" Lili asked, feeling a sense of déjà vu.

"All doppelgangers, dead eyes. No soul, only body. Like a mask. Cynthia different. Still life in eyes. Don't trust her. Hid. Always hid from her."

Lili shivered. "So she's still alive?" she whispered.

"Alive? No. Here? Yes. Don't know how. Different."

Lili looked at Kaidyn, distraught. This wasn't answering her question. If anything, it was making things worse. Her mother wasn't alive but she wasn't dead either? She would prefer one or the other. What made it worse was his description of her looking different but still having life behind her eyes, unlike Aidyn when he changed. Grant's description fit her childhood memories perfectly.

"What tree are you talking about?" Kaidyn asked, resting a hand on Lili's shoulder and gently moving her aside so he could stand between her and the man.

Grant simply pointed in the direction he was referring to, at the far end of the level. "Big tree. See from here. Never go. Scary. Any who go, don't come back. Monsters kill them. So many monsters. Most dead now. Still hunter. Giant. Both guard the tree."

"We've heard that before." Kaidyn sighed. "So why do people go to the tree?"

"Don't know." The man looked Kaidyn up and down. Lili felt Kaidyn tighten his grip on her shoulder.

"You want to go? Won't come with you." Grant's eyes shifted to Lili and narrowed. "You went to the tree?"

"No," she said. "Though based on what he's said, we might have to go to it if that's where everyone else went. It might be exactly what we're looking for." In order to destroy the forest, they might have to burn the tree...or talk to it the way Grant said her mother did.

"It sounds like they didn't succeed in whatever they were doing, so maybe following the crowd isn't the best idea," Viktor commented from the doorway.

"We should ask the man more questions. He's been here for years. If anyone knows how to survive down here, it's him," Kaidyn said. "If what he says is true, he's the only one left."

"Works for me." Leon sat down against the wall and Viktor did the same, motioning for Kaidyn to continue the interrogation.

"How have you avoided dying?" Leon asked, pulling a protein bar from his pocket and taking a bite as he stared at the strange, thin man.

"Hiding," Grant answered bluntly.

"How many monsters are there?" Kaidyn asked, leaning against the wall and staying by Lili's side. "And do they have any weaknesses we can exploit?"

"Only three left. Soldiers killed the rest. First is the village monster. Here when I came." He pointed in the direction of the village where the blob resided. "Can't move. Trapped. I don't approach. Next, the giant. Also here when I came. Big and scary but slow. Has a pattern. Easy to avoid."

"I don't know about that," Leon said. "He followed us pretty quickly."

"Though to be fair, we didn't really know where we were going," Viktor added.

"And the third?" Kaidyn asked.

"Two soldiers in one. The hunter. An assassin from the east, a knight from the north. Also here before I came. Very fast, very stealthy. Blind. Don't make a sound and you survive."

"How did two soldiers from different parts of the world come down here?" Lili asked, catching his remarks about a European knight and what sounded like a Japanese samurai, just like the book said. "How did people from across the ocean enter an unknown forest in Canada?"

"Moving forest. My own theory. Many years in Canada but moved before that. Traveled the world. Different shrines, different architecture, different languages, different armor. Very old." The man pointed at the walls and for the first time, Lili noticed hundreds of different drawings and writing carved into it. Some were in English, some in various European and Asian languages, and the rest she couldn't read or recognize, though they did look familiar. The drawings were labeled maps of the area or poorly drawn faces. One of them was of her parents. Grant must have drawn that one.

Seeing her parents, drawn by someone who probably knew them better than she did, filled her with an aching wish to meet them again.

"So you're the only human here?" Leon asked. "You haven't seen a little boy, have you? About this tall and blond?"

"That's a stupid question." Viktor elbowed him. "The entrance was covered by the lab. Unless he managed to fall through one of the other holes without a rope, he's dead."

"Saw him, yes. Two days ago," Grant said, making everyone gasp.

"Wait, you really saw him?" Leon leaned forward, grinning for the first time in a while. "Where was he?"

"Leon," Kaidyn warned but the older man didn't seem to hear.

"Saw him in the woods, near the tree."

"That tree again," Kaidyn muttered.

"But boy was doppelganger. Not person." Grant pointed to his eyes. "Empty eyes, no soul."

"What are doppelgangers?" Kaidyn asked. "How do they come to be?"

"Some who die aren't turned into monsters," the man answered, his speech slowing and tone becoming even more serious. He sounded less insane for a moment. "The forest takes them for itself and makes their bodies start walking about, acting like they had before, but they do the forest's will. There was one soldier who died and we couldn't behead him. Then the next day, he returned to our camp acting like nothing had happened."

Kaidyn frowned. "Like my siblings. Did the soldier try to kill you after he returned?"

"Yes, he did. So we freed his body." The man dragged his finger across his neck and tilted his head.

Leon looked down at his feet, his food forgotten. "So, Billy's not real? He's just a...walking corpse pretending to be human? But he didn't try to kill any of us."

"Sometimes waits. Forest gets bored. Plays with us like toys. Sometimes used to lure people in and down." His stuttering speech came back and Lili stopped listening. At least her mother wasn't described like that. He seemed to think her mom was different, that she might still be alive and wasn't just pretending to be.

"Okay, now you leave." Grant suddenly stood and pointed at the door. "No room for five. Room for one. Too much noise brings monsters."

"Uhh..." Leon looked to their unofficial leader, who sighed and got to his feet.

"Sorry, sir, but we can't leave just yet. Not until we figure out our next step." Kaidyn lowered his head. "Are you really okay with throwing four kids outside to be eaten by a giant?"

"Not eat. Behead. Giant doesn't eat. Tries to free you with death. So old it must pity us." Grant glared at Kaidyn, then turned away. "Fine.

Won't send you out but can't get attached. Will lose you. Always lose everyone. Not even children safe."

"He's afraid of living with us because he doesn't want to watch us die," Lili translated, feeling sympathy. He must have been so lonely down here, alone, cursed to remain the sole survivor.

"You don't need to worry about us, sir," Leon said, pumping his fist in the air. "I'll protect my friends. I'm willing to risk my life for them."

"Besides, if my gut is right, we'll be heading out tomorrow." Kaidyn looked to the others. "I think we need to take a look at this tree. Besides, there's nowhere else to go."

As soon as he said it, Lili could feel herself being pulled in that direction. She knew he was right. That tree was their last stop, their final destination. Plus, that was where her mom had gone. If she was still alive, that was where they'd find her.

Episode 23

Lili knew tonight was the last time she'd be able to dream. They'd decided over a dinner of protein bars and dry fruit, alongside cooked rabbit and weeds for the man, that tomorrow they'd find a way around the monsters and investigate this tree. They only planned to look at it from afar and figure out why it was so important but Lili knew they'd end up getting closer. There was nowhere else to go at this point.

After Lili went to sleep, listening to Viktor ask the man questions late into the night, she saw her mother again. Her childish body climbed down from the tree, just like before. Then, while her uncle called her name, Lili's mother touched her chest. There was a lot of pain—a hot, searing sting in her chest. This hadn't happened last time.

Instead of responding to her uncle, Lili turned toward her mom this time and when she looked up, she noticed tears streaming down her mom's face. Her fingers were digging through Lili's chest, cutting right into her. They were the cause of the sting that was so painful. At the same time, her mom was using her other hand to grab her own wrist. It was like she was trying to pull her cutting arm back, to prevent herself from harming her own daughter. She was struggling against herself, like she wasn't the one in control.

"Mom?" Lili whispered, confused. The pain in her chest was immense but she was more worried about the tears streaming down her mom's face. She had never seen her cry before. Her head felt fuzzy too, like it couldn't comprehend the fact that her mom's hand was supernaturally digging through her chest and into her heart.

"Lili," her mother sobbed, removing her hand and leaning away, squeezing her eyes shut. "I'm dead, Lili. Don't come after me. Don't come in here."

"...What?"

Before she could explain, her mother's eyes widened in fear, like there was something within the walls behind her and it was about to kill her. Then her mouth opened unnaturally, her jaw dropping low. "Come find me," she told Lili robotically. "Save me, Lili."

Lili's eyes went wide but the dream ended and she awoke in the dark cave, the pain in her chest dulling but never fully going away. Leon and Viktor were asleep beside her in their sleeping bags and the survivor was on his rabbit pelt in the corner. Kaidyn was the only one missing.

Rubbing her eyes with shaking hands, Lili looked toward the entrance. Where was their leader?

After venturing beyond the safety of the cave with a knife in hand, she found him standing next to one of the shrines. The stone bowl sat atop a tree stump and he was resting his hands on its edge, staring into it.

Lili stepped forward, opening her mouth to call out to him, but he suddenly kicked the stump, his abrupt movement making her jump. After kicking the stump a few times, he tried to grab the bowl and yank it from its post, muttering unintelligible words under his breath as he tried to destroy the thing with his bare hands.

"Kaidyn?" she whispered. He turned toward her with mud and tears streaked across his cheeks. "What's wrong?" she whispered. It must be about Aidyn. Seeing him act this way brought back her own pain from her father's death.

"I'm telling the bastard who took my blood that I want it back," he muttered, giving the shrine another kick but barely leaving a mark.

"I'm asking God to take it back for me. I don't want whoever's behind this place to have a single piece of me."

She stepped closer but maintained a foot long distance. "Kaidyn, do you want to...talk about what happened?"

"No, I don't." He gave another kick, avoiding eye contact. She could see tears dripping from his jaw. "I just want to find that tree or whatever it is and burn it to the ground. Whoever made this forest deserves to die."

"I agree...but only if that means it will free everyone and prevent more people from entering. We can't act rashly and waste our one opportunity." Seeing him so angry about revenge was a little scary. "Focusing on only vengeance could make you take risks that put everyone else in danger." She needed to ensure they were all thinking clearly going forward. If they made a mistake, it could cost the lives of every person in the three levels, including Jacques and Meriel.

"I..." He sighed and motioned for her to leave. "You should go. I don't want to end up saying something I regret again."

"I can take it. It didn't stop me last time, remember? Tell me."

"It was nothing of consequence." He groaned and finally stopped hitting the bowl once it became clear it wouldn't fall. "I don't want to hurt you like I did before...You and the others are all I have left. I don't want us to die hating each other."

"I don't hate you," she said. "And don't worry. I know you don't hate me. Technically, we haven't even known each other longer than a week anyway, so it's not like our opinions of each other mean much."

He smirked, then started laughing, raising his head to the level's ceiling as the last of the tears slipped from his face. It felt strange to hear him laugh after everything they'd faced but she was glad she got to see him smile. It might be the last time any of them could.

His laughter woke up Leon and Viktor. A few seconds after his shoulders stopped shaking, they both came out of the cave to join in.

"What's going on?" Leon asked. "Having a party without us?"

Kaidyn pointed at the shrine. "Trying to break this. Whoever built it made sure it couldn't be destroyed. Explains why they're the only things left standing around here."

Viktor looked past the hills, toward the tree of the fallen angel. His chin quivered. "Are we sure we want to do this, Kaidyn? We could spend a few weeks investigating this level and talking to the crazy man again, then we could go when we're more prepared—"

"We only have enough food for another week," Kaidyn interrupted. "Two at the most. And I don't want us losing our minds like that guy did."

"Then we'd better make our final days count," Leon said, patting both Viktor and Kaidyn on the back and making them double over from the force. "But I'm confident we'll all make it out of here alive, so there's no need to be worried about food. We'll be fine as long as we stick together."

Viktor rubbed his back, his mouth lowering into a scowl. "If we *do* make it out," Viktor said hesitantly, "I want to carry all the level's plants into the real world. I'll become famous for discovering them and name them after myself...and you guys too, if there are any extra."

Lili chuckled. "Unfortunately, my name is already taken."

"And I'm not sure someone will want to pick flowers named Jacques or Viktor," Kaidyn added jokingly, his tense stance finally relaxing.

Viktor scowled at them. "Fine! I'll just name them all after myself and you'll regret missing out on this opportunity," Viktor said defiantly, then sighed. "*If* we make it out, that is."

Leon noticed his friend's somber mood and immediately tried to cheer him up by joining in on the wish-making. "After I release the footage and become famous, I'll pay for my family's hospital bills." He pulled out his camera. They had already dropped some of the film off with Diego for safekeeping, just in case. "Then I'll find a new place to discover—one just as cool as this...but less dangerous."

"You really think this place is cool?" Kaidyn asked doubtfully.

"From an objective point of view," Leon answered with a cheeky grin. "The plants and animals are, at least, and the people. I'm not referring to the monsters." He glanced nervously at Kaidyn, afraid to insult him and his family. The twin didn't seem to mind.

"When I get out, I'll return to my parents and apologize for leaving them," Kaidyn said to save Leon from the awkward silence. "And maybe I'll convince Jacques' parents to fund some kind of relief group for the survivors in here."

"Lili. What will you do after this is over?" Leon gestured toward the hills and far-off giant. "After we find your mom?" He sounded like the only one who believed she was still alive.

"I'll reunite my mother with her brother—my uncle—and apologize for leaving him." Lili smiled sadly. "And then my uncle can finally explore this place. He always wanted to enter the forest but refused to leave me behind to fend for myself."

"Do you think he followed us in, then?" Kaidyn asked and she realized she hadn't considered it in a while.

"Maybe but...I feel like we would have seen him by now, right?" she said. Part of her hoped he had followed her, bringing an army with him like he mentioned wanting to do dozens of times before. She was the reason he hadn't done it in the past.

No one answered.

She didn't want to think about how her uncle must have felt to find her gone the day she left. Her heart aching, she changed the subject. "Maybe we should go back to sleep. It'll be hard to solve a mystery when we're sleep deprived."

Leon nodded and pushed them back toward the cave, checking over his shoulder one more time to look for Billy. "She makes a good point. Let's enjoy our last night together."

Lili knew she wouldn't, since that dream of her mother's hand digging into her chest still lingered. She hoped to never see her mother like that again. Her face and speech had felt so...wrong. Robotic. Possessed.

They reentered the cave. Lili could tell Kaidyn wanted to break down and cry again—to completely give up—but he was pushing himself for one more day, doing so for the sake of his friends. He wouldn't last beyond that. She could feel it. If they didn't go now, they wouldn't live long enough to get a second chance.

Leon stationed himself at the cave entrance while everyone else settled in. She noticed him muttering to himself a few times and even stepping out once, as though he'd seen something. It reminded her of when Aidyn continued claiming to see his siblings.

"Did you see Billy?" she asked him once, determined to never ignore the warning signs again.

Leon looked her way, his eyes red. "I thought I did a few times but...it's so dark that I can't be sure. Best not to risk going out alone to check, right?"

"Right." They couldn't have a repeat of what happened last time with Aidyn. "Try to get some sleep," she told him, then rolled over and shut her eyes. It felt like tomorrow might be their last day down here. They'd either find a way out...or meet their end like everyone else.

Episode 24

"**D**anger," the survivor told them as they drank from their water bottles and finished the last of Viktor's dry meat. "Do not go. Danger."

Lili turned to the older man. He was drinking from a wooden bowl of water he'd procured at the waterfall. It came straight out of the wall, which didn't bode well for the liquid's safety. Accompanying the water were dandelions that had somehow grown on the rocks despite the lack of sunlight, hence their pedals being grey instead of yellow.

"Do not go," Grant continued. "Find new cave. Not die young."

"Thanks, old man," Leon said. "But we have to find Lili's mother and maybe Billy too if we're lucky."

Kaidyn looked ready to counter him on that final point but didn't.

"Why don't you come with us?" Viktor asked Grant, who immediately started shaking his head like a child. "We could use the help," Viktor added slowly.

"No. Never listen to me. Always see friends die." Grant started quivering and biting his nails. "No. Can't go. Must live. Warn more. Some may listen."

"That clearly hasn't worked for you before," Kaidyn said bluntly, wiping his hands on his pants, his meal done. He stepped toward the door. "You regret allowing others to go out and die, right? Because they wouldn't heed your warnings. Well, maybe the reason they died is because you didn't go with them to help."

"That's a little harsh," Lili started but Kaidyn didn't acknowledge her. He was too focused on Grant, who was finally listening without his eyes trailing away or clouding over as they had before.

"We need all the help we can get," Kaidyn continued. "We're kids, right? We need your guidance. Aren't you tired of sitting around, waiting to die of old age by yourself? You can help us destroy this forest and end this torment." He paused. "You can finally go home."

The man sat up, opening his mouth...then he leaned against the wall, waving Kaidyn away. "I told you what I know. I can't go with you." His voice was normal again. "I've seen enough of my friends and comrades die. Seeing the same happen to a bunch of bright-eyed children will drive me over the edge."

"Then help us," Kaidyn insisted. Leon and Viktor grabbed his arms, holding him back.

Grant still wouldn't move. "I'm sorry." He turned away, staring at the wall and his carvings of Lili's parents. "I'm sorry."

Kaidyn looked ready to continue his rant but Leon grabbed the back of his shirt and dragged him out the door. They'd heard enough arguments to last a lifetime. Viktor left too, sheepishly avoiding eye contact with the older man. Now it was just Lili, alone with the last person who saw her parents alive.

"It's okay." Lili tried to smile at him even though he wasn't looking at her. "Thank you for doing what you could." She waved goodbye. She hoped they could come back for him someday but this would likely be their last meeting.

The man didn't reply.

Lili didn't sigh until she exited the cave, hating to leave him behind like that. The others were standing outside in the grey light, pointing out the giant's current location. It was at the far end of the level and wouldn't pass by for a while. It seemed to have a set pattern, in which it circled around the village, then past the hills where they currently were, before patrolling around the forest in front of the angel tree. If they left now, they'd have enough time to avoid its route.

In front of the tree was a thick forest of pines. They were so close together that Lili could barely see through to the other side. If Grant wasn't lying, that was where the blind hunter resided—the only other monster the villagers and soldiers hadn't killed. They would have to avoid the hunter at all costs but that meant chancing the giant instead. If they went through the open, barren lands between the wall and the forest to reach the tree, they'd be exposed to the colossal beast. But the giant at least had a predictable path and was so slow it would offer a few hours of leeway. The only risk was being spotted. If it took an interest in them and chose to run, which they weren't sure it could do, they'd be done for.

"We should get moving," Kaidyn said, pointing at the barren area where the giant was walking. "By the time we reach that spot, it should be near the village."

"Shouldn't we form a plan of attack?" Leon asked. "Just in case?"

"Of course, but we can do it while we walk." Kaidyn slid down the hill and the rest were forced to follow. Now that Kaidyn was in charge, he was quick to act.

The land was eerily silent as they walked. They only heard the occasional skittering of black mice and the constant stomping of the giant from afar.

Lili tried to stay as quiet as she could, softening her steps while also keeping up with the fast pace of the taller boys. They kept their voices low as they went but each high-pitched word they uttered made her glance first at the giant, then at the pine forest. If the hunter heard them, they'd have no way of knowing. Those woods were so cast in shadow that it might as well be night.

"Do you think you could climb the giant?" Leon ventured, since Kaidyn and his brother used to do all the climbing on their previous escapades. "To cut its throat?"

"I doubt it. Its skin looks ready to fall off at the slightest touch," Kaidyn answered. "I might be able to jump onto its shoulders from one of the taller trees." He shrugged. "But that's a long shot and he'd need to be in the perfect position."

While Lili listened, her eyes trailed after a black rabbit with white eyes as it hopped across their path. It had leapt from a hole in one of the hills and was chasing a piece of fluff from an old dandelion.

"Maybe we can burn the thing." Viktor showed off a growing collection of weapons in his pack that he'd either brought from home or took from the soldier's castle. He'd acquired several packs of matches, grenades, flares, Molotov cocktails, and oil.

"Maybe, but Dr. Ana said killing monsters with fire doesn't work, remember?" Kaidyn said. "If the head is still attached, it could writhe around in agony forever." He cringed, as did the rest of them. Lili imagined poor Aidyn, burning alive in a monster's body. She would hate to wish that fate on anyone.

"The beheading thing still doesn't make sense to me," Viktor muttered. "It's not like the monsters heal or anything, right? Why can't we just cut them in two?"

Kaidyn looked to Leon, who had been the one to interview the soldiers the day before they left. Leon shrugged sheepishly. "I didn't think to ask about that," he admitted, turning red.

"We could always go back to Grant and ask him," Lili ventured to cover for him.

"Too late." Kaidyn suddenly stopped in his path and stared at the warrior's forest, which was less than three hundred feet way away. They all did the same and Lili froze when she saw a dark figure twice the size of a man zip through the trees at an inhuman speed. The shadows were too dark to see what it was but they could picture it regardless.

Lili's rabbit hopped past them, blissfully unaware of the danger it was in.

They'd ventured too close to the forest, and they'd made too much noise. Now, it was coming for them.

The bunny came to a halt as the flower it had been chasing floated away. Lili saw it raise its nose to the sky and sniff, then it started frantically digging into the ground, like it was trying to make a tunnel.

"Nobody move," Kaidyn whispered, though no one was.

A black figure suddenly darted from the top of the trees toward the rabbit. The grey light around them finally revealed the creature's form. Lili studied it, her lips wobbling as she listened to its gurgling groans.

The entirety of the warrior's body was inky black, including its clothes. She could barely make out any human features besides the limbs and holes in the face where the eyes, nose, and mouth should have been.

It had a long blade in each hand. The left held a silver longsword with a red hilt and the right's blade was thicker, with a golden hilt and the crest of a shield on the end. They clearly originated from different countries and cultures yet were wielded by the same beast. It was just as Grant said: it held blades from both the east and west.

Lili hadn't understood what the survivor meant when he said the creature was two different men fused together, but now she understood. The first body, the bigger one, had only a faceless head and seven-foot-long arms that were being used as legs. They held up the entire being, using spindly fingers to dig into the ground. The second body was jammed into the chest of the first. It had no head and while it did have legs, they were stubby and couldn't touch the ground. They dangled below the torso, useless. This second being's arms were long too and they were being used to hold up the two blades.

The blackened clothes hanging off the bodies further showed that they were from two different countries and times. These once-human warriors from Europe and Japan had been melded together to form a single guard with four unnaturally long arms.

The warrior gave an inhuman shriek as it zipped through the air toward the rabbit, then it spun itself around several times, its blades spinning through the air with it. It reminded Lili of a deadly helicopter.

Lili steeled her body as the swords cut through the rabbit, shredding it into three pieces. Blood splattered the ground near their feet. Its prey now dead, the monster came to a sudden halt in front of the animal's corpse and leaned down next to it, as though listening for a heartbeat.

So this was the being that had wiped out those villagers over a hundred years ago. If it killed all the villagers at the same time, they may have come together to form the blob afterward. Lili held her breath as the beast moved its head around, listening through the holes on the sides of its skull.

Everyone remained still, barely breathing, until the monster finally shrieked at the ceiling, then retreated to its forest home.

Nobody moved.

They shouldn't have come this close to the forest. The slightest sound might attract it now.

Lili looked to her right to see where the giant was. It was nearing the village walls. If they waited too long, it would eventually turn around and spot them. The giant was slower than the alternative. They'd at least stand a chance against it. This Hunter moved at lightning speeds, treating the air like one would water.

"What do we do?" Leon eventually whispered. She'd never heard him speak so quietly before.

Kaidyn nodded to the right. They all knew what he meant. It was better to risk the giant.

Each step they took felt like they were being brought closer to death. When Viktor accidentally crushed a piece of dry grass under his heel or Leon slipped on the dirt, they froze, waiting to see if they'd alerted the hunter. A few times, they did. The trees would swish as the blurry shadow zipped between the trunks, but then nothing would happen.

There would be no shrieks, no blades spinning toward them, and no eyeless face peering out from between the branches. Lili was honestly surprised their earlier conversations hadn't attracted its attention.

The group was halfway around the forest—about a half hour into their walk—when Kaidyn tapped Lili's shoulder and nodded behind them. Peering over her shoulder, she saw the giant making his slow march around the village. They were running out of time and this slow pace wasn't helping.

Then Leon gasped, making everyone freeze again, and he pointed at the forest. Something else was moving in there, something full of color.

Lili nearly gasped too when she spotted a little boy with blond hair running through the trees toward them. It wasn't hard to tell who it was. They'd seen him less than a week ago.

Billy. He was as pale and thin as he'd been the last time they saw him, though he wasn't injured in any way. She reached out a hand reflexively when he tripped over a log and squeaked in pain, face-planting loudly in the dirt and making plenty of noise as he collapsed.

Lili's heart had already been racing but now it was on fire. That child was going to get himself killed.

But...didn't Grant say he wasn't real? He was just a doppelganger. If that were the case, they shouldn't move to protect him.

The question was, would Leon believe Grant's warning?

She looked at her friend, who was reaching for his axe and had taken a step toward the forest. He looked ready to protect the child, even if it was a trap. She was sure he was visualizing one of his sickly sisters in Billy's place, vulnerable and in need of his protection. He would never forgive himself if he let the child get shredded by the warrior, even if he put himself in danger.

"Leon," she whispered, touching his arm. When he turned, she shook her head, desperate for him to know it was too risky. She didn't want to see him die.

Leon looked down at her, scrunching up his face to resist the urge to help the boy, but then they both saw the child leap into the clearing, sobbing. There was blood streaming from a fresh cut on his arm and Lili realized the monster must have gotten to him after all. If the warrior was willing to hurt him...did that mean Billy was human?

Before Leon and Lili could move, she saw another dark flash in the wood behind Billy, darting past his tiny form on the ground. It was moving around him, not toward him, but a second later it course-corrected and jumped straight for the boy.

"Billy!" Leon shouted, going against his instincts and Lili's warnings. "Get down!"

The boy did so, pressing his forehead to the ground. Not a second later, the warrior pushed itself off the tree trunks as it had before to reach the rabbit. Billy ducked and its blade narrowly missed his head but when the monster landed in front of the child, it immediately turned around, blood dripping from its mouth in long strands. Lili saw its long fingers scratch the ground, digging in preparation for another leap.

It leapt into the air once more, but instead of aiming for Billy, it spun around, charging at Lili and Leon instead. Leon's shout had alerted it.

Episode 25

A lot of things happened at once. Leon pulled his axe off his back and pushed Lili to the ground while Kaidyn drew his sword and lunged to the side. Meanwhile, Viktor pulled out one of his Molotov cocktails and struggled to light a match. By the time he'd created a spark, the monster was upon them. Leon shoved Viktor out of the monster's path before doing the same.

The hunter flew over them. Lili and Viktor stayed on the ground, unmoving and hiding their heads under their hands. Leon and Kaidyn stood on either side of the creature, readying for an offense of their own.

The hunter landed on the ground behind them, its blades narrowly missing Lili's legs, then it angled the side of its head toward them, listening for movement. It didn't have ears but that didn't seem to matter. It was trying to find out where they'd landed so it could tear them apart. Its top head twitched and twisted, like a curious bird.

Lili's eyes darted from her friends to the giant. It was facing their direction now and if it got close enough, its booming steps might offer enough of a distraction. The sound would make it possible to slip away from the blind hunter. However, the giant wasn't close enough yet. They'd need to stall until it was.

Their world stood still for a moment, waiting for the Hunter to make a move. Then Viktor, still lying on his stomach, struck the match and lit the string jutting from the top of the Molotov. The sound of the match scraping against the box and lighting up made the creature whip its head in Viktor's direction. Hissing, it sped toward him.

"Now!" As soon as the monster passed Kaidyn, he leapt into the air and tried to bring his blade down on the thing's neck. Leon did the same on the other side with his axe. Viktor threw the lit weapon at the creature and rolled away from the blast, whimpering as he did so.

Lili saw the creature's head snap from side to side as Kaidyn, Leon, and the cocktail flew toward it. It swung its long arms around itself, spinning like a top, and hit Leon's legs and Kaidyn's chest. Its blades didn't manage to cut through their armor, but it did force them to jump out of the way. They fell while doing so. The explosive hit the creature's chest, just below the neck, and burst into the flames. Unfortunately, the fire didn't reach its head so the creature didn't even acknowledge the Molotov while it tumbled to the ground.

Viktor grunted as he rolled to a stop. The flames were already going out, doused by the blood pouring from the hunter's cuts and mouth. After it landed, the hunter snarled at the four of them, ready to try again. All three boys had fallen so it was Lili's turn to distract it.

The monster raised its sword, giving Lili half a second to react. She crawled to her feet and shouted. "The giant's coming," she warned the others, which was true. However, she wasn't actually shouting for the sake of her friends. She was trying to get the giant's attention, which she did. As soon as she made a loud noise, the colossal beast started jogging toward them. Its huge feet pounded against the ground, sending the dirt below their boots into the air.

"Lili, stay quiet and get out of the way!" Kaidyn shouted back, using his blade to push himself upright. There was blood draining through his chest piece. If it weren't for his armor, he might have died from the warrior's cut.

The hunter listened for them, giving itself a few seconds to choose a target. While it did, the pounding of the giant's feet got closer. It was loud enough now to block out the other sounds, creating the perfect cover for escape. If the warrior couldn't see or hear, it would have no idea where they were.

"Maybe we can get the monsters to kill each other," Leon shouted, swinging his axe at the creature, then leaping away again when it lashed out. The footsteps seemed to be disorienting it.

Kaidyn growled and ran toward Viktor to help him up. "As far as we know, monsters always work together against us."

Lili tried to guess how long it would take for the giant to reach them but judging by the distance and its speed, it might be longer than five minutes.

The warrior swung its sword toward Leon, snapping the handle of his axe in two and narrowly missing Leon's neck. She knew they wouldn't last five minutes with this thing, even if it was deaf.

"We'll keep him busy," Kaidyn shouted to Lili and Viktor. "Run to the tree."

Lili looked to the far end of the level where she could see a large tree with a grey trunk and pink leaves sprouting from its branches. The fallen angel tree. It was the only bit of color in this bland wasteland. It would take at least an hour to reach it. Half an hour if they ran. There was no way Leon and Kaidyn would survive that long against the hunter.

Lili ran to Viktor, who was on his feet again, while Kaidyn and Leon circled the creature, narrowly dodging its attacks but missing it in return. She grabbed two grenades from Viktor's pack, which was still unzipped and losing some of its contents.

"What are you doing?" Viktor hissed. "He told us to run."

"If we separate, we're dead," she answered. "You and I can't hit it with swords but we can throw stuff at it."

Viktor's mouth lowered into a firm line. He glanced at the hunter. "We might die."

"We'll die either way," she said.

To prove her right, the warrior finally managed to land a hit.

Leon and Kaidyn had continued taunting it, jumping between its "legs" and trying to cut them off, when the monster's long blade finally caught Leon's right leg with one of its long hands and crushed his foot between its fingers. Leon shoved himself away from the monster but slammed into the ground, smashing his nose and leaving a trail of blood in his wake.

"No way," Viktor whispered as Lili pulled the grenade's pin and threw it at the creature. She bit her lip as the pain in her shoulder, caused by the cannon's earlier bruising, intensified from the movements. The explosion went off a few feet away from it but the sound was enough to make the warrior turn away from Leon, leaving him spitting blood and crawling away with a broken leg.

The four-armed hunter's attention shifted toward her, leaving Leon alive. Gritting her teeth, Lili lobbed a second grenade at him. This one bounced off one of its shoulders. The explosion was too far to do any real damage but it did wound the shoulder.

"Die, you bastard!" Viktor screamed, lighting a second Molotov cocktail and throwing it at the beast's face. It arced down and only hit one of its hands. "Stay away from my friends!"

Kaidyn grabbed one of the warrior's arms and swung onto its back, but when he raised his sword to slice off its neck, it used its unburned arm to grab him by his throat.

"No!" Lili threw another grenade at its other hand and managed to hit it, but the explosion severed the arm completely, making it drop to the ground and Kaidyn with it. He landed on his side with a loud crunch and his sword flew from his hands.

Even though it was now missing an arm and was continuing to lose blood, the hunter still didn't look hurt by any of the flesh wounds or burns. It refused to slow down.

Lili reached into Viktor's pack again, praying she'd find something stronger than a grenade, but she already knew it was hopeless. This hunter was unstoppable and she had no idea what she was doing.

Her fingers wrapped around another grenade, its round surface rough against her palm, but as she pulled it out, she heard a loud gunshot and turned, surprised.

Her eyes widened as a bullet cut through the samurai's throat and it fell sideways, blood spurting from its blackened skin and soaking Kaidyn, who was lying beside it and trying to pull himself up. Kaidyn's arm was hanging at his side, limp.

"Who did that?" Viktor asked, looking to Leon, who was still lying on the ground, crippled.

Lili struggled to pull the pin on the grenade, ready to throw it but having difficulty with her weakened arm. There came a second shot. It followed the first through the monster's neck. This time, she could tell where it came from. Turning, she spotted a man sitting in one of the trees, firing from the branches with a sniper rifle. Grant had joined them after all.

The crazy survivor slapped his own face with one hand, then shouted at them. "Lead it toward the giant!" he ordered, his voice speeding up from insanity until he slapped himself again. "If we can agitate it enough, it might fight the other one. The older they are, the more independent they become."

"Right," Lili whispered and threw the grenade at the warrior to get its attention. She then charged toward the giant. As she ran past Viktor, he dropped his pack and joined her, only pausing to grab his shield and hold it over his head. Lili wished she had one of those too. She did manage to pull the helmet she received at the castle from her pack and slip it on before dropping her pack too. They'd need to be as light as possible if they were going to lure the hunter toward the giant.

"I'll slow the hunter down with gunfire," Grant continued as they ran past. "But I only have five bullets."

"That might be enough," she told Viktor. The giant had run half the length of the third level, slowed by its giant swords and sickly form.

Lili's ears rang as she charged across the dirt and grass, kicking up ashes as she ran. The giant's blades made a horrible screeching sound as they dragged across the stone ground. There were two more gunshots behind her, adding to the chaos around them. A second later, she heard a crash and knew the warrior was scrambling to catch up with them. She estimated it to be ten feet behind.

Viktor was panting, already tired, but he was pushing through his exhaustion, his face red but eyes wide, focused on the giant ahead. Nothing would stop him now.

"When it's a hundred feet away," Grant's voice continued behind them, followed by a third shot, "Run to the hills at your right. The uneven ground will slow him down."

"If he knew all this, why didn't he attempt this earlier?" Viktor hissed between deep breaths.

"Maybe he did," she said, glancing over her shoulder. She wished she hadn't a moment later.

The hunter's empty eyes were less than two feet away from her head and it took everything in her to keep going. She wanted to drop to the ground so it would leap over her again, but the giant was almost in front of them now. She'd need to turn soon to avoid both creatures.

There was a fourth shot, then a shout from Grant. "Now!"

Lili's boots left skid marks on the ground as she swerved to the right, aware that if she wasn't quick enough, the hunter would behead her and Viktor in one slice. It was a struggle to focus on breathing, moving her feet, and preventing a fall at the same time. She leaned so far right that she had to press her hands to the ground to prevent landing on her face.

The giant's feet hastened as she changed directions, retreating to the hills where they'd started their journey. She felt the wind of the warrior brush past her and ducked just in case, already wondering how it would feel to have her head removed. This was the first monster that seemed set on beheading them. Like Grant said, perhaps the giant and hunter were so old and independent that they'd regained enough humanity to behead people. They had lived in these flesh cages for decades so they surely wanted to avoid giving others the same fate.

There was a final gunshot from Grant. She turned to look over her shoulder, still running.

Grant's final bullet cut through the back of the hunter's neck, pushing its head forward, but it still wasn't dead. It dragged its blade across the ankles of the giant, slowing the lumbering beast's steps for one second.

"Please," she heard Viktor whisper as they ran. "Let this work."

If it didn't, they'd be dead. Jacques would be the only survivor left in their group, just like Grant.

The world stood still for a moment as the giant directed its attention at the two-torso hunter, then it wheezed and raised its left hand, swinging its sword toward the warrior.

"Get down!" Lili shouted, grabbing Viktor and pulling him to the ground with her. They both screamed as the giant's blade came within a few feet of their heads, then it struck the side of the warrior, cutting its entire body in half. Blood splattered the ground around it, sinking into the dusty ground.

After cutting the warrior down, the giant lifted its leg to crush it underfoot. The warrior's two halves started to move on their own, still alive and reaching for their dropped swords. But before they could rise, they were crushed under the behemoth's heel.

"We did it," Lili whispered, tears springing to her eyes. "It's dead."

"There's still the giant," Viktor warned, grabbing her hand and pulling her up. They continued toward the hills. Now that the biggest threat was out of the way, the giant had noticed them again. Lili could already imagine getting crushed like the hunter. A memory of roadkill filled her brain.

They continued running. The giant veered toward them. She looked back at Grant.

"Keep going!" Grant shouted, throwing down his gun and starting to climb off the branch he was perched on. She could tell he was smiling. He'd finally overcome his fears and protected others.

But her victory was short-lived. She noticed something else move nearby. Squinting, she realized who it was. Billy was standing at the base of the tree, looking up at Grant with wide eyes. The child had stayed out of their way during their previous fight against the hunter and Lili had completely forgotten about him.

"Grant!" she shouted as the survivor crouched, ready to jump from the tree. Leon shouted warnings at the same time, unable to move due to his broken leg. "Wait! Billy is—"

But it was too late.

Lili could do nothing as Billy's jaw dropped, lowering itself far beyond what should be physically possible. As soon as Grant fell to the ground, too focused on the giant to realize he was in danger, Billy grabbed him by his legs and bit a chunk out of his back. Grant screamed maniacally, waving his arms as the little boy took a second chunk out of his neck with his teeth.

Lili screamed as she watched Grant slump over, dead.

The trees around his body began to stretch their branches and roots toward him, ready to turn his corpse. The forest had claimed another victim.

Episode 26

Kaidyn screamed and ran toward the slack-jawed child, his one arm swinging limply behind him. The other still held his sword. Before Billy could finish chewing on the meat he'd ripped from Grant's body, Kaidyn cut off the boy's head. Lili gasped as it fell to the ground, the last of its blood draining into the dirt.

"Is this what you want?" Kaidyn screamed at the trees, dropping his weapon. "Are you happy now?"

"He's losing it," Viktor whispered, panting as they fled the giant. "If any more of us die, he might end up just as crazy as that poor guy." Viktor's eyes darkened, realizing he was speaking ill of the one that had saved them.

"He has us. We won't let that happen," Lili said, but as she and Viktor reached the hills, the giant still stomping after them, she knew their odds weren't good. Right now, Leon seemed most likely to become a victim. He'd essentially lost his legs.

Viktor looked over his shoulder at the giant. "There's a rope of some kind around one of his hands," he told her. "He can't raise his hand because the weapon is tied to it."

"Yeah. So?" Lili didn't see where this was going. As she pulled Viktor back to his feet, she saw the giant getting closer. He was moving his other hand toward them, the blade leaving a long cut through one of the hills, slicing through it like butter.

"If we tie his other weapon to his other hand, he won't be able to raise either arm," Viktor added, scrambling after her and sounding ready to collapse. "Then Kaidyn can jump from a tree and reach his neck without fear of getting hit."

She looked up at the giant's neck, ready to explain how it would take too many slices to behead it, but then she realized she was wrong. Up close, the giant's neck was actually quite thin. Perhaps it was thick a hundred years ago, but most of the muscle was gone now, rotted away. Only the bones remained solid. The village people didn't stand a chance of killing it, but thanks to time and the labor of those who had come before, Kaidyn might be able to change that. "That...might actually work."

"Unless we have some kind of cannon or something, there's not much else we can do." Viktor grit his teeth. "Oh! Or we could make a trip wire and try to knock him over. Then Kaidyn could reach him."

Both ideas sounded valid but risky. There was no guarantee either plan would work.

Now that he was close, she could see several holes in the giant's chest and arms from cannon fire and other ancient forms of heavy weaponry. If the people who came before had all failed, four young adults wouldn't do much better.

"Hey!" They heard Kaidyn screaming at the behemoth from the trees. "Hey! Over here you big bastard! Kill me!"

"He's trying to lure it away from us," Viktor whispered, pulling a grenade from his pocket. She was surprised he had the guts to carry one on his person. He didn't bother to answer her questioning look as he pulled the pin and tossed it over his shoulder in the hopes of tripping up the monster. "But it doesn't seem to be working and I don't have many more of these things."

"Then let's head into those trees." Lili studied the arms of the creature. They were still thick, some red muscles visible through the loose skin. The wrists were thin, barely big enough to wield the blades. "Maybe we can blow off its hands so it can't use those swords."

"It can still punch us though." Viktor ran past her, heading toward the thick forest like she suggested. It wasn't a threat now that the warrior was dead. "None of these plans will work," he said, frustrated. Without Jacques and Kaidyn here to offer ideas, they were struggling.

"Then let's just get the giant to the trees. Kaidyn can climb one of them and jump onto its head like you said." She could already see Kaidyn climbing the tree Grant had jumped from, his sword strapped to his back. He was still using his injured arm so it must not have broken in the fall.

"Do you have any rope in your backpack?" she asked Viktor, pointing at the pack they'd abandoned several feet away.

"No." He jerked his thumb toward his pants, showing her how he'd used the rope as a belt. "I was using it for this, but it won't be thick enough to stop that thing."

"I'll give it a shot anyway," she said. "Give it to me."

They charged toward the trees, nearly inside the forest now. Viktor started tugging the belt from his waist. He'd wrapped it around three times, so it took a while.

"Are you that desperate to keep your pants up?" she asked in frustration as they reached the tree line.

"Leon likes to steal my pants sometimes as a prank," Viktor said defensively, finally getting the last of it off and handing it to her. "Are you planning to trip it?"

"Yes." She glanced at the giant to ensure it wasn't upon them yet, then ran around the nearest trunk with the rope. She circled it three times, just like Viktor's belt, then tied one of the knots her uncle had taught her years ago. "Keep going, Viktor. Make noise so it comes this way." She pointed in the right direction, then carried the rope between this tree and another one.

"Got it!" Viktor darted away, screaming as he always did.

She ran, nearly tripping over the piles of bones littering the grey grass. Some were clearly the remains of humans, while others were so stretched and deformed that she knew they were the remains of monsters that had been killed by the generations who had come before. She was standing in a graveyard, soaked with layers upon layers of blood.

"Kaidyn!" she shouted when she found a suitable tree and started circling it, tightening the rope to create a makeshift trip wire. "Get ready! If this works, you can cut off its head!"

There was no answer but she knew he was close enough to hear—the only worry was the giant's footsteps drowning her out. A tree crashed ten feet away, pushed over by the beast's legs.

Realizing she'd get crushed if she stayed, Lili dashed out of the woods. If the giant did end up tripping, she didn't want it falling on top of her. She stayed quiet as she moved so it would continue following Viktor and his screams.

The forest wasn't big, but she kept stumbling across skeletons as she went, all of them missing heads. She often found the skulls several feet from their bodies. Some of them still had skin on them, filling her nose and throat with the stench of old meat. Part of her was glad the Hunter had spared them from the forest's control. Only a few of these bodies had been turned into beasts and used to kill their friends. At least they found peace.

Lili eventually reached the edge of the forest and circled around, headed toward Leon's fallen body. She couldn't hear Viktor's shouts anymore. His throat must have given out. Luckily, he didn't need to draw the giant in anymore. It had reached her rope.

Kaidyn was crouched at the top of his tree, visible above all the shorter ones. The giant's head swiveled toward him, noticing his hiding spot. It took one step further, changing its course to reach Kaidyn, but then it looked down. It must have noticed the trap.

"Please fall," she whispered. "Please."

Kaidyn leapt from the tree, risking it. As he flew through the air toward the monster's neck, it started to lean forward. It was collapsing.

"Yes!" She cheered as she watched Kaidyn reach the creature's neck. He would have missed it if it hadn't fallen, but now the back of its head was exposed and ready to be sliced.

There was complete silence as Kaidyn jumped past the neck, leaving a huge cut in his wake and losing his blade in the flesh. Then he landed in another tree and started falling through the branches. She breathed a sigh of relief when he managed to catch one with his good arm and came to a stop.

"Did he do it?" Leon whimpered. He was thirty feet away, kneeling on his good knee with his other foot twisted under him.

"I don't know." She looked up, hoping to hear the giant fall. Instead, there was a loud crash and the colossal raised its head again, returning to its standing position. The crash must have been the sound of it breaking the rope. Not only that, its head was still on its shoulders, though it was slouching forward now. They would need to cut it one more time to kill it.

"Get my pack," Leon ordered, pointing to his bag a few feet away. He was already dragging himself toward it but wasn't making much progress. "I only have this pistol." He pulled it from its holster and pointed it at the giant. The chances of hitting it from this far away were low, though it *was* a large target.

Lili ran toward his pack, then looked up when she heard Viktor's voice again. This time, he was screaming from genuine fear, rather than as a distraction.

More trees started collapsing, including the one Kaidyn was on, and a few seconds later, Viktor broke through the branches and charged toward them, screeching and sobbing at the same time. His bravery had reached its limit.

"Don't worry, guys," Leon said, raising his gun and closing one eye as he peered down the pistol's sights. Lili cringed when he fired the weapon and missed.

"That won't do anything, you moron!" Viktor shrieked, trying to pull Leon up by his armpits. "We need to get out of here!"

It was no use. Without his legs, Leon couldn't flee and was too heavy to carry.

Lili started digging through Leon's pack, pulling out some knives, a sword, and two grenades. The only other items were snacks and a picture of his family.

"Move, Viktor! Go!" Leon shoved his smaller friend away and fired at the giant's head. The bullet hit its cheek but did nothing. "Stay out of the way so I don't shoot you by accident." He fired a third time.

"We're all gonna die!" Viktor screamed. Lili couldn't disagree as she held up the grenades. The only consolation was that even if they died, Kaidyn would survive. If he hadn't been killed by the fall, he could hide long enough for the giant to forget about him and continue its endless march. Then he could reach the pink tree...albeit alone.

Then again, if that happened, he might end up like the survivor, insane and rotting in a cave. Grant and the scholar's book said the tree couldn't be destroyed. They didn't even know what it was. So leaving Kaidyn alone would no doubt drive him to end his life.

"Viktor!" She ran back to Leon and Viktor and handed each of them a grenade. "Can you...throw these thirty feet high?" she asked, knowing it was impossible.

"We can at least hit its leg," Leon said confidently, preparing to pull the pin. "On three, release the pin. One—"

Lili looked up at the giant. It had almost reached the edge of the tree line. Ten more feet and it would crush them.

"Two."

Viktor whimpered but held his arm behind his head, ready to throw.

"Three!"

They threw their grenades. The explosives hit the ground, rolling just far enough to reach the giant's feet. Lili shut her eyes when they exploded. The giant grunted loudly, swinging its arm toward them, but then its knees buckled and it started to fall, its ankles bleeding. They had weakened it.

"Get away!" Leon shouted, firing his pistol at it again. "Save yourselves!"

Viktor clearly wanted to run but groaned and tried to pull Leon instead. "We're not leaving you! I couldn't live with myself if I did!"

Lili glared at the goliath. It had fallen to its knees but was gradually swinging its sword at them, determined to see them all beheaded. It had no other goal.

"Mother," she whispered as she realized she was about to die. "I'm sorry."

It was over.

Then Kaidyn emerged from the forest, silently speeding toward the monster. His wounded arm looked even worse, bleeding and covered in purple bruises under his torn sleeve. His sword was gone, still embedded in the giant's neck, but he had a knife. When he reached the back of the beast, he used it like a pickaxe, climbing the beast's leg.

It turned its head toward him.

Lili's stomach dropped as its massive blade stopped a few feet away from her. It was distracted...but for how long?

The giant couldn't turn its neck or move its arms without injuring itself, so it had to shake its entire body instead, trying to get Kaidyn off its back. The skin swung off its bones but Kaidyn was determined to hang on.

She laughed in relief, then turned to Viktor. "We need to distract it long enough for him to reach its head. Do you remember where we dropped our packs?"

Viktor stared at her, out of breath and terrified. "Of course I do," he said, though it sounded like he wasn't pleased about going back to get them.

"Come on," Lili said urgently.

Kaidyn stayed quiet as he climbed. He'd gotten past the goliath's chest and had almost reached the shoulders. Lili could see him digging his knife into the bones now, since the skin was too loose above the waist.

While he climbed, Lili and Viktor found their packs and pulled two pistols and a crossbow from them. Fully armed, they ran back to Leon. Viktor hefted his bag onto his back while they went.

Leon had run out of ammo but was still fighting, screaming at the beast and waving his arms. He was just as lively as ever, even with a broken leg.

"Look at us, you dumb giant!" Viktor screamed as Lili emptied her gun, firing at the giant's legs. Then she pointed her crossbow at its neck.

"Why don't you pick on someone your own size?" Viktor continued.

Lili shot her first arrow at the creature and smiled as it lodged itself in the skin around its throat, drawing more blood. Not a second later, Kaidyn reached the same spot. Everyone watched as he dug his knife into the monster's neck to hold himself steady. Then he climbed right into the massive cut he'd created and started pushing up, trying to shove the head away from the neck from the inside.

"He's insane," Viktor shouted, then laughed at the absurdity of what they were seeing. He handed Lili another pistol. "Don't worry about ammo. I have five more."

Lili grinned and aimed down the barrel. By this point, their enemy couldn't be distracted. It had dropped its sword and was reaching for Kaidyn, desperate to yank him out of its neck.

"Stay back," Leon repeated. "Kaidyn can do this. I know he can. You can't be here when it falls."

Viktor stopped in his tracks, twenty feet from the goliath, but Lili kept closing in. Was there really nothing else she could do to help? What if she retreated and it cost Kaidyn his life?

The monster patted the back of its head, feeling around for Kaidyn, then Lili heard the loud squelch of flesh being ripped. The giant's head snapped forward. Lili covered her eyes as the giant's skull detached from its neck and slammed into the ground.

They gasped as a blood-drenched Kaidyn rose, standing atop the now headless neck. His face was raised to the sky, taking a breath of relief from his victory. Lili cheered as the goliath's head settled with a crunch, sending up clouds of dust.

They'd done it. They won.

Episode 27

"Watch out!" Viktor grabbed Lili and yanked her away from the giant as its body started falling forward. Kaidyn crouched again, preparing to jump off the beast's neck right before it hit the ground. But as Lili stepped away from the falling body, she realized it might hit Leon.

"He's gonna die!" Viktor shrieked as they stared at their crippled friend, too far away to reach him. Leon's legs were both limp beneath him, useless. When he looked at them, they could see it in his eyes; he knew he couldn't escape.

Lili's heart clenched as Leon raised his hand and waved at them, smiling with that same huge grin he always showed for the camera. He opened his mouth to say something, probably to give them one more encouraging word, then the shoulder of the monster landed on him.

"No!" Viktor fell to his knees as dust and ash rose around them, stinging their eyes. They didn't see Kaidyn land but heard him shouting Leon's name. He must have rolled off the body.

Viktor started sobbing, beating his fists against the ground. Lili wanted to curl up in the fetal position, but when she heard Kaidyn start screaming, she chose to remain strong. It sounded like his guts were being dragged out. She scrambled toward him. After the dust settled, she found him pressing his forehead against the giant's corpse, right where Leon was sitting a moment ago. His shoulders were shaking with sobs, just as they had when Aidyn died.

Lili wanted to do the same. Leon had always protected them and this had finally been her chance to help him. She should have dragged him away, should have planned ahead, should have known this would happen and done more.

Now he was dead. The only consolation was they wouldn't have to see him turn like Aidyn.

She reached a hand toward Kaidyn, heart pounding painfully and ears still ringing. Then she hesitated. Would he want to be left alone? He was crying like a child and Viktor was doing the same a few feet away. Every part of Kaidyn was drenched in crimson and he reeked of ancient blood.

No. They needed comfort now more than ever. If they gave up, they would never be able to avenge Leon and Aidyn.

She placed a hand on his shoulder and squeezed, pursing her lips. She had to remain strong for them. "He died protecting us," she whispered.

Kaidyn muttered a prayer under his breath, then turned toward her, his tears leaving trails through the blood on his face.

"It should have been me," he whispered.

She was thinking the same about herself. "He died so we could finish our mission."

Kaidyn nodded, then walked over to Viktor and wrapped his arms around him.

Only after Lili joined them did Kaidyn raise his head. "Let's get to that tree. Leon and Grant cleared the way for us. Let's make it count. Leon would want us to make it home so we could help his sisters."

He had recovered faster this time. They were all becoming de-sensitized to death. A week ago, Lili had been an average eigh-teen-year-old—normal in every way. Now, she had witnessed the deaths of two people her own age and walked over countless corpses, both living and dead. This forest had changed something inside her.

But she hadn't lost her humanity yet. She was still determined to find her mother, though this wasn't just about her anymore. It was about saving lives—Jacques, Meriel, Diego, the soldiers, the villagers, and any other poor soul who wandered in here. They needed her help and this might be the only opportunity any person had, or would ever have, to end this. They were the first to reach the tree without its guardians to protect it.

Thanks to the sacrifices and battles of countless generations that came before them, they had made it. Lili just hoped they could figure out how to destroy the tree.

Breathing out to release the tension in her chest, Lili looked past both of her friends at the village behind them. "Kaidyn. Viktor." She pointed at the village walls.

"What is it?" Kaidyn asked as Viktor wiped his cheeks.

Lili frowned. The walls of the village had previously stood tall. Now they were destroyed, lying in rubble. Either the giant had crushed them without their notice or the blob had been so determined to kill them that it had broken through on its own. She could see the large mass of flesh gradually moving toward them, its numerous limbs tumbling over each other as it rolled forward.

"The blob is coming," she warned, nearly choking on the coppery stench in the air, mixing with all the ash floating around their heads. "We need to keep moving."

Kaidyn helped a recovering Viktor to his feet and Lili turned around to study the tree. It was exactly as it had been—the beautiful pink leaves and flowers contrasted by the black walls and grey grass surrounding its trunk. She felt like it was waiting for them, taunting them with its appeal.

They were free to reach it now, with only the blob left, but if this ended up being a trap, Kaidyn and Viktor wouldn't be able to fight back. Viktor was trembling like a leaf and Kaidyn's arm was practically useless.

Viktor was staring at the giant's shoulders and the blood splatter beneath it. "Leon's body is under there," he said. "We can't just leave him." His voice cracked.

"We have to," Kaidyn replied quietly. "We'll come back for him. I promise. Can you walk?"

"I can." Viktor nodded, steeling himself before retrieving his pack.

Kaidyn yanked his sword from the giant's corpse and cleaned the dark blood from its blade.

"I'm sorry, Leon," Lili whispered as they prepared to leave him behind. "We'll make this count." His sacrifice wouldn't be in vain.

Weak and wounded, the trio readied themselves and ran toward the tree. They could reach it in twenty minutes if they went as fast as they could, even though it was at the top of a slight incline. There was no telling how soon the blob would reach them and, just as Leon said, it would be nearly impossible to kill it with only one fighter among them. Destroying this ominously beautiful tree was their only option, and they had to do it quickly.

Because the land around them was so dark and dreary, it made the tree's glow look welcoming in comparison. Perhaps that had been done intentionally. If Lili grew up in this murky and blank land, she would have easily been drawn to this spark of light.

The grey light from the walls reflected off the pink leaves, casting a pale sheen on Lili's face as she ran toward it with shaking legs. There was also a faint scent coming from the tree, a mix of strawberries and cherry blossoms. It made her realize just how filthy and smelly the three of them had become.

The spot would be beautiful if it weren't for the stone statues they found lining the bottom of the hill, frozen in poses resembling a running or defensive stance. It was clear Lili and her companions weren't the first to reach the tree. The trio hesitated when they reached the statues, afraid of stepping forward and meeting the same fate, but then

Lili looked back up at the tree and noticed something that changed her perspective.

Her throat closed with fear and then elation. She could see someone kneeling beside the tree, her back familiar and nostalgic. Even in a crouched pose and despite their years apart, Lili recognized her.

It was a single person, a woman with long black hair, dark skin, and a grey dress with a bark-like pattern across it. Lili felt a shiver run down her spine as the woman turned toward them. Lili saw, for the first time in six years, the face she had dreamed of. It was her mother, her face unchanged from that day at the wall. There wasn't a single wrinkle on her forehead or under her eyes. Instead, green sprouts crept from her skin and lips. Her eyes used to be a chocolate brown but were now a mix of deep green, the color of poison and rot.

"You finally arrived," the woman cooed.

Led by her emotions rather than her mind, Lili stepped past the statues. She had to reach her mother, despite the risk. To her great relief, her legs didn't turn to stone once she passed the threshold, and this encouraged Kaidyn and Viktor to follow suit.

Lili's mother smiled when they stopped a few feet away from her. Her long hair was pulled back into messy braids that framed her forehead, completely withdrawn from the plain ponytail she used to sport.

Her voice was sweet too, like a parent soothing a crying child. Lili's initial response was to be calmed by the voice, but then she felt frightened. Her mother's cheeks were stretched up in a smile but her eyes didn't match. Instead, she looked horrified. Lili couldn't tell if she feared them or herself.

Kaidyn held up his sword defensively and Viktor put both hands into his pack, reaching for weapons Lili couldn't see. She was the only one who didn't arm herself. Even though she was scared and Grant had warned that something was wrong with her mother, Lili couldn't bring herself to do more than rest her palm on her knife. It felt counterproductive to threaten someone she had spent years hoping to find. Plus, her heart was resisting. Even though she'd told Kaidyn she could do this, in the heat of the moment, she struggled.

"This is your mother?" Kaidyn asked. It didn't sound like a question. They had all expected this.

"Yes," her mother answered before Lili could speak. "I knew you would come for me eventually. Now that you're finally here, we can be together again." Her words sounded like they should be directed toward Lili but the woman was facing all three of them when she spoke. It felt wrong.

Luckily, Kaidyn wasn't willing to play games. "Tell me about this tree. Why is it here? What does it do?"

"This?" She pointed at its branches carelessly. "It's just a decoration, like everything else here."

"Those monsters weren't just for decoration." Kaidyn took one step forward, readying his sword to stab her if she made one wrong move. "Answer my question or I'll cut it down."

"Yeah," Viktor added, hyping him up. The loss of Leon had destroyed his shy disposition.

"If you have any questions about the forest, you may ask me now, but I can't answer anything in regards to the tree. It's just a decoration, as I said. I'm not lying to you. After all..." Her voice changed, shifting from a soothing mother to a higher, faster pitch like that of a child. "I've waited six years for both of you to arrive."

"Both of you?" Lili glanced at Viktor. There were three of them.

"Okay." Kaidyn glared at her. "First question. How are you still alive and why are you standing here?"

"I speak for the forest...and the forest is ready to give you an opportu—"

"What are the shrines for?" Kaidyn interrupted every time her voice changed to that creepy, childish one. "The ones that took our blood."

"Oh, those? I haven't used those in over a hundred years. They were just a means for my people to offer me blood. Once they stopped giving offerings, I had to...find other means to feed." Her voice switched from soothing to childish in every other sentence.

"So, the shrines don't do anything?" he clarified.

"They do. They feed me." She smiled unnaturally, her lips stretching so far they cracked and bled.

Lili decided to reach for her knife after all. This didn't feel like her mother. Was Grant wrong? Was it just another copy, like Billy was a copy of the couple's real son?

"It's not my fault the people stopped using them," the woman continued. "If they just gave blood to me of their own accord, I wouldn't have been forced to take it. They're fully capable of giving blood in their human forms. If they weren't so lazy and selfish, I wouldn't have had to twist them up like I did."

"Let me get this straight," Lili interrupted, sure that whoever was using her mother's voice was someone else. Her real mother would never speak like this. "The reason you kill people and turn them into monsters is to get blood? That's it?"

"Of course. What else would I need? Well, I do enjoy the entertainment your kind brings, but blood is the priority." She pointed at the giant's dead body behind them. "He gave me enough to last a hundred years. In return, I kept him alive for a thousand. I can do the same to you, if you agree to serve me like your mother did."

"What?" Lili pulled out her knife, her heart racing with fury. "My mother would never agree to such a thing. She would never serve a murderer."

"Why do you think she's still standing here and hasn't aged a day?" Her mother, using that childish voice, sneered. "She was the only one who didn't die to my defenders, just as planned, and since I didn't have many servants left, I offered her the opportunity to become my voice for as long as I could keep her alive. Now, I am offering that same chance to you two." She pointed at Lili, then at Kaidyn. "And since you've killed my two protectors, I'll need a new one to defend me from any future attacks. Your big friend would have done nicely but I can settle for this one." She pointed at Viktor, whose eyes widened in fear. "Since you love plants so much, I would love to turn you into one, Viktor." His name sounded filthy on her tongue.

Kaidyn glanced at Lili. "Why do you want us specifically? Don't you already have Lili's mother?"

"I don't need someone to simply stand here and greet visitors. That's not particularly productive. I need messengers now, people who can bring in new humans for me to...meet. A thousand years ago, my villages were full of carefully chosen humans, those who respected me and gave offerings like I was a god, but then they got cocky and thought they could kill me, so I had to use the bodies of their loved ones to defend myself. It was horrid, having people I considered friends turn on me so quickly." She sighed dramatically, as though she were the victim. "But if you two manage to bring in more people and teach them to use the shrines and treat me like a god once more, no one will have to die. I can keep you alive for centuries too, like I did with my defenders."

"Do you really think we'd believe that lie?" Lili shouted and pointed at the blob of humans rolling toward them, then at the statues surrounding the hill. "We know what you do to people who live here. You torture them without mercy, then turn them to stone when you're done with them."

"Weren't you listening?" The speaker groaned and ruffled her own hair in frustration. "I just told you, I had to kill them because they weren't giving me blood. Without it, this whole forest would dry up and the walls would collapse, killing everyone inside. Is that what you want?" She pointed at the red veins running along the walls, confirming that they were bringing big blood from the levels above, all the way down to this single tree. Its roots were tinged red, just like the pink leaves. "Besides, once you become my servant, I cannot turn you to stone. We become one, sharing pieces of my heart. Killing you would harm me too."

"Letting your forest die sounds like a good idea," Kaidyn said.

"Trust me, boy. If you don't join me, someone else will. There are always more. You two were just chosen because you'll connect to the most people. Lili here will convince her uncle to enter and bring in all those fresh humans who constantly patrol my walls. She'll give them some lie about glory and honor in battle against me, then they'll be trapped down here forever and become a nice little army to defend me for the next thousand years."

"Mom...Why are you saying such horrible things about your brother?" Lili whispered, horrified.

"I'm not your mom!" the voice shouted, then gasped and cleared her throat. "But she is in here, see?" She pointed at her own eyes. "Her soul is still here and I'll let it go once you give me what I want."

Lili frowned, trying to subtly study the tree and see if there was anything that might help them defeat this forest demon or whatever it was.

"Kaidyn is who I'm really banking on," the demon continued. "I couldn't have the blond one, since he's too smart and cocky, and the big one is too dumb to be believable. And you Viktor...you agitate me, so you won't do either."

Viktor glared but didn't say anything. His hands were slowly rummaging around in his pack.

"But Kaidyn is the perfect presenter to bring in new humans. He can spread his moving pictures to every country in the world and I can even travel to some of them when the time is right. I haven't lingered long in this part of the world but wouldn't mind relocating once more." Lili realized she must be referring to the online videos the Rural Rangers published. "Plus your voice will continue for generations, even after you're dead. You are the perfect example of a sole survivor, a tragic hero who lost his brother and defeated giants." Her voice turned theatrical. "You finally made it out, alive but traumatized, and need more people to join you on your journey into the lower levels. You'll claim there are more than three and that whoever comes with you and follows in your footsteps will surely discover all the mysteries and treasures below."

"There's no way I'd do that," Kaidyn hissed.

"Even if it means I can bring back your brother? And your other siblings? I can still save them, you know. I kept them alive all year for you. Then you selfishly decided to kill them on your own, which was quite rude. Not to worry. I can still bring them back. Their souls are still within my possession."

Kaidyn looked down, faltering. "That can't be. I saw their eyes. They were...wrong. It wasn't them."

"It was," the forest insisted. "You were just too blind to see it. Join me, and I'll agree to bring them back."

Lili was confident she was lying about Aidyn and his siblings. She believed Grant when he said the eyes of every monster were dead. Only her mother was supposedly still alive...alive but controlled.

Her mother shrugged. "Or you can reject me and I'll make you do my bidding anyway."

"How exactly will you do that?" Viktor asked, finally speaking up and moving slightly to the right as he addressed the woman. "We killed your two warriors and all you have on your side now is some middle-aged woman. Nothing can stop us from burning this whole place to the ground."

"Nothing except the giant group of villagers who are fast approaching," the woman answered, rolling her eyes. "As well as the monsters above. Even without them, I am not defenseless. The statues should attest to that."

"Then why haven't you done it to us already?" Viktor asked.

Lili's mother smiled, as though the forest was eager to answer.

Before waiting for a response, Viktor lifted two lit Molotov cocktails and threw them at the tree, followed by a grenade. His questions had distracted Lili's mother long enough to let him light the weapons inside his pack. Now the bottles of liquid were shattered on the trunk of the tree, bursting into flames and lighting up the branches faster than should be possible.

"No!" Lili's mother ran at Viktor, knocking him down the hill. She pulled a knife from her gown and dug her feet into the ground to chase him and finish the job.

Lili shouted for her to stop and Kaidyn moved to block the woman's path. Viktor landed on his back and groaned in pain. The pack slipped off his shoulders.

The tree's leaves were a bright orange now, burning like paper. If the tree's current state had any impact on its control over her mother, it made no show of it.

"Don't kill her!" Lili shouted at Kaidyn, trying to grab her mother's arms from behind. Her mom wouldn't be able to live with herself if she killed someone. She was sure of it. In Lili's dream, her real mother had been crying, begging Lili not to come. Now Lili knew why. She knew it was a trap and had tried to warn Lili before she lost control.

Kaidyn stopped, his sword an inch from her mother's face. He glared at Lili. "You heard her. She plans to kill us. We need to defend ourselves."

"We still don't know how to destroy this forest," Lili countered. "At least wait until we figure it out."

"Do you really think the forest would tell us the secret to killing it?" Kaidyn asked, then sighed. When he did, lowering his guard, her mother suddenly stomped on Lili's foot, attempting to crush her toes with her boot before shoving her to the ground.

"No!" Lili screamed as her mother leapt on top of her, knife poised to slice her chest open. Once Lili went still, her mother turned around, holding Lili hostage so Kaidyn couldn't attack.

"Lower your weapons or I'll kill you and turn her to stone," the woman screamed in that childish, sing-song voice. It still seemed determined to turn them to her side.

Lili stared at her mother and saw her eyes rebelling against her mouth. Her mom was still in there, fighting back against this force possessing her.

Kaidyn frowned, unwilling to drop his weapon. He looked as unsure as Lili was about why they hadn't been killed yet.

A tear slipped from her mother's eye.

"Mom," Lili whispered. "Please, fight this thing that's controlling you."

"I...can't..." she whispered, gripping the knife with both hands now. It was pressing against Lili's neck but wasn't drawing blood. Kaidyn tightened the grip on his weapon. He was staring at Lili, asking for permission to kill. He wouldn't take her mother from her, as his brother was taken from him.

"Please," Lili whispered. "Let us save you."

There was a second tear, then her mother suddenly screamed, the smile vanishing from her face. Lili's heart stopped as her mother reversed the blade into her own chest. Blood splashed Lili's chin as her mom flopped onto her side, sighing with relief before the childish voice returned.

"You fools! This was your final chance to become my friends. Now I'll have to take you by force, just as I did with her!"

The voice trailed off as her mother started panting, gripping the wound on her side to stop the bleeding. Lili rushed to put pressure on it, kicking the knife away so the demon couldn't use it against them.

"You'll be okay, Mom." Lili was crying now. "You're safe now. I'll protect you. I won't let you leave me again."

Her mother raised a bloodied hand and touched Lili's cheek.

Lili desperately wanted to hug her but couldn't let her lose any more blood.

"I'm tying her up," Kaidyn said and did so, using rope from Viktor's pack. Viktor got back to his feet and pushed Lili aside.

"I'll take care of the wound. You two focus on that." He pointed at what remained of the tree. During their fight, it had burnt so quickly that it was nothing but ash now. Even the stump was blackened and looked ready to crumble at the slightest touch.

All three of them were shaking, aware of how quickly they could die. The tree's only way of fighting back now was turning them into statues. Lili wasn't sure why it hadn't done so and what it meant by using force to turn them. Was it summoning monsters from the top level, as it claimed it would do earlier?

After Lili got to her feet, wiping her mother's blood from her chin with a sleeve, she noticed a hole beneath the tree stump. "Is there something under the tree?"

"I'll check it out." Kaidyn tightened his grip on the sword and stepped toward it.

As he went, Lili noticed blood pouring from her mother's side. It touched the ground, then sank into the grass and dirt before vanishing. The forest was drinking her blood, just as it did with everything else that bled here. The forest was still alive and hungry. Burning the tree hadn't been enough.

Kaidyn stood over the tree's remains, then kicked the black stump. It crumbled under his boot, revealing more of the hole. "There's a tunnel down here," he called back to Lili. "I'm going down. You coming?"

"Whatever you're doing, do it fast!" Viktor shouted back. "That blob is still on its way."

"Okay. Stay here, Viktor. We'll check it out." Lili ran to Kaidyn's side but glanced back at her mother once more to make sure she was okay. She was pale and her forehead was wrinkled in pain, but she was still breathing. "I'll be right back, Mom," she promised.

The hole Kaidyn had found beneath the tree was only wide enough to fit two to three people. It led into a tunnel that continued west, toward the walls of the forest. Strangely, this tunnel's walls weren't grey or brown like the rest. Instead, it was the deep red of arteries. It smelled sweet and coppery, like rotting flesh.

"I'll go first," Kaidyn said, patting her back. "Take this knife. There might be more monsters down there."

"Got it." She accepted the weapon he handed her, then watched him jump into the hole. When he confirmed it was safe, she joined him, feeling an uncharacteristic swell of excitement in her chest.

The ground was squishy beneath her feet and the bottom of her boots turned red as soon as she landed. Everything smelled strongly of pungent rot and it was enough to make her head fuzzy. The air was stale, like it had been locked away for decades.

The tunnel remained dark until Kaidyn pulled a flashlight from his belt and turned it on. When he shined the light down the tunnel, she realized why everything smelled so rotten.

The tunnel wasn't very long, maybe forty feet at the most and seven feet high. However, the walls themselves were ten feet wide, built that way to fit all the bodies sticking out of them. Lili covered her mouth as she beheld dozens of people trapped within the walls, their torsos buried in the dirt. Only their faces and arms were free, though it didn't do them any good. They couldn't dig their way out.

Every person was in a different stage of decay, starting with the freshest person next to Kaidyn. He was a man wearing a black soldier outfit and hat. Lili recognized his Nazi uniform, though the man looked forty at the oldest, which shouldn't be possible. His skin was grey like her mother's and there were green leaves and branches sprouting from his skin, nose, and mouth, filling his throat so he couldn't make any sounds besides muffled groans and wheezes.

"This is barbaric," Kaidyn whispered as he shined his light into the empty eyes of each person. There were people of every race, culture, and time trapped in the walls, some of them slumped over but still breathing. Others reached toward Kaidyn and Lili with moss-covered, bleeding hands. All of them were bleeding from some part of their body. When Lili stepped closer, she spotted bloody veins running from each body into the walls, like an IV drip.

"Do you think this would have been my mother's fate if we didn't save her?" she whispered as she and Kaidyn continued down the tunnel, moving slowly to avoid the grasping hands. "Locked in here for eternity?"

"It said it couldn't kill its servants, so it makes sense that the forest keeps them here," Kaidyn said. "I'm glad I killed my brother so he wouldn't have to suffer like this...if beheading even works. Now that I think about it, maybe the beheading was just a trick of the forest, making us believe we were saving our loved ones from eternal torment, only to have their bodies reused later so we wouldn't know."

Lili wasn't sure. Kingsley had been confident about it and he'd been here for nine years.

"It's all a game for the forest," Lili whispered, feeling a headache form. The stench made her lightheaded. Her legs started to wobble. "Watching us fight to get down here. Making us kill each other. Spying on us so it could copy our mannerisms later when we became its puppets." She always felt like she was being watched and had assumed it was her mother. Now she knew it was the forest watching her instead, enjoying the game of cat and mouse.

"Well, I'm putting a stop to it." Kaidyn paused, his light finding the end of the tunnel. The bodies became older as they proceeded. At the very end, the people were no more than mummies, their skin so drained and lifeless that they could pass as skeletons. If it weren't for their ragged breaths, Lili would have assumed they were dead.

There was another thing at the end of the tunnel, too. It was what they'd been searching for this entire time.

All the veins running along the walls—all the blood from the victims—it channeled into a single, beating heart suspended from the ceiling. It looked like a human heart, except every part of the red organ was covered in wide, reptilian eyes. As the light passed over it, the pupils shrank and turned to study Kaidyn and Lili, shivering as more blood pumped into it.

"Found you," Kaidyn whispered with a tired smile. "Finally. I found it, Aidyn."

Lili tightened the grip on her knife. "What are you going to do?"

"What else?" Kaidyn raised his sword and took a step toward it. "Cut it in two. Then we'll burn the tunnel so every person can be put out of their misery."

Lili gulped and followed him. Her heart rate increased. "But if we do this, it might make the entire forest cave in. It'll kill Viktor and Jacques and everyone else."

"But it will save future generations from falling into this trap," Kaidyn said and raised his sword. "There's no changing my mind, Lili. Just stand back so you don't get hurt."

Her head was pounding so loudly now that she could barely register what she was doing.

"Very well," she said, a dark chuckle rising from her throat without her permission. "At least you came down here alone."

She raised her chin, an unnatural smile stretching across her face. Then she wrapped her free arm around his chest. Her body was moving on its own, disobeying her mind.

Kaidyn paused and glanced at her. "What are you—"

Lili pulled him toward her and drove her blade into his side.

Episode 28

"Lili?" Kaidyn doubled over, dropping his sword as she twisted the knife, another chuckle bubbling up inside her. She didn't know why she felt the urge to do this. Was she trying to protect the soldiers who were still alive? No. It couldn't be. She had planned to kill the tree too, a minute ago.

At least she had missed his heart, intentionally moving her arm at the last second to hit his side instead. He would be okay, so long as he didn't bleed out. His heart had been her original target but...why would she try to stab him in the first place?

What was happening to her?

Kaidyn gasped in pain as she yanked the knife from his back, then dug her hand into the wound she'd created. He gasped, his face scrunching up in pain. She felt something climb out of her palm and into his wound, like bugs crawling across her skin. Any attempts to pull her hand out and save him from this agony were futile. Her body had a mind of its own and as she opened her mouth, she realized what was going on. She hadn't instructed her body to do any of this. She wasn't in control...just like her mother hadn't been.

Kaidyn realized it at the same time, his tired eyes widening.

"The forest already got to you," he whispered, coughing up blood. "When?"

Lili's body shrugged without her permission. Then that same childish, high-pitched voice her mother had used exited her own mouth. "Six years ago. I led her mother out, hoping to lure in a few unsuspecting soldiers, but ended up finding this one instead. She was too small to be of much use, but I decided it would be fun to hide inside her for a few years and try to lure the entire army in."

That had been the pain she experienced when she was a child, though her memories of it became foggy. Her mother must have reached inside and placed something in her heart, something to let this forest control her and see through her eyes.

She didn't know why she'd forgotten. Maybe the forest wiped her memory or the trauma of seeing her mother deformed and zombie-like made her forget on her own—done in a desperate attempt to preserve the memory of her original mother. Either way, she was horrified that this thing had been living inside her for six years, watching her every move and taking advantage of the love for her mother, using it to trick her into coming here.

Now, she would do the same to her uncle. He had spent ten years trying to protect her, warning her to stay away from the walls. Ironically, she would be the one convincing him to finally come inside. She would give this monstrous place more innocent people to feed on. Then the cycle would continue, twisting more children into murderous, bleeding servants living unnaturally long lives.

"So, you've been controlling her this entire time?" Kaidyn hissed, attempting to step toward the heart but Lili wrapped her other arm around him, her grip tightening without her permission.

"Not really. I used her once or twice, just to see what would happen, but most of the time her simple and boring motivation to save her mother did all the work for me. I barely had to lift a finger. It helped that she had barely any hobbies or personality to interfere with my plans, similar to you. Her desperate desire to save her mother and your silly plans of revenge made you walk right in without question." Lili finally pulled her hand out, her fingers sticky with blood. Kaidyn screamed in pain and she could hear Viktor shout from outside, asking what was going on.

"It was fun to see you discover this tunnel. The looks on your faces were quite entertaining. Seeing so much hope get snuffed out was exhilarating," the forest continued through Lili's mouth. "But now it's time to end this."

Kaidyn grunted, struggling against whatever she'd placed inside him. "I'm not turning into one of your puppets."

"You're too late. Any minute now, you'll be under my control."

Lili could feel Kaidyn weakening under her grip from both the wound and the forest's power. By the time Viktor came to see what was going on, Kaidyn would be the forest's tool and Viktor would be next.

Lili couldn't let this go on. She had to retake control of her body.

She tried to steel her arms and prevent any more movement but the more she tried, the more she felt herself grin and laugh. The forest knew she was trying to rebel and found it amusing.

"Just to be clear, this isn't Lili talking?" Kaidyn pulled himself up onto one knee, pressing one of his hands against his wound and sneering at Lili, or rather the person controlling her. "This is the forest talking, right?"

Lili laughed. "Yes. It is I, your soon-to-be master." She sounded like a child acting out a role.

"How long until you have complete control?"

"Less than a minute."

"That's all I needed to know," Kaidyn whispered, cringing from the pain.

Then he raised his leg and kicked Lili with the last of his strength.

Sharp pains shot through her chest as she was launched across the tunnel and hit the wall behind her. The pain was nothing compared to the relief she felt, though, as she watched Kaidyn push himself to his feet and grab his sword.

"You must have forgotten the person you were controlling was a weak girl," Kaidyn said, running toward the heart and raising his blade. "No offense to Lili, but you should have picked a stronger puppet if you wanted to stop me." And now that he was part of the forest, it couldn't turn him to stone without harming itself.

"No!" the forest screamed from Lili's mouth and every other body in the tunnel. Every hand reached for him but he was faster and stronger. He'd come too far to be stopped now.

"Lili! Get up!" the faces on the walls screamed at her but Lili had hit her head on the wall and was in too much pain to rise. "Move this cursed body!"

Lili smirked, glad being useless had finally paid off.

"Stop him!" The forest's voices shrieked like a child but it was too late.

Kaidyn used the last of his energy to bring his sword down on the heart. He sliced it cleanly in two, detaching it from the veins hanging from the walls. He then chopped it thrice more, screaming in outrage as he finally avenged his lost family members.

Years of stolen blood spurted from the open heart, drenching Kaidyn and even reaching Lili's boots. Kaidyn continued to shout, taking out his anger on the selfish demon. When the heart was nothing more than a heap of red flesh at his feet, he finally stopped, his head drooping and chest rising rapidly from frantic breaths. She heard him pray under his breath, thanking his god for the strength to continue this far. If he'd given up earlier, Aidyn would have died for nothing.

As soon as Kaidyn cut through the heart, every person hanging from the walls slumped over, dead, and Lili regained control of her body. Tears had stained her cheeks, a reaction from the forest's defeated cries, but now she was smiling.

The forest was dead.

Everyone in this cursed forest was free.

Kaidyn put away his bloody sword, panting heavily, but when he turned toward Lili, he finally looked happy. The weight on his shoulders was gone and his eyes weren't pained as they'd always been. "Are you okay?" he asked softly, clutching his side again and stumbling toward her. "Are you hurt?"

"No." She ran to him and pressed her hands against his wound. "More importantly, are you okay? I stabbed you—"

He shook his head and leaned his head against her shoulder, wrapping his other arm around her in a tight hug. She tensed as he squeezed her, as though he was afraid of losing her. Only after the pain became too great did he let her go.

"I think we should leave. The monster from the village might still be coming," he said quietly, leaning on her as she practically carried him to the tunnel's exit.

"Right." Lili led the way, shouting for Viktor to help them up. Luckily, the young man was already at the hole, looking down with the expression of someone expecting to find the worst.

"What happened?" he shouted down as Lili tried to lift Kaidyn out of the tunnel. "Your mom was freaking out a second ago but now she's fast asleep." She must have been screaming along with every prisoner in the tunnel.

"We won." Lili forced a sad smile. "Is the village monster still coming?" she asked as Kaidyn climbed out with Viktor's help.

"Yeah." Viktor sighed. "We may have won, but we're still gonna get eaten by the blob. This isn't how I wanted to go out."

Once Kaidyn and Lili were above ground, Viktor started pouring liquids on Kaidyn's wounds and patching him up. "How did you get stabbed like this?" Viktor asked. "What was down there?"

"The heart of the forest," Kaidyn said, lying on the ground with his arms spread out like a snow angel. "And as for the wound..." He glanced at Lili, then up at the third level's ceiling. "The forest tried to kill me before I could kill it."

"Well, at least it didn't hit anything vital," Viktor commented as he bandaged the wound. He then pointed back the way they'd come. "Let's get moving."

Lili ran to her mother's sleeping body. "Mom?" She pulled on her shirt. There was a bandage under it now, a gift from Viktor. They were lucky he'd survived to deal with all their wounds. They might have bled out without him, though his healing would do them no good if they died to the blob anyway. "Mom. Wake up. We need to go." Panicking, she looked past her mother at what remained of the giant. Beyond it, the blob of bodies was still creeping toward them, moving like a caterpillar. It would take a while to reach them, but if they became cornered, they'd be in trouble.

"Help me carry her," Lili told Viktor, who did so without question.

The four of them headed back as quickly as they could, though their pace was agonizingly slow compared to before. Lili could tell from the look in their eyes that Viktor and Kaidyn were already deciding whether they should kill or avoid the monster. It was huge but it wasn't indestructible. Human flesh was easy to cut through, as she'd now learned.

"It's slow," Kaidyn commented as he limped after her and Viktor. "Maybe we can circle around it and climb back up the rope before it catches us."

"And you're sure we won't turn to stone?" Viktor asked.

"There's nothing else we can do," Lili said. "Let's try it. If things get bad, Viktor and I can try to burn the blob instead."

Viktor looked scared but nodded. "I've always wanted to participate in battles anyway," he said as they passed where Leon's body lay.

Lili looked at Kaidyn, whose skin was greying from the loss of blood. She gulped. The wound was worse than she originally thought. He wouldn't make it very far in that condition. It would take hours to walk all the way to the exit and maybe even longer if they kept traveling this slowly.

"Kaidyn, hide behind the giant's body with my mom. Viktor and I will go ahead." She turned toward Viktor. "I think we'll need to start with plan B."

"That's not what a plan B is," Viktor muttered but didn't protest. Kaidyn did, though.

"We can still try to sneak past it..." Kaidyn insisted, then groaned in pain. He couldn't climb a rope in this state. "Fine." He nodded at her mom. "I'll take care of her. Just get back quick."

Lili nodded, forcing a tight-lipped smile. *Be strong. Just a little longer. You've killed giants. What's one more?*

"Hero time," Viktor whispered as he tossed things out of his pack to lighten the load, only keeping what they'd need for the fight. Lili helped Kaidyn pull her mother to a safe spot behind the giant. Once she knew they'd be okay, she instructed Kaidyn to stay put.

"I can still help," he said, but his ragged breathing and the blood seeping through his bandages proved otherwise.

"You need to be the survivor," she said stubbornly, touching the hilt of the sword in his hands. "Plus, you need to protect her. If we die, you're all she'll have left."

Kaidyn scrunched up his face, resisting. "I don't want to be left alone," he whispered, breaking Lili's heart.

"You won't be," she told him confidently, punching his chest lightly in an attempt to lighten the mood. It was what Leon would have done. "I promise."

He looked ready to hug her like he had in the tunnel, but Viktor called out to Lili from the side before he could. All Kaidyn could manage was a quiet, "Come back safe."

"We will." She said, then waved goodbye as she rejoined Viktor, who was now armed with all the weapons and tools he had left. "Are you ready to do this?" she asked.

"Y-yeah!" Viktor's voice was shaky but he was ready. "Let's go."

The two weakest members of the party turned and walked toward the blob, too tired to run but ready to give their lives protecting their friends. They would die heroically if need be.

It took a while to reach the monster and the closer they got, the more it towered over them, blocking their view of their surroundings. The blob's heads growled, shrieking and groaning in pain as it rolled. The noises it made blended in with a loud groaning, creaking noise from the ceilings and walls. The forest was no doubt collapsing around them.

Lili felt her stomach churn when she got close enough to make out the human faces. She could feel dozens of empty eyes on her.

This would be their final stand. Her mother and Kaidyn's survival hinged on this moment.

"Ready," Viktor said when they were close enough. He didn't sound ready, but they had no choice.

Lili steeled herself, trying to remember everything she could from the training she'd received on this journey. She gripped Kaidyn's knife, egging herself on...

Then there was a sudden explosion behind the blob and it burst into flames.

Viktor and Lili ground to a halt, gasping as the entire mass of flesh wobbled and screamed.

"What's going on?" Viktor whispered as a second explosion sounded, then a third.

When the blob stopped moving forward and tried to turn around, a small tank appeared behind it. There were three soldiers standing atop the vehicle, carrying large rocket launchers. Lili watched slack-jawed as they unleashed their rockets onto the beast.

Her heart leapt and Viktor fell to his knees beside her, sobbing from relief.

The cavalry had finally arrived. They'd been saved. She would never have to fight again.

Episode 29

The tank continued firing at the blob, but as there were still countless bodies within it, the monster didn't die right away. Instead of keeling over, it instead rolled toward the tank, forcing the newcomers back.

"You need to behead every person inside it!" Lili shouted at the soldiers standing on the tank. Her voice alerted them and they waved, then a second tank appeared, speeding toward her and Viktor.

Shocked that some tanks had managed to make it through the human-sized hole they'd used to enter, she looked up at the ceiling. To her shock, the hole had been enlarged, made large enough to fit a tank. There were more small holes in other sections too and each had ropes hanging from them.

Lili realized that all the sounds she'd heard hadn't been the forest collapsing but the soldiers breaking in. She'd been so focused on the blob that she hadn't thought to look up.

The pair raised their pistols, wary as the tank came to a stop before them. They were still on edge after everything they'd seen.

The top of the tank opened and a man in a grey military uniform climbed up to face them. As soon as Lili saw him, she screamed with joy.

"Uncle Gabriel!"

"Get in here!" he cut her off, pointing to a ladder on the tank's side. "Are you the only two left?"

"No. Mom and one of our friends are next to that giant corpse," she answered as even more soldiers came into view, several armed with rocket launchers or swords. Among them were the soldiers from the castle, led by Diego, but the more surprising additions were some of the guards from the village, led by Kingsley.

As Lili and Viktor climbed onto the tank, the blob continued rolling about. Before they finished climbing in, her uncle started driving the tank away from the monster.

Once Lili was inside the cramped space, surrounded by grey pipes and dials, she was surprised to find someone else inside the tank, controlling the gun. When Viktor landed next to her, the person moved away from their post to greet them. It was Meriel, wearing a soldier's uniform and looking happy for the first time in their acquaintance.

"Glad you're okay," Meriel told them. Lili had never felt more thrilled to see her.

"You decided to come after all," Lili told her with a relieved smile.

"Only after the army arrived," Viktor commented glumly as the tank continued grinding forward.

"When did they get here?" Lili asked.

"A day after you left. They've been on your tail since the beginning," Meriel answered. "Your uncle said he entered the walls two days after you did, bringing every man, weapon, and vehicle he could."

"We lost a lot of men on that first level," her uncle called from the driver's seat. "Lots of vehicles too. Those that didn't shut down struggled to get through the terrain. We're lucky we managed to get these two tanks through."

"If you had all this stuff, why didn't you do this sooner?" Viktor grumbled.

"I tried to convince others to go in for years but couldn't go myself. With Lili relying on me, I couldn't bear to leave her behind and without me leading the charge, very few people were willing to risk their lives."

Lili gulped as she realized what his arrival meant. If they had waited in Kingsley's village for a few more days, everyone might still be alive. Aidyn, Grant, Leon. None of them would have been killed. What a horrid thought.

Her stomach convulsing, Lili climbed back up the ladder to look outside. She watched as her uncle drove the tank toward the giant's corpse, ready to pick up the other survivors.

"Once Lili's uncle arrived to save her," Meriel explained as they drove, "Jacques woke up and convinced the other soldiers to go with him. He's...very good at persuasive speeches." She frowned, turning away shamefully. "I'm sorry for not coming with you."

"Better late than never," Lili said, too tired and relieved to care. If the soldiers were here, that meant doctors were likely coming too. They could help the others. No one else would have to die.

Lili thought she had no more tears to cry but after seeing the unbridled joy on Kaidyn's face when the tank arrived, she started sobbing all over again, as did Viktor. While she ran out to hug her mother, she saw drones zipping down from the holes. The soldiers had set up secure ropes and were hauling things up and down now, as well as bringing down more people to secure the area. By the time Dr. Anna had brought out her tools, the blob behind them had been destroyed and burned. The battle was over.

It took several hours for the soldiers to form a camp and start burying the bodies. The blood no longer disappeared into the ground to feed the forest, so the entire level stank of it. It was a relief to know that they weren't being spied on or consumed by the demon but, in its absence, the land around them had become dark and stale. Luckily, with their forces combined, the soldiers numbered over a hundred, along with the two tanks they had lowered through the hole above, so clean up didn't take as long as it could have.

During that time, Dr. Anna and her assistants inspected Lili and Viktor's bodies for wounds, then quickly moved on to the others. Lili mentioned having something inside her heart—a remainder of the forest's corruption—but Dr. Anna didn't view it as a priority when compared to the two stab wounds she already had to deal with. Lili's current state was pushed aside until a later hour, though the soldiers were instructed to keep an eye on her, her mother, and Kaidyn just in case.

"I'll get back to you right away," Dr. Anna said with feverishly curious eyes as she packed up her tools, headed for a different tent. "I've never seen such a case before. It's fascinating. I can't wait to dissect you."

"She creeps me out," Viktor whispered about the doctor as she left. They were both seated on wooden tables the soldiers had procured in the abandoned village. Their filthy clothes had been replaced with clean green uniforms Lili's uncle had brought. Viktor was currently filming the chaos with their last remaining camera, its lens only slightly stained with blood. He didn't mind the stain, since Jacques would claim it added a spooky touch.

"Well, at least she's saving our lives," Lili said, then snapped to attention when she noticed her uncle approaching her. He had spent the last two hours dealing with the other soldiers, so she'd managed to avoid his inevitable lecture about entering the walls despite all his warnings. Now there was nowhere to run.

By the time he reached her tent, his glare had turned into a frown. She cringed when he placed his hands on her shoulders...then he wrapped her into a warm hug. "I thought I lost you," he whispered, his voice cracking. "Every time I encountered a corpse, I feared it was yours. Now I have both of you again. I'm so glad."

She smiled and squeezed him back, feeling him shake from sobs. "I'm sorry for leaving."

"And you're going to get the lecture of your life once we're out of this place," he grumbled, pulling away and looking down at her like a disappointed father.

Lili looked up at the hole in the ceiling. There were dozens of men climbing up and down without turning to stone. That meant Lili could leave this place anytime she wanted. The villagers on the first level had most likely left already, eager to meet the family and friends they left behind when they entered this prison.

"Just keep an eye on us," she warned her uncle quietly. "The forest put something in us to control our bodies. Until the doctor can investigate, maybe you should tie us up."

"I'll keep a lookout," he said but didn't sound concerned. "The forest's barriers are gone now, so whatever you did brought its reign to an end. What did you do, by the way?"

She pointed at the tent where Kaidyn was being patched up. "He destroyed its heart." She wouldn't mention how he kicked her in the chest before doing so. She had no idea how her uncle would react to that.

"Heart?" Her uncle scratched his head, confused. "I'll take your word for it."

She nodded, knowing he'd get the whole story from her eventually. She didn't want to talk about it yet. She was more worried about the others. Jacques was still on the second level and she wanted to see how he was doing. Viktor and Kaidyn were also eager to get up there and ensure he'd survived.

None of them would risk going up until the soldiers had killed every monster on every level, though. That might take several hours or days by the looks of it.

"So, what's the plan?" Viktor asked Kaidyn as he joined them in the tent, his wounds wrapped in white bandages and skin regaining its color. This was the calmest he'd looked in days, though his eyes still held the darkness his brother's death had left. "I take it the Rural Rangers are disbanded?" With Aidyn and Leon dead, there were only three people left. "Not much of a crew now."

Kaidyn nodded at Lili. "We have two new members if Meriel is willing to join."

"It's just...without the others, it'll feel a little...empty." Viktor looked down, devastated.

"We'll get used to it with time." Kaidyn had the same look. "Leon and Aidyn wouldn't want us to separate just because they're gone. They'd want us to watch each other's backs."

Viktor and Lili nodded.

"Thank you," she whispered, tears springing to her eyes. These were her first real friends. "I'll try my best to become useful."

"You already are," Kaidyn replied. "And I can train you with a sword if you'd like. Both of you," His entire aura had changed now that they were no longer in danger.

"Lili!" Her uncle called to her from one of the tents, interrupting. "Your mother wants to see you."

"I'll be right back," she said and stood, patting both of her friends on the back before heading out.

"Take your time," Viktor said, leaning back on his table. "We're not going anywhere."

"We'll be waiting for you," Kaidyn said, taking a seat on her abandoned table and imitating Viktor's position. By the time she left, they had both covered their heads with hats or sweaters and fell asleep despite all the shouting soldiers and doctors.

"I'm coming," Lili called to her uncle, who was standing beside her mother in one of the other tents. She was draped in a blue medical robe and had several IVs sticking out of her arms. She was smiling, though, despite the strange green growths protruding from her body. As Lili ran toward her, glad to see her in good health, she knew this had all been worth it. She just wished so many hadn't died to achieve this reunion.

Epilogue

Three years later

What used to be the lab on the second level was now nothing more than a slab of concrete with an elevator and ladder in the center, granting researchers access to the third level. The ground beneath them shook with the rumble of generators.

The air was fresher now than it had been three years ago. In the aftermath of the forest's death, the dirt and stone ceilings had caved. However, the soldiers and scientists had assured Lili and her friends the area was safe to enter now due to all the supports they had installed. The forest was basically a corpse and the researchers didn't want to lose access to this new and strange lifeform.

Lili was well-armed this time, wearing a bullet-proof vest, steel-toed boots, a pistol, a shotgun, and a sword. She had permanent scars on her chest and back from where Dr. Ana and a plethora of other researchers had cut her open and extracted the piece of the forest's heart to study it. The same was done to Kaidyn and her mother. She hadn't received many updates on what they found yet but hoped they'd keep it safe and secure, never allowed to grow again. The most Dr. Ana claimed to find was evidence of the forest existing in other countries in the past, which should be impossible. "Signs point toward it being supernatural," Dr. Ana had said, sounding flabbergasted by her own theory. "The creature, if you can call it that, appears ancient, even alien. We'll need years to study it before we even begin to understand what it really is."

Kaidyn had asked the doctor to keep him informed, but Lili didn't expect him to receive many updates in the future. Every survivor had been told that the forest was completely eradicated and the only ones who knew about the forest's heart pieces were forced to sign documents promising to keep it a secret. Kaidyn had been resistant but Lili was just glad to be done with it all. If she never heard about the forest again in her lifetime, she'd be happy.

Viktor wasn't as well armed, carrying only his giant pack full of food and cooking utensils, just like last time.

"You never know. There might be a cave-in and we'll have to learn to survive like we did back then," Viktor had said while preparing for this trip. He was the only one worried now. Since dozens of storage rooms and research facilities had sprung up in the forest, they'd have more than enough food, water, and weapons to dig their way out.

Jacques was seated in his wheelchair beside them, his useless legs dangling off the edge of his seat. The ecstatic look on his face while he filmed everything was worth the struggle to get him there

Kaidyn was standing a few feet away, shoveling the last of the dirt onto the four graves they'd spent the entire day digging. A monument rested behind them, the words "To all who were lost to the forest. May they rest in peace" engraved on it.

Behind them was another monument listing the names of all the researchers who died in the lab when it was overtaken four years ago. The government had promised Lili and her friends they'd leave room for the graves of Leon and Kaidyn's siblings. Their funerals had occurred outside the forest but Kaidyn had insisted they be buried here. He never explained why and Lili hadn't asked.

As the twin threw his shovel aside and joined them, Lili spotted Meriel walking down the road toward them. She had left early this morning to bury her husband elsewhere, preferring to do it in private. She must have finished earlier than expected.

"Am I late?" Meriel asked, her hair long and pulled back in a no-nonsense ponytail. She still had the scars on her face and the grief behind her eyes, but she had regained some confidence.

"You're just in time," Kaidyn answered as he stopped beside Lili and took her hand in his, gripping her a little too tight for support.

"We didn't have any ceremonies planned anyway," Jacques added. His body may have been broken but he still had his showman's manner of speaking. "We just came to say goodbye."

It would be wrong to begin their next adventure together without telling Aidyn and Leon where they planned to go.

"I still can't believe I'm joining a group of people ten years younger than me," Meriel commented sarcastically as she stopped beside Jacques.

"No one's forcing you," Jacques teased her. They all knew she had joined of her own free will, though she still liked to complain about it, even after two years of working together.

Everyone fell silent as they stared at the square stone lying before the four graves. On it was written:

In memory of Leon Sullivan, a great warrior and even greater brother.

In memory of Aidyn Myer, whose big dreams and even bigger heart live on.

In memory of Max Myer, a loving brother and mourned son.

In memory of Minnie Myer, a beloved daughter and wise sister.

"We added something while you were gone," Lili told Meriel, pointing at the bottom of the stone. She could tell Meriel had already seen it because the woman's shoulders were shaking from sobs and her head was lowered to hide her tears.

In memory of Daniel Smith, a cherished husband and son who died protecting the one he loved.

"We will honor their memory," Jacques said, staring at the stone. "And continue their legacy."

Lili nodded, squeezing Kaidyn's hand as he lowered his head too. "Wherever we go, their spirits will be watching over us," she added.

"Yeah." Viktor covered his eyes with his fists. "We're heading to England, Leon. We heard rumors of a two-layered tunnel system under London and are planning to investigate. We'll visit your sisters while we're there."

Lili forced a smile for Leon and Aidyn. "We'll make you proud." She felt something stir in her heart, a feeling that Leon and Aidyn were still here with them. "You were lost too soon but we'll do our best to ensure it never happens again. We'll protect each other, as you did for us."

They spent ten more minutes in respectful silence, taking the time to mourn their stolen family and friends. Then, once all was said and done, they headed out together, ready for their next adventure.

Author's Notes

Gratitude

I have a lot of people to thank but first, I'd like to thank the readers. Writing can be a lonely and exhausting process (especially when I try to actually publish something rather than let it sit on a shelf forever). I appreciate everyone who took time out of their day to explore this forest and witness its end.

I have a few other people to thank: God (who gave me my creativity and inspiration), Victoria (who reads my stories, critiques them, and sometimes creates art to represent them), and my editor (for pointing out all the plot holes and trying to keep the story flowing properly).

The writing process

This story came about when I watched an anime (which will remain unnamed) and I came out of it unsatisfied. It had a super interesting concept but I didn't like how the questions were answered and how characters were handled. I wanted to see a twist where the monsters used to be humans and the setting itself was the villain, so I decided to do it myself.

This story was one of the harder ones to complete. I spent a while writing up to the point where they reached Kingsley's town, then I hit a roadblock. I originally had them flee the village and try to find another hole rather than confront Kingsley. It was at this point that I knew something was wrong. The story felt boring and there was no real conflict. While the setting still kept me intrigued, I just didn't care about the plot. So I shelved the book and forgot about it.

Months later (or at least I think it was months), I realized how to fix this. I needed to make the characters fight back against Kingsley and force their way down, all while revealing some secrets about Kingsley himself. Of course, because time had passed, I chose to start writing from the beginning again. (My writing style changes and adapts over time, so I don't like to go back and reuse older works. It's a personal preference).

This time, the story reached its conclusion. After that, the next drafts came a little more smoothly.

Book Trivia

- Lili's original name was different. She used to be named Zilla but I found it too silly for the setting so I changed it to something more simple. The name Zilla was reused in one of my romance novels instead (The BFF Role).

- The Rural Rangers were inspired by a group in a kid's film, *Red Shoes and the Seven Dwarves*. It's stupid but I thought it would be fun to take the silly-looking dwarves and turn them into more fleshed-out, horror characters. For context, there are 7 heroes who turn into dwarves: two English (one being the male lead), one French, one German, and three Italian triplets. I whittled this down by getting rid of the male lead (since I already had Lili) and changing the Italian triplets to two Japanese twins (sorry Italy). Then I fleshed out their personalities. They basically weren't the same at all by the end but I thought it would be fun to share the original inspiration behind them.

- Meriel was originally going to be a controlled monster but that role was replaced by Max and Minnie instead.

- The book was originally titled "The Forest Within the Walls".

- I originally planned to write a sequel where Lili kept the heart in her chest and later became a forest of her own, but decided I wanted to do something else with the tree heart in a later book so I let Lili and Kaidyn have a happy ending.

Inspirations/Recommendations

There were other stories that inspired me when writing this book. I'll list and recommend them below. If you liked this book and want more, you can read/watch/play these to scratch that itch.

Books: The Call, Maze Runner, The Luminaries, The Dark Between the Trees

Movies/Shows: Attack on Titan, The Ritual, Coraline

Videogames: The Forest, Darkwood

What's Next?

I'm always working on something new but in terms of horror, I'll let you know about three projects I'm currently working on that are similar to this. (Will they *actually* come out? Who knows?)

Ossuarium: Coming out in October 2023, this is a science fiction horror story about two people crash landing on a water-covered, alien planet. As they try to survive against starvation and monsters, they discover alien ruins to explore and follow in the footsteps of two researchers who came before them.

The Crimson Ticket: Willy Wonka meets Saw and Squid Game in this factory tour gone wrong. It's equal parts thriller, murder mystery, and horror.

Skeleton Crew: An unofficial sequel to The Vanishing Forest, this will be a trio of novellas about a young woman terraforming a planet in the far future. While prepping the planet for human life, she stumbles upon abandoned underground labs filled with zombies and mysteries.

This book is still in the outlining stage, so I can't guarantee anything yet.

Unnamed Project: In a world similar to Earth, four children must learn to survive in a world falling apart from the inside. Travel from a walled city of cannibals, to a farm guarded by a mad scientist, and eventually a mountain of human guinea pigs enslaved by a rogue AI. This is also in its early stages (and has been delayed in the same way The Vanishing Forest was) so I don't guarantee anything for this title either.

If you liked this story, please buy a copy (if you haven't already), leave a review on Amazon, and share it with your friends. My dream is to one day sell enough copies for the books to pay for themselves (so I can invest in more editing, proofreading, and maybe even audiobooks someday). Thanks again for reading. I appreciate your support and hope to see you again soon.

Horror

Action-packed plots, atmospheric settings, & horrifying monsters

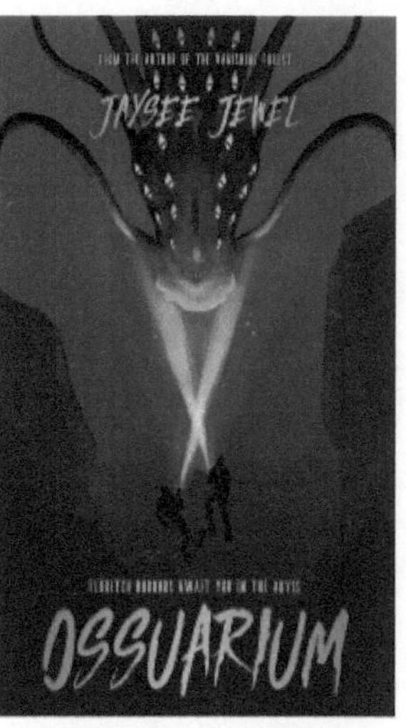

A dark fantasy adventure filled with horror, eerie monsters, and a deadly mystery to solve.

An unlikely pair crash land on a flooded planet with alien ruins to explore and sea monsters lurking below

Fantasy

Slow burn romances, political intrigue, and brutal magic systems

In a world where an immortal Arbiter reigns supreme and the trickster gods are growing bored, Neia and Kairon become two unlikely souls brought together by tragedy

A young heiress set to inherit her mother's empire falls for an enslaved insurrectionist

More from Jaysee Jewel
SCIENCE FICTION

Humanity was wiped out by an oceanic parasite. Now it's up to cowardly Indi and 99 other children to retake their homeworld

Terraforming a planet isn't easy when there are abandoned experimental labs and zombies under your feet

More from Jaysee Jewel

Romance

A high school graduate realizes she's a side character in a cheesy romance and decides to upend the author's plans.

Cooper can see ghosts and is horrified by them, but one girl won't leave him alone no matter how much salt he throws at her